DESERT INQUISITION

Afterward, he had the captive brought out and pegged to the ground so that he could use nothing but his lungs, and even these inside a corseting of ropes. Then Jalisca drew a line of molasses from the hole of red ants and ran the line to the head of the prisoner. The face of the prisoner he smeared with the sweet.

"They are coming, *amigo*. All the little red ants. They've eaten a mouse for me, but that only gives them an appetite for meat. You should see them coming, like a big broad pen drawing a red ink mark across paper. That's the way they look. But they'll feel differently.

"They are going to climb on your face. They'll start eating the tender places first. They have sense enough for that. The lips and the eyes are the tender places...."

> "*The Song of the Whip* is so well written, so exciting, and so thoroughly readable, that we advise even non-Western fans to go for it."
> —*New York Herald Tribune*

*Books by Max Brand
from Jove*

OUTLAW'S CODE
THE REVENGE OF BROKEN ARROW
MONTANA RIDES
STRANGE COURAGE
MONTANA RIDES AGAIN
THE BORDER BANDIT
SIXGUN LEGACY
SMUGGLER'S TRAIL
OUTLAW VALLEY
THE SONG OF THE WHIP

WRITING AS EVAN EVANS

THE SONG OF THE WHIP

A JOVE BOOK

This Jove book contains the complete
text of the original hardcover edition.

THE SONG OF THE WHIP

A Jove Book/published by arrangement with
the author's Estate

PRINTING HISTORY
Original hardcover edition published 1936
Penguin edition published 1957
Jove edition/December 1986

All rights reserved.
First published in Argosy Magazine.
Copyright © 1936 by Frederick Faust.
Copyright renewed © 1964 by Judith Faust, Jane F. Easton,
and John Frederick Faust.
This book may not be reproduced in whole or in part,
by mimeograph or any other means, without permission.
For information address: The Berkley Publishing Group,
200 Madison Avenue, New York, N.Y. 10016.

ISBN: 0-515-08885-4

Jove Books are published by The Berkley Publishing Group,
200 Madison Avenue, New York, N.Y. 10016.
The words "A JOVE BOOK" and the "J" with sunburst
are trademarks belonging to Jove Publications, Inc.

PRINTED IN THE UNITED STATES OF AMERICA

CHAPTER 1

Among the peons "The Song of the Whip" was known long ago and always cherished. They never dared to sing it except when they were alone, beyond earshot of their lords and masters, the rulers of the state, the rich *hacendados*, the overseers, the *Rurales*. The reason for this caution lay in the words of the song, not in the rich rhythm of its music. The original is a little too strong for translation, but, removing some of the more Gargantuan language, the poem goes line by line something like this:

> I am weary of slaves;
> Their hides are too tough;
> Many blows have thickened their skins;
> I must cut deep, very deep,
> To open the peon's heart
> And let out the screaming.
>
> But I could make music flow
> From bodies more tender.
> A song of howling, a shriek
> From delicate lips I could draw.

And the last four lines, with a liberty taken with the words, here and there, easily go into English rhyme like this:

> Give me no more the tough back of a peon,
> A Juan or José, a Pedro or Leon,
> But give me a lord from a lordly terraza,
> A Diaz, Angeles, or a Lerroza.

This was the song which a *charro* was singing on the bank of the Rio Grande. He sang it loudly and he sang it well, for he was very drunk with *mescal*. The special point of the song, for the Mexican cowboy in his silver-spangled suit of yellow leather, was that he was singing in a little town which belonged, every inch of it, to that same lordly family of the Lerrazas. The peons left their work to come and listen. They looked over their shoulders to make sure that no representative of the owners was near, and then they grinned, slowly, turning their heads and staring at one another, drinking a deep and quiet joy in the insults thrown at their masters, while the charro still rode back and forth, yelling out his song, and refreshing himself from time to time with a pull at a bottle with which he beat the time.

Verse followed verse. All Mexican songs are long. This was almost an epic, the greater part of it too filthy for any but peon ears to endure.

And on the other side of the narrow old Rio Grande, in the patio of the tavern which looked south towards the Mexican town opposite, Montana listened to that singing with a very faint smile while he sipped cool beer and smoked cigarettes.

A tall man, loose-hipped, stiff-kneed, a true horseman of the West, came up to Montana's table and pushed his hat on to the back of his head. This exposed a crimson mark left by the heavy hat-band. From the redness, sweat began to roll down.

"You Montana?" asked the tall man.

"Some folks call me that," said the Kid, looking up with that same faint smile.

"My name's Riley. I come from this here."

"Give your feet a rest," said the Kid, and pulled a chair around. Riley sat down.

"Drink?" asked Montana.

"After I finish talking, maybe."

"Go ahead."

"Some of the boys been talking things over with me," said Riley, as he sat down and slipped his belt so that the Colt in its holster hung in a commodious position, well forward and under his hand. "And what they wanta know is how long you figure on staying here in this town."

"Till I'm rested," said Montana.

"What some of the boys was figuring was that you don't look particular tired."

"Don't I?" said Montana.

"You look fit to take a jump over the moon," said Riley.

"Looks are mighty deceiving," said Montana. "There's many

THE SONG OF THE WHIP

a man with a smooth face and a smile whose heart is bowed down with care.... Have a smoke?"

Riley accepted the makings and twisted the wheat-straw paper around some Bull Durham tobacco.

"How they make this stuff, anyway?" asked Riley. "Chipped weeds soaked in old tobacco juice?"

"Anyway, it's the habit," said Montana.

"It's the only thing I like," said Riley. "It's queer how people take to habits. Some live on fresh air and a fine view, and there's some that hanker after flap-jacks and desert dust, and then again there's some that seem to live on trouble."

He looked steadily into the blue eyes of Montana.

Montana said: "Sure. Some people take to *pulque* and some wouldn't feed it to pigs."

"But then again," said Riley, "you'll find five or six people all in one patio with only a single idea in their heads.... Look right around here. That scrawny greaser, over there, all by himself, and those two charros in the corner drinking slow and talking soft, and that other pair by the gate of the patio pretending not to notice us. What you think they've all got on their minds?"

"Mañana," said Montana.

"The hell they have. They've got the Montana Kid on their minds.... How old are you, Montana?"

"You count the years, and they're not so many. But you count the care and the trouble I've been through..." said Montana, with his smile.

"Yeah, I know about that. You've raised some fine hair on your head, too, and all those greasers would like to lift it."

"Would they?" said Montana, running his long fingers through the hair that had been mentioned.

"Chihuahua offers five thousand dollars for the Montana Kid. 'El Keed' is worth ten thousand pesos in Sonora. Mexico City will pay down ten thousand more."

"I don't think those fellows are looking for my hair," said Montana, with the greatest good nature. "But I'll find out."

He stood up and called: *"Amigos!* Attention!"

The Mexicans, when they heard the ring of that voice, were startled violently.

"Friends," said Montana, when he had their attention, "are you looking for my hair?... You, there, with the broken nose, take your hand away from your gun.... You with the red scarf, I can see your hands under the table.... Now that I look at you again,

I see that you're a flock of greasers, with dirt worked into the grease.... Get up and get out. I need your room for my elbows. Vamoose! Move!"

The man with the broken nose leaned far forward in his chair until his right hand was out of sight behind him. Riley had slid under the table with a gun in each hand. But the hands of Montana rested on his hips as he smiled upon the Mexicans.

The man with the broken nose got up, slowly. He began to move with sidelong steps towards the gate of the patio. He was framed against the blue and golden mountains of the day's end. Then he disappeared with a leap. After him went the rest of the Mexicans, one by one, silently.

Riley got up off the ground.

"My Gawd Almighty!" he said.

The waiter ran out, his white apron tossing up and down above his knees.

"Where'd they go? Hey, where'd they go without paying?" he shouted.

"Those drinks are all on me, brother," said Montana.

He sat down again. Riley picked up the makings and began to roll another cigarette.

"They think a whole lot of you, the greasers do," he said.

"South of the river I've got a lot of—friends," said Montana.

"You can have 'em," said Riley. "The point I was making was: How long before half a dozen, or half a hundred of those greasers sneak across the river, one night, and lift your scalp; and while they're lifting your scalp and the bullets are flying, how many bystanders are gunna go down and cash in their chips at the end of the game? That's what the town's been thinking about, and that's what the boys want me to put up to you."

"Suppose I don't care to move?"

"Some of the boys was thinking of making up a party and calling on you."

"Well, I'm staying here till I feel more rested," said Montana. "How long will that be?"

"I can't tell.... Hearing that charro sing on the other side of the river refreshes me a lot, though. But I can't tell."

"Montana, why not be reasonable? Why go around singing the declaration of independence every day of your life? The boys don't want any trouble with you. They'd rather have a hundred and eighty pounds of wildcat to move. But they're worried."

"Give me some time," said Montana, "and I'll take myself off

THE SONG OF THE WHIP

your hands. But I've been pulling a big load uphill and my shoulders are sore. The whip only makes a tired horse baulk. Besides, I'm an American citizen, and I've got a right to rest in the shadow of the old flag."

Riley could not help grinning. He said: "You're a tough hombre, Montana. You been pretty far south, that last trip of yours, I guess."

"Why do you think I've been far south?" asked Montana.

"Those golden spurs of yours never were made north of Mexico City. And that silver wheel-work around the brim of your sombrero came from pretty far south, too. That blue silk shirt looks damned hidalgo to me, and about five years of needlework went into the embroidering of that sash you've got around your hips. . . . Some people might say that a pirate ought to put his loot in the hold and not keep it on deck for everybody to see."

"I never know what to do with fancy clothes except wear them," said Montana.

There was an outbreak of yelling from the farther shore of the Rio Grande. The charro in his brilliance of silver-spangled leather disappeared, bent far over the windy mane of his horse. A half-dozen riders had burst out from behind the village houses. Two of them pursued the fleeing cowboy. The rest reached with lariats or whips at the peons who had formed the audience. The lariats were swift; the whips flashed like striking snakes. But the peons scattered like dead leaves in a whirlwind. Only one of them tripped, fell, was up again instantly, and that moment was snared by a noose.

The captor, his horse at a run, took a turn with the raw-hide rope around the pommel of his saddle and dragged the peon headlong, whipping up the dust in a huge cloud.

When he came to a halt, the peon dragged inert at the end of the lariat.

"You brained him on that stone," said one of the riders.

"Well, what of it?" asked the man of the lasso.

He trotted his horse back, the peon bumping over the irregularities of the ground, his arms and legs flopping up and down.

The Montana Kid stood up from his table, stretched himself with care, like a cat after sleeping, and sat down again. The dark blue of his eyes had grown paler, the color thinned by excessive light.

"Kind of mean, those greasers," said Riley. "But they can take it. They're used to it. They got leather hides, and their bones is made of hard rubber. You can bend 'em but you can't break 'em."

THE SONG OF THE WHIP

Montana said nothing. He began to hum a song, the words of which declared:—

> I am weary of slaves;
> Their hides are too tough;
> Many blows have thickened their skins...

A tall, blond Castilian who commanded the horsemen gave commands. His voice came small but clear across the narrows of the river.

"Wake him up. Tie him to the tree and wake him up."

They triced the peon to the tree. He hung limp. They rode by him at a trot, at a gallop. Each, as he passed, struck with his quirt at the back of the peon. Some of them expertly snapped their lashes, cutting through the cheap cotton cloth; others rose in the stirrups to give greater force to the strokes.

"Who's the fellow with the blond moustache?" asked Montana. "Do you know him?"

"That's the majordomo of the Lerrazas in this part of the world," said Riley. "That's Emiliano Lopez. Some people say that he's going to marry Dorotea Lerroza, and get half the Lerraza millions."

"Millions? Is that what he's going to get?" said Montana.

The agony had roused the peon. He began to scream. He leaped up and down, dancing with pain. Then, as though realizing what he was doing, and where he was, he mastered his voice and stood silent.

Thin, rapid, they could hear, across the river, the whip strokes.

Don Emiliano waved the others aside. He shouted something. He dismounted from his horse and stood before the peon. He rolled up the sleeve of his right arm, after he had handed his brightly-embroidered Mexican jacket to one of his men. Then he selected a whip and measured his distance. He began to strike slashing strokes. The shirt, the entire back of the peon, turned crimson.

"Kind of sickening, ain't it?" said Riley.

"Dogs get what dogs deserve," said the Kid.

The peon lifted his head. He suddenly sang in a great voice "The Song of the Whip":

> I am weary of slaves;
> Their hides are too tough;
> Many blows have thickened their skins...

Don Emiliano shouted with rage. He redoubled his blows.

The Montana Kid stood up. "Ah?" he said. And he watched and listened.

Riley stared at him. He said, afterwards: "He seemed to like it!"

But all that Montana said was: "There are at least a hundred peons in that village."

Afterwards he stretched himself, cat-like, and sat down again. The evening was closing in, the voice of the flogged peon came screaming across the river:

> "Give me no more the tough back of a peon,
> A Juan or José, a Pedro or Leon,
> But give me a lord from his lordly terraza,
> A Diaz, Angeles, or a Lerraza."

As he finished the chorus, the peon slumped. He hung dangling from the rope that tied his wrists to the tree. His whole body had turned into a helpless rag of flesh.

CHAPTER 2

The stars glimmered in the slack water at the edges of the old Rio Grande. A hunting owl slid down the air at the verge of the stream, on the watch for any small, living thing that might have come to drink in the safety of the night. But no human eyes saw Montana swimming his mustang across the shallows of the river, or wading it up the farther shore. He made the horse lie down under the side of the bank; then he went on to the whipping-tree. The peon had not been released. He had recovered from his fainting-fit and now stood sloped against the tree trunk, with his legs shuddering under his weight. Before long, exhaustion would make his legs give way and he would hang again by the arms, in exquisite agony.

Montana stood behind him and heard the prayer: "Mother of Heaven, forgive my sins. Forgive Julio Mercado. Have mercy on his mother. Melt the heart of Don Emiliano with a little pity. Mother of Heaven, forgive poor Julio Mercado. Forgive him for singing the song. Forgive..."

Montano said: "Hey, *muchacho*, it was a good song. Why are you sorry you sang it?"

Julio Mercado straightened a little.

"Are you one of Don Emiliano's men?"

"No, *amigo*."

"Then I am glad that I sang the song. I had to sing it, because when I came to my wits I heard my own voice screaming. I sang the song to make my throat clean again. A man should not howl like a dog."

"I heard you howling, and then I heard you sing. You *are* a man, Julio Mercado."

With a touch of his hunting-knife he cut the rope that tied the hands of the peon to the tree. Julio Mercado sank to his knees.

"What have you done, señor?" he groaned. "Tie me up again

to the tree. If they come in the morning and find me free, they will flog me to death; they will turn my mother out of her house. Mercy of Heaven, tie me up again or I am a lost man——"

"If I leave you here," said Montana, "you'll be free before the morning in spite of them. You'll be dead, Julio."

"No. I have counted the moments. It is almost morning."

"The night has only begun."

"Mercy—Jesús!" said Julio.

"Lie down on the ground, on your face," said Montana.

The peon obeyed. Montana pulled the ragged shirt from the back of Julio. Here and there the blood had dried, gluing the shredded cloth deep into the flesh. The body of Julio shuddered as the shirt was drawn carefully away, but he made no sound. He merely began to make a slight snoring sound, he was drawing in his breath so hard over his swollen tongue.

Montana put a flask of brandy and water to the lips of Julio. He lifted up the head so that the man could drink more freely.

Julio said: "Now, after this—to die after this—to die is a happiness, *Valgame Dios! Valgame Dios!* Tell me your name, my father!"

"I am only a gringo, Julio."

"Whatever the color of your skin may be, God has put a good Mexican heart under it."

"Lie still," said Montana.

He began to cleanse the back of Julio with alcohol.

"Ai! Ai! Ai!" whispered Julio Mercado as the stuff burned his raw flesh. "Jesús! Jesús! This is a liquid fire!"

"Now," said Montana, "you're clean. There will be no infection. You understand, Julio. No pus will form in the flesh. There will be no running sores for the flies to get at."

He rubbed in an ointment, gradually, with tender hands.

"I sleep!" murmured Julio. "The pain goes. I sleep. I shall sleep forever. In heaven there is nothing but sleep for poor peons. That is enough.... No feet aching with frost in the morning.... *Valgame Dios,* how the frost had burned my feet to the bone!... No burning sun in the summer. But sleep. Nothing but blue sleep in heaven. Señor, you are my father and my grandfather. May God fill your hands with gold, since that is the gringo's heaven."

"Stand up," said Montana. "Can you stand, Julio?"

He put his hands under the pits of the Mexican's arms. Mercado heaved up, strongly. The muscles under his arms, stiffening in great slabs, stood out hard as wood against the fingers of Montana. The Mexican stood before him.

"Now this," said Montana, "and we will shut out the cold and the damp of the night air from the wounds."

He swathed the body of Mercado in thick, soft bandages, rich in downy lint.

"Ah-hai! I could laugh!" breathed Julio. "There is no more pain. I could dance."

"Here's the last of the brandy and water. Drink it."

The peon drank. He blessed Montana and gave him back the empty canteen.

"Now what will you do?" asked Montana.

"I get my old mother and we run away to the mountains as fast as the *burro* can carry her."

"Is there nothing to do before you go?"

"There is to thank you, señor. Here, on my knees—"

Montana gripped him and held him up.

"I want you to be man, Julio. I don't want you to kiss my feet like a poor, beaten dog.... Listen to me. Because I heard you sing 'The Song of the Whip'—that's why I came to you tonight. Now, if you are a man, you will see that there is one thing for you to do before you leave the lands of the Lerrazas."

"Do you mean the killing of Don Emiliano? Señor, he knows that the peons hate him, and he sleeps at night surrounded by his men. They are all fiercer than Rurales. They all are devils."

"Suppose that I help you to get at him?"

"Señor, you are a brave man, but no two of us could do it, even if you were El Keed."

"I *am* El Keed!"

"*Valgame Dios!*" gasped Julio. "Are you that man?"

"I am he."

"Then let us go—together! I know that Mexican bullets cannot touch you, and Mexican hands cannot hold you. Let us go together. You first. If you will help me to take him, I would hang him at this same tree with a gag between his teeth, and beat him as he beat me!"

That northernmost *hacienda* of the great Lerraza estates was like most of the other country dwellings of the rich family. It was low, with great wings spreading back and to either side. The walls were four feet thick, to keep in the warmth of fires in winter, the

THE SONG OF THE WHIP

cool of shadows in summer. Beyond the main building lay the outhouses; beyond the outhouses lay the corrals; beyond the corrals stood the little village of white huts where the peons lived, those who worked the lands closest to the house. The majordomo, Emiliano Lopez, slept in the eastern wing in a great room where once a conquistadore had slept before him. It had a huge four-poster bed with a canopy over it, the floor was tiled; there was a hearth on which eight-foot logs could be burned. The furniture of chairs and couch was covered with moth-eaten red velvet. In the ceiling appeared two or three angels in plaster, badly cracked and broken away by the hand of time. And under the canopy of the bed Emiliano Lopez slept sound and smiled at his dreams.

He was a handsome man, young, in the prime of life, with that gentle prospect of Dorotea Lerraza and her millions before him. This helped Don Emiliano to smile in his sleep; also he smiled because of the sweet after-taste of the flogging of the peon.

Don Emiliano believed in a firm hand with the peons, and he used one. There were no runaways from his administration. Once he had chased two runaways for three weeks and caught them, and flogged them to death in front of the hacienda, with all the other peons grouped about to see the justice done. After that there were no more desertions. The peons looked upon the will of Don Emiliano as the will of God, and therefore the receipts increased each year and the heart of the great Tomás Lerraza was gladdened so that he smiled on the suit of Lopez for the hand of Dorotea. Don Emiliano, in short, was an efficient administrator.

He secured the safety of his body—and of his administration—by keeping about him men who were the material of which rurales are made. That is to say, he recruited them from the jails, giving liberty to murderers in case they were willing to do no more murders except at his commands. They were devoted fellows. Each of them had at least two killings to his credit. Each of them enjoyed a string of four tough mustangs, plenty of rifles, revolvers, and ammunition of the best, flashy clothes, pulque at will, and brandy on feast days. They ate roast kid twice a week, and in general they were lords of the land. Nevertheless, the discipline was strict, and the refractory were discouraged by the hand of Don Emiliano himself. He had them brought before him and pistoled them with his own gun.

Four of these men slept in the room at the right of that of their master. Four of them slept in the room on the left of Don Emiliano.

Under his window, which opened high from the ground, a ninth man walked up and down, relieved twice during the night. In this way, Don Emiliano kept his person sacrosanct and laughed at the hate of the peons.

On this night the guard under the window as one Juan Torres, young, strong, swift, with the morals of a tomcat and the fighting virtues of a jaguar. When he saw the shadowy figure walking towards him through the night, he lifted the sawed-off shotgun to his shoulder and bade the stranger halt.

The man walked straight on: "Hurry! Hurry!" he commanded. "Don Emiliano wants you at once."

"About what?" asked Juan Torres.

"About the girl, you fool!" said the other.

Juan Torres started. He thought of many girls, because there were many to think of. He wondered which one was in the mind of Don Emiliano.

He lowered the shotgun and said: "Who are you?"

"El Keed!" said Montana, and struck at the same time with the heel of a Colt.

Juan Torres fell. In falling, he pulled both triggers of his gun and blew a great channel in the dust.

The roar of that gun was an unexpected thing, and Montana paused for an instant, uncertain.

Julio Mercado did not pause. He ran past Montana. He leaped, caught the rim of the open window, and hauled himself through it. On either side of the room of Don Emiliano had commenced a stampede of footfalls as his guards rushed to get out of the house to the scene of the explosion. They were all good fellows, according to their lights, and not one of them held back from the prospect of a fight with guns.

Don Emiliano himself was rising from his bed when he saw the silhouette of a man climbing through his window. Immediately behind this first intruder loomed the head and shoulders of a second man, who leaped down into the room like a great cat.

"Don Emiliano!" cried the first comer, panting. "It's an attack—a surprise attack—bandits!"

"The devil!" exclaimed Don Emiliano, and rushed for the window.

He had not recognized these two good fellows who had swarmed through the window to his assistance. Now he plunged past them to have a view of things outside. In the back of his mind there was grim cursing. Somehow, he told himself, he always had expected a descent on the ranch, but not in the middle of the night. That was indecent and un-Mexican. Your good Mexican, bandit or otherwise, fights by day, and by night, like a true gentleman, he does his sleeping. He is a fellow of regular habits. So Don Emiliano with his brain in a whirl charged for the window, and as he went by the taller of the two men something was thrown over his head, he was jerked to the floor, and all in a trice his arms were bound and a gag of wadded cloth was thrust between his teeth.

He still attempted to struggle, but struggling choked him rapidly, now that he could not breathe through his mouth. Besides, something hard jabbed into the pit of his stomach, and he heard the tall man say: "We don't want to murder you, Lopez. Come quietly and oblige your humble servant."

Lopez went quietly. There was something in the manner of this speech that discouraged resistance.

He was walked into the room at the right; and outside his window he could hear, in the garden, the babbling voices of his men, his true and trusted guardians exclaiming: "Juan Torres! Juan Torres! What's happened? Wake up!... *Por Dios!* He's dead!"

"I hope not," murmured the tall man at the side of Don Emiliano. "I didn't mean to hit him that hard.... Julio, help yourself to those guns. Not too many, but a couple of belts of ammunition and a rifle or two, and a pair of revolvers.... That's the system!"

Julio loaded himself quickly with some of those most modern weapons which Don Emiliano always provided for his private police. He threw over his left shoulder four belts of rifle and revolver ammunition. And then he led the way to the rear hall, which led to a door at the back of the house. Footfalls—the pattering of bare feet, the thudding of bare heels—ran everywhere through the mansion of the hacendado. But to the bewilderment of Don Emiliano, no one came near him.

They stood under the stars. There was not a sound near them— only the babble of voices on the farther side of the big house.

"We'll need horses, Juliano, and good ones," said the tall man. "Where are the stables? Where are the stables of Don Emiliano's own horses?"

There was a good deal of fear in the heart of Don Emiliano, but there was horror, also. The horror was greater than the fear, for it was a sacrilege which the two intruders had committed when they laid hands upon his aristocratic body; but it was to Lopez almost a greater sacrilege when he saw the two breaking into that wing of the stable where his choicest thoroughbreds were kept. In fact, they were not his. They belonged to the great Tomás Lerraza himself!

CHAPTER 3

"Light a lantern," directed the tall man.

Julio found one. Before he lighted it, he protested, "But if he sees our faces, señor—"

"Don't you want him to know who is doing this to him?" asked the tall man. "Let him see you, Julio. As for me, he can't see past my mask."

"But if the light is seen by any of the servants—"

"We have to take chances. There's no comfortable way through life unless a fellow takes chances, Julio. Light the lantern."

It was lighted. The flames ran across the wick. The chimney was clamped down with a squeak of rusty iron. The flame rose. It leaped once or twice, then it settled into a steady glow that showed Don Emiliano the face of Julio Mercado. The heart of Lopez sank and it seemed to him that he could feel again the handle of the quirt in his hand. He made sure of his death. There would hardly be time, even for these cool devils, to torture him long. But he would die in some frightful way.

And yet, such was the singular nerve of Don Emiliano, he was able to feel rage and scorn and hatred and shame when he saw the two of them peering into the capacious box stalls where the horses of Don Tomás were kept—the horses fit for a king—the horses which no man on the hacienda except Don Emiliano himself was allowed to bestride in the long absence of the real owner.

"Tell me, which are the best ones?" asked the tall man behind the mask.

"This one. This mare, señor," said the traitor Julio. "You can see her—how beautiful she is—with a head like a deer, and such eyes. I have seen her run like the wind. Take her, señor, and I shall use one of the mustangs in the corral—"

"Take the bay mare for yourself, Julio," said the tall man. "She doesn't fill my eye."

15

The heart of Don Emiliano had leaped, when he heard the first words of Julio. It was a tribute to Lopez that he could suffer, at this moment of personal danger, at the thought of seeing thoroughbreds in the hands of bandits. His heart fell again at the answer of the tall man. But still, neither Julio nor the tall man would be able to guess the great secret.

"Here's a better thing," said the tall man, looking into the next stall.

There was a big gelding in there—a great grey gelding capable of carrying two hundred pounds all day long through mountains. A very valuable horse, and yet the heart of Don Emiliano leaped again when he thought that this was all the robbers might seize upon.

"Yes," said the masked man, "this horse might do."

"Then take it, in the name of God!" panted Julio Mercado. "Do you hear them? They are coming, señor!"

He pointed. A stir of voices was pouring up the hill from the hacienda, at that moment.

"Let us take a little time," said the tall man. Behind his mask, Lopez saw that the eyes were blue, oddly luminous, set well apart. He saw, also, the weight and power of the shoulders and the long arms and the lithe narrows of the hips. He noted even the fine embroidery of the red sash about the hips of the stranger.

It was some great man, he was sure, some power in the specially Mexican realm of banditry.

"We mustn't hurry, once we're sitting under the wishing-gate," said the tall man. "Let me see—"

He took the lantern and looked into stall after stall. His comments ran: "I like a Roman nose. The devils generally have plenty of bottom. We might look at this one again.... This dish-face won't do.... No withers here ... Over in the knees, over in the knees; and that's not for mountain work.... Hold on! Ah-hai! ... Let me look again! Do you know this stallion, Julio?"

The heart of Don Emiliano sank into his boots. For that was the horse of horses.

"I've seen him, señor. He was brought in not long ago. You see how his ribs stick out. He is nothing. His feet are too big. His chest is nothing for width. His lips are two elbows thrusting out."

"True," said the tall man, nodding. "He is not a horse at all. He is a sword-blade. I think there is the sort of steel in this ugly

THE SONG OF THE WHIP

devil that I could use. He has the blood-stain in his eye. Savage devil, eh?"

"Señor, he almost has killed two grooms."

"He's not for the hands of grooms. He's for hands like mine," said the tall man, haughtily.

"Quick then, señor! And God forgive me for letting you take such a bad horse! They are coming, surely."

"There is still time. As long as we have two such horses under our hands we have won the game already.... This saddle for you, and this for me.... So! You stick out your belly to cheat me, do you? What's the name of this narrow-chested devil, Julio?"

"El Capitán, señor," gasped Julio as he pulled hard on the cinches.

"El Capitán?" said the tall man, putting his knee into the ribs of the chestnut and waiting. "There was a great stake horse not so many years ago called 'The Captain'. And that—"

Here he saw his chance and jerked the cinches up suddenly. El Capitán, caught unawares, stamped in his anger, and switched around his ugly, snaky head. The tall man slapped his nose.

"In a little while you'll come to know me, *amigo*," he said, and laughed. "Not let's bring our friend, here, down to the whipping-tree."

Don Emiliano—suddenly brought back to his own concerns—was led out into the open night. The tall man, shading his eyes, peered down the hill. All the village danced with lights. People were running here and there on the bank of the Rio Grande with lanterns.

"That way is shut off to us," said the tall man. "I see that I shall have to stay on this side of the Rio Grande for a day or two. But the chief thing is that we can't take Don Emiliano back to the whipping-tree. To the devil with such luck! However, there's a tree right here beside us that ought to do.... Tie him up.... So!"

Don Emiliano found himself bound fast by the wrists to the trunk of the tree. His eyes swam with fury and disdain. And down there by the river were the many men, the many fools, the trusted guards in whom he had invested so much money, so much thought in picking and choosing them from hundreds of villainous criminals. The dogs had false noses. They were running the wrong scent.... Ah, for two or three of them at hand, here! But they all were far away! Useless as the stars in the sky!

He heard the tall man saying: "His nightshirt is no thicker than the shirt that you were wearing this evening. Here is the whip and there is his back, Julio. Help yourself."

And the traitor Julio was saying: "Ah, God, if only my father and his father before him—may they rest in heaven!—could see me now! Be their hands with mine on the handle of the whip! Now—now—now!"

The blows struck through the body of Don Emiliano, searing strokes of pain; but he hardly felt them. He stood up straight. Fire consumed his brain. The whip—the whip was on his own body, and wielded by less than a dog! He felt those strokes upon his soul.

"Good!" said the tall man. "Very well laid on, Julio. Wait till I get the gag out of his mouth, and then we'll hear him howl a time or two."

He pulled the gag from between the teeth of Don Emiliano.

"If he cries out, they will come for us!"

"They never will reach us, with such horses under our saddles. And what's a meal without music? Let me hear him howl!"

The whip fell again, a shower of cutting strokes. Down the back of Lopez flowed the warm blood. He felt it. He felt the agony leaping through his body, but it never reached his brain. The shame that lived there was far too great to admit any other feeling.

"Wait!" said the tall man.

The flogging ceased for the moment.

The tall man stood before Don Emiliano and looked closely into his eyes.

"He breathes a little hard, but there is still plenty of heart in him, Julio."

"Let me kill him!" panted Julio. "I see his blood running already. To have drawn blood is the same as to have killed him.... Let me finish him!"

"Wait!" commanded the tall man. "Don Emiliano, do you hear me?"

Emiliano Lopez said nothing.

"I talk about the little matter of your life," said the tall man. "Do you hear me?"

"I hear you," said the strangled voice of Lopez.

"You are a little too brave to die under a whip. You should at least have a gun in your hand when you finish. Suppose that I give you that chance now?... No, your hand would be too unsteady. Now, listen to me. Julio Mercado, having wiped out the score, a flogging for a flogging, teaches you that even a peon is a man. He is leaving your service—for mine.... In the meantime there remains behind him his mother. She is an old, good woman. You will be tempted to put hands on her in revenge. Well, Lopez, I'll have your sacred oath that she shall go free, untouched by you, when her son leaves. Will you swear?"

Don Emiliano could hardly speak. No pain but rage was choking him.

"I'll swear," he said.

"By your own saint—by San Emiliano—and by the blood of God—will you swear?"

"I swear."

"Speak the oath out in full."

"I swear by San Emiliano and by the blood of God—"

"Go on!"

"That I shall not harm the mother of Mercado."

"That is enough. But I'll add this. If you break your oath, Lopez, I'll come to you through hell fire and deep water and cut your throat for you to the neckbone. Do you hear me?"

Don Emiliano was silent.

"Do you hear me, you blood-sucking rat?" said the tall man through his teeth.

"I hear you!" said Don Emiliano. "And may the time come when I can hear you *and* see you again—when my hands are free."

"You talk like a man," said the tall fellow. "Come on, Julio. We have a bit of riding ahead of us.... This will please the hired men of Don Emiliano, when they have to cut down their master from the tree. First put the gag back between his teeth so that they won't find him here until the morning. The hours will be something for him to remember.... *Adios,* Don Emiliano!"

CHAPTER 4

Mexican news, unless it has to do with oil or silver mines, or promising revolutions, gets small space in American newspapers, even in Southwestern ones, but something in that episode on the Lerraza hacienda struck fire to the fancy of reporters. That was why young Richard Lavery, junior, bowed his dark head over the front page of a journal and read with a puckered brow:

"A peon flogged ... cut free in the night by an unknown man, probably an American but speaking perfect Spanish.... The majordomo of the hacienda stolen out of his bed at night ... one of his guards left badly stunned, in danger of dying, without memory of what had happened.... The finest of the Lerraza horses stolen. ... Emiliano Lopez tied to a tree and flogged as the peon had been ... the peon himself whirled away to safety ... a strong guard set along the river for leagues to keep the American and the peon from escaping to United States soil...."

Young Richard Lavery jerked up his head with a sudden fire in his Irish-blue eyes and shouted: "Montana! Montana! No other man could do it! Now he'll go south to Rubriz!"

He went to the window of his room and looked across the vast natural terraces of his father's ranch dotted with the grazing cattle by thousands. It was not a ranch. It was a kingdom, and Richard Lavery was the heir apparent. And yet as he lifted his head his eyes were dim with memories of an open camp fire, unshaven, fierce men squatting about it, a guitar twanging somewhere, a voice singing an old ballad.

Enchantment drew the feet of Richard Lavery out of the house, towards the stables, into the pasture where his own horses grazed, eagle-eyed racers made of hammered iron, bronze, and burning fire. Then he turned suddenly away and went into the saddle-room and took a lariat from a peg on the wall.

• • •

THE SONG OF THE WHIP

Benito Jalisca, squat, bow-legged, scarred by battle like a bull-dog, heard the story during the noon halt of his detail of Rurales. Of all that hardy lot of criminals who had been given a chance to lead new lives if they were willing to serve the law, Benito Jalisca was the hardiest member. He was eating his beans, sopping them up with *tortillas*, while the story continued. Then he took one swallow of the sour red wine, stood up, saddled his horse, looked to his rifle, and mounted. The lieutenant said: "What's up, Benito? And where do you think you're bound now?"

Benito Jalisca merely pointed towards the man who told the story.

"El Keed!" he said, and reined his horse away.

The lieutenant was a violent man. He shouted an oath and reached for a gun, even, when he saw Jalisca canter away, but one of the other Rurales held his hand. "You can't take Benito from that trail!" said the Rural. "He's followed it before. He has two scars from it. He would rather meet El Keed than an angel from heaven, even if he has to die for it."

The lieutenant bit at his moustaches and grunted. Then he waved his hand and dismissed Benito Jalisca towards the far horizon.

Brother Pascual, his huge walking-staff leaning against the wall of a shepherd's hut, was setting splints on the broken leg of the shepherd when the son of the shack came in and told the story. And Brother Pascual, lifting his shaven, sun-bronzed sconce, wondered over the story.

"What gringo would do such a thing for a peon?" he muttered.

He kept on muttering until he had finished the bandaging which would hold the splints in place. Then he leaped up and grasped his great walking-staff which would have been a burden rather than a help to anyone other than a giant. "El Keed!" thundered the friar. "El Keed has returned!" And he went off with immense strides, heading towards the mountains, pulling up the flowing skirts of his robe over the heavy cord that belted him round.

The bishop ate, on this day, not in his palace, but in a little restaurant frequented by muleteers, because his charitable visits had just finished an exhausting round through the poorest section of the town; and he was accustomed to entering a little restaurant and eating his black *frijoles* and black bread; the muleteers never were overawed for more than two minutes. For first they recognized him as that good man who was a true father to the afflicted, and afterwards they forgot him altogether, for his wan face and his abstracted eyes were more like a picture on the wall than like ordinary human flesh. And that was how the bishop heard the story. A faint shadow of earthly thought and care crossed his face. He lifted his gentle eyes. And then, smiling inwardly, he whispered: "El Keed!"

Rosita, the dancing-girl, had finished her dance and sat with her legs crossed immodestly, breathing a little from exertion, and making herself smile around the rose which she held between her lips. Young *cabelleros*, seeing her from a distance, came suddenly and eagerly towards her, but then behind the smile and the rose they saw the dangerous bright devil in her eyes and checked themselves again.

It was from one of these that she heard the story, filled with exclamations—a gringo—a flogged peon—banditry at the hacienda of the great Lerraza—the high-born Emiliano Lopez flogged—and who could have done it?

Rosita jumped on to the window-sill and sprang into the street. She began to run. As she ran, a gendarme thought she was drunk, because she threw back her head and staggered so. But when she came closer he saw that it was laughter that made her reel. And as she went by he thought he heard her singing "El Keed! El Keed!"

Mateo Rubriz sat at the big oaken table with his red skullcap on the back of his head and his sleeves rolled up to the elbows. He had a leg of mutton before him, and with a razor-sharp hunting-knife he whittled off slices and slashes of the meat. Some he crammed into his own huge mouth and washed down with draughts of wine from a beautiful jewelled chalice; but most of the meat he tossed over his shoulder and one of the dogs leaped and caught it out of the air. For the tale Mateo Rubriz was hearing had made him lose his appetite. It was told him by a tall young man who had a blood cloth tied around his head and who mumbled when he spoke, because he had been shot through the cheeks. So he mumbled, and little bubbles of blood kept forming and breaking on his lips. He had escaped in this condition. The other two had been killed. It seemed as though everyone had been forewarned that bandits were coming! There had been no chance even to make a good fight of it!

Rubriz kept saying: "So! So! So! If the three of you had gone quietly—but no. I understand what happened. You made as much noise as horses. If you had neighed, people might have thought that you really had four hoofs and weren't dangerous except to the furniture. Get out of my sight! I used to have men. Now I have only boys and fools around me. Now I have only—"

It was at this point that a tremendous outcry started in the dusk of the evening, outside the mountain shack where Rubriz made his headquarters, above the law.

This uproar continued; guns exploded; Rubriz started to his feet and stared sternly around him; and then the cook, who in the midst of fumes of smoke was stirring a great iron soup-pot in the corner of the room, leaped to his feet and waved the great iron ladle which he was using.

"El Keed!" he shouted.

And at that moment the Montana Kid entered the room, surrounded by shouting men and with Julio Mercado behind him, pinioned by the arms.

Mateo Rubriz uttered a great cry and sprang forward. He was less than middle height. He had bowed legs. He was built like a bulldog. And now he grasped Montana by the elbows and lifted him, bodily, well above his head, and carried him, and thrust him up so that Montana was standing on the table in the middle of the room. The jewelled chalice from which Rubriz had been drinking, he refilled, and placed in the hand of Montana. In his own hand he caught up the great leathern bottle from which he had filled the cup.

"We drink—we drink—we drink together, *amigo!*" shouted Rubriz. And he lifted the bottle towards his lips.

"We drink—we drink!" yelled the others.

Hastily each man provided himself with a tin or a cup or a glass of wine, still shouting: "We drink—to El Keed—we drink—"

But here Montana shouted: "What of my friend? Does he drink with us? Is he one of us? I offer you Julio Mercado—a peon—flogged by the whips of the gentry after he had done their labors all his life—I offer you Julio Mercado.... Will you take him?"

Rubriz put down the wine-bottle. Some of the wine had sloshed across his mouth and was dripping down his chin. He wiped it off on the back of his arm and his hand.

"Here—give him to me," he said.

They pushed Julio Mercado forward to him. With a vast left hand Rubriz gripped the peon.

He said, staring into the eyes of Mercado: "If you go back to the law, what will happen to you?"

"I shall be whipped to death," said Mercado.

He was frightened, but he was telling the first truth that came to his lips. The companions of Rubriz shouted.

"Will the Rurales be your friends?" demanded Rubriz.

Mercado turned his head, looked at Montana, and then groaned.

"No, señor."

"Tell me who I am."

"You are Mateo Rubriz."

"What do you know about me?"

"You are a great devil, señor."

A shout of laughter commented on this.

"Have heart for everything," said Montana, loudly.

Mercado turned a yellow-green face and tried to smile.

"Will you be one of us?" shouted Rubriz savagely.

"Señor, my master has brought me to you," said Julio Mercado.

"You fool," said Rubriz, "in my band, there are no masters except me."

"Then I cannot be one of you," said Julio. "I have found my master and I shall not change him."

There was another shout at this, but whether it was applause or anger poor Julio Mercado could not tell.

He lifted his head and took a great breath when Rubriz yelled: "You have looked in on us—you have spied out our secrets—and now you say that you will not be one of us?"

"I shall not leave my master!" said poor Julio.

Rubriz flashed out a great knife. He waved it before the eyes of Mercado.

"Will you not?" he roared.

Mercado shut his eyes, but he shouted, desperately: "No! I shall not leave him—señor. My master—help me!"

But to his dismay, El Keed spoke not a word. A desperate effort made Julio Mercado, then, but powerful hands were laid upon him and mastered him instantly.

The knife flashed again before his eyes. He made himself ready for death. And then he felt, across his forearm, the drawing of the keen edge of the blade. The warm blood began to run.

"Oh, my God, receive my spirit!" groaned Mercado.

Someone touched his arm—and not with a knife.

He opened his eyes, and he saw them, one by one, all those desperate faces, come close, and each with a hand touched the slow drops of blood that ran down his arm. Then, horrible to tell, they lifted their fingers and licked the blood from them.

He heard Mateo Rubriz shout: "Is his blood our blood?"

"Yes!" shouted the many voices.

"Is he one of us?" yelled Rubriz.

"Yes!" came the yelling answer.

"And forever?"

"Forever!" they roared.

A great hand gripped that of Julio Mercado.

He saw the grinning face of Rubriz.

"You fool!" said Rubriz. "Do you think that El Keed is not with us as much of a master as I am? Now, friend, your battles are our battles, your friends are our friends. Take care that you introduce us to no weaklings!... Now drink.... Hai! Where is the wine?... Give him to drink.... All of us, with open throats, till the cups are dry.... El Keed and his friend, forever! They are ours!"

CHAPTER 5

The lovely lady, Dorotea Lerraza, was so blonde, so blue-eyed that no one would take her for a Mexican. No one in Paris did, at least, in spite of the size of her diamonds and the length of her strings of pearls. She was not only lovely in face, but she was made for a one-piece bathing-suit, and no man since the Greeks can say more. If there was anything strange about her, it was her way of stopping smiling, suddenly, and looking a man straight in the eyes. Some men did not stay for a second look, but tall and handsome Emiliano Lopez had stayed, and eventually he had become the accepted one.

Don Tomás, lord of the Lerraza millions of land, of cattle, and of *pesos,* had accepted Don Emiliano as a future son-in-law without misgivings. He always had been afraid that his beautiful daughter would desire a title abroad, whereas, he well knew, as all Mexicans do, that there is no title so important as the old Castilian blood coupled with a residence in Mexico of some three or four centuries. Like the Lerrazas, the Lopez blood was old, Mexican, and pure.

Tomás Lerraza sat at the window and looked out into the patio where a peon hung by his wrists from the whipping-post, his knees dragging the ground, his weight swaying slightly from side to side.

The white overseer had knelt by the peon and pressed his ear to the man's back.

"How soon will he be able to take more strokes of the whip?" asked Don Tomás.

The overseer rose and bowed as to a lord.

"He will not be able to stand again, señor," he said. "The man is dead."

"Dead?" said Señorita Dorotea. "Dead?"

She came closer to the window and opened her blue eyes wider.

"Who could have expected that—so soon?" she said, and looked with surprise at the bleeding back of the peon.

The blood was no longer running. She remembered, from detective stories, that blood would not run after a man was dead. Here was the singular confirmation before her eyes. She had learned at school that nothing is so well learned as that which has a physical demonstration. How true some lessons may prove to be!

So thought Dorotea Lerraza.

Don Tomás lifted his head so that his white spike of beard thrust out like a silver lance-head.

"The old, true breed, it has vanished," he said, regretfully. "This many lashes, in the old days, would only have begun to oil a peon's tongue. Now it has killed a man and cost us some money. Economy becomes a difficult matter in these days, eh, Emiliano?"

Don Emiliano bowed. He was a brave young man, and proud of his blood, but like everyone else in the world, he was more than a little afraid of the only head of the Lerraza family. Yet he considered Don Tomás an ideal to be aspired towards—an ideal which, when he married Dorotea and claimed the fortune, he wished to copy closely.

A house mozo came in and bowed towards Don Tomás.

The Lerraza was saying in a clear voice: "Cut the man down and bury him. Did he confess nothing?"

"Nothing, señor," said the overseer.

"And yet he was the best friend of that Julio Mercado. He must have known that there was rebellion in the heart of Mercado. Yet he would not speak?"

"He swore, still, that he had nothing to say," said the overseer.

"His death be on his own stubborn tongue and not on my conscience," said Don Tomás. "Take the body away."

He turned towards the mozo, who still was blowing. Lady Dorotea was still at the window, watching the body being dragged away. The head fell over to one side, and the legs sprawled in a silly manner. She smiled a little, innocently. She felt very young, seeing how much there is to be learned in the world.

Don Tomás stroked his lean, hard, brown cheeks, finishing each stroke with a caress of his white spike of beard.

He said to the mozo: "What do you wish to say? Did *you* know Julio Mercado?"

"God forbid, señor," said the terrified mozo. "God forbid that I should know such a scoundrel—beyond seeing him and loathing his face. God forbid that I should know him."

He began to bow and back out of the big room.

"Wait a moment," said Don Tomás. "What did you come here to say?"

"Ah, señor, I came only to say a little thing. That a Rural is here at the house, begging for leave to speak with Your Excellency."

"I am not an Excellency, fool."

"No, Excellency," said the mozo.

"Therefore, don't use the word 'Excellency' when you speak to me again."

"No, Excellency."

Don Tomás was not angered. He merely smiled.

"Such fools!" he murmured. "The teaching of a few centuries they cannot forget after a generation of the new régime.... Well, my boy, bring in the Rural, if you will."

In fact, the Rurales had entrée everywhere. They were the chosen police force of Mexico, and if they were all as savage as blood-hounds, if they were all guilty of bloody crimes, for that very reason their importance could be doubted the less. Don Tomás accepted them as a national institution in which, as a good Mexican, he was bound to be proud.

The mozo came back, presently, with a short, bow-legged stub of a man with scars on his face. He made a bow to everyone in the room. Then he came forward and bowed again to Don Tomás. All Rurales were not so well bred. Don Tomás almost smiled his pleasure.

"What will you have?" he asked.

"Senor," said the Rural, "I would have a few words with you alone."

"You are speaking," said Don Tomás, "to me alone." He added, when the Rural looked towards Dorotea and Emiliano: "And the others are my blood, or soon will be."

The mozo had vanished from the room.

Still the Rural looked for a moment towards Emiliano and Dorotea Lerraza. At last he collected himself and said: "I am Benito Jalisca, a sergeant of the Rurales."

"I see your decorations," said Don Tomás, still warming with amiability.

"My work," said Jalisca, "is to trail a gringo marauder, gunman and murderer and thief, one called in our country El Keed."

"I have heard of the American dog," said Don Tomás. "What brings you here on his trail?"

"Because he has been here before me," said the Rural, bluntly.

"Who has seen him?"

"Don Emiliano," said the Rural.

He bowed towards Don Emiliano.

"What the devil are you talking about, fool?" asked Don Emiliano.

The Rural lifted his head with a slight jerk and looked again at Don Emiliano, with a slight difference.

Lady Dorotea glanced at her lover also. She smiled. She liked to hear certain pungencies from the lips of a man to whom she would entrust her heart. Nothing pleases a woman more than to know that a man is a man.

"I am talking," said the Rural, slowly, "of a night which Don Emiliano also may remember." The Rural was blunt, but no Mexican lacks courtesy. He added: "It was a night on which certain fine horses of Señor Lerraza were stolen."

Don Emiliano did not carry a knife, and yet he made a significant move with his hand. He was just as blond as Señorita Lerraza, and yet he was just as Mexican.

"What do you mean, you dog?" he demanded.

"Be still, Emiliano," said Don Tomás.

Emiliano was still. But he glanced in apprehension towards his lady.

She turned her lovely face full towards him, and smiled. One could not have told whether she understood that her lover had been helpless in the hands of ruffians, or whether she delighted in the thought of pain, even if her beloved had had to be the sufferer.

Don Emiliano shrugged his shoulders, and then regretted the gesture, for his back still was very sore.

The Rural was saying: "The bandit who came here was El Keed, the gringo."

"Ha!" said Don Tomás.

"It was he," insisted the Rural.

"How do you know that? Who has talked to you?" asked Don Tomás.

Don Emiliano had come two or three paces forward in his eagerness.

"I know, señor," said Benito Jalisca, "because I have followed the trail of this man for a long time."

"For how long?" asked Don Tomás.

"As long as this, and this," said the Rural, and touched two of the white scars which were inscribed on his face like capital letters.

"That is all very well," said Don Tomás, "but it is not proof."

"I tell you, señor, that no other man could have done the things which he accomplished here."

"Explain that," said Don Tomás.

"Señor, it would be a bitter thing to hear."

"Nevertheless, I wish to hear it."

The Rural looked once, briefly, towards Don Emiliano. Then he said: "What is the value of the life of a peon?"

"A few pesos. Why?"

"Consider then, señor, what manner of man it would be who would take great offence because a peon was flogged—even to death?"

"True," agreed Don Tomás, stroking his sharp white beard again.

"But when this Julio Mercado was flogged, and not even killed, a gringo crossed the river and entered Mexico without a passport, and cut the man down, and then—"

He paused.

Don Emiliano said through his teeth, "Go on!"

"Thank you, Emiliano," said Dorotea, sweetly.

The Rural continued: "Well, I shall tell the story, although you know it. He cut down the peon. He went with him to the guarded house and room of Don Emiliano. He struck down the guard outside the room—and the poor guard still lies between life and death. He entered that room. He took away Don Emiliano at the extreme peril of his life. He took time to select the best horses of Your Excellency, and then, before he left, he did certain things to Don Emiliano."

"True," said Dorotea.

Don Emiliano looked suddenly at her with burning eyes, but he saw that she was smiling.

"And out of all this," said Don Tomás, "what proves to you that the criminal was El Keed?"

"He was a man who did something for nothing," said the Rural.

"Many a man is capable of doing that," said Don Tomás, smiling.

"Señor, he was able to breathe the breath of manhood into a peon—a peon who had been flogged!" said the Rural.

"True," said Don Tomás, "but even other men would be capable of as much as that."

"Señor," said the Rural, "finally he spent time in the stable while many armed men were searching for him and endangering his life, yet he waited in the stable until he had found the *best* horse."

"Ah!" said Dorotea.

"Be still!" commanded her father.

"Senor Rural," said the girl, "is this man, El Keed—is he one who knows horses so well?"

"Señorita," said the Rural, "he is one who knows perfectly two things, horses and—"

He stopped himself by striking a hand across his mouth. He looked guiltily at Don Tomás.

"And what?" asked Dorotea.

"Pardon me, señorita," said the Rural. "He is one who knows horses very well."

The girl turned to her father.

"This Jalisca is a man of sense," she said.

"I don't know what you're talking about," said her father.

"Of course you don't," said the girl, "but—": And here she laughed, and looked towards Don Emiliano. "Do you know, dear Emiliano?" she asked.

He stared back at her.

"I hope not, Dorotea," he said stiffly.

"Ah, but you know," said Dorotea, and laughed very merrily. In fact, she was a very merry girl.

"You deduce," said Don Tomás, "that there is only one man in the world who could have done all these things—a daredevil who knows horses extremely well—"

"Horses—and other things," said the Rural. "But this, I swear, is El Keed. I have heard the description that Don Emiliano gave of him. Don Emiliano, let me ask you—"

"Ask and be damned," said Don Emiliano.

"Continue," urged Don Tomás.

"In fact," said Jalisca, "when you saw him did he seem like a big man?"

"He did," said Don Emiliano.

"Heavy in the shoulders?"

"Yes."

"And yet, somehow, even in his slightest movements, did he seem light enough to run up a tree?"

"Yes," said Emiliano Lopez, "light as a cat—very like a cat when he moved."

"He wore a mask?"

"Yes."

"And therefore you were not able to see his eyes clearly?"

"No."

"Nor the color of his hair?"

"It was black," said Lopez.

"And the color of his eyes—was it by any chance blue?"

Lopez started for the first time.

"Yes, blue, blue, blue!" he cried. "My God, the man knows! It *was* El Keed!"

"Ah-hai!" cried the girl. "How I should like to see him—"

"Dorotea!" said her father.

"In chains, with a rope round his neck," she ended.

"And what does all this come to?" asked Don Emiliano, passing his hand inside his shirt-collar to make the breathing more easy.

"It comes to this—that when he left this man swore that, if any harm came to the mother of Julio Mercado, he would come down like a hawk from the hills and have vengeance for it."

"He said those things. But how the devil do you know it? I've told only one person," said Emiliano Lopez.

"Señor, there are words that run like quicksilver through the body and pass into the open air," said the Rural.

"No matter where you hear—it is true," said Don Tomás, impatiently. "But what does all of this lead to?"

"It leads to a simple and beautiful thing," said Benito Jalisca. And he ran the red tip of his tongue across his lips.

"Continue," said the Lerraza.

"No harm, heretofore, has happened to the mother of this Mercado?" asked Jalisca.

"She is an old woman," said Emiliano. "She had nothing to do with the insanity of her son."

"Still, suppose that she were thrown into the cells? Suppose that she were taken and whipped, just a little, and then confined behind the steel bars?" suggested Jalisca.

"Ah?" said Don Tomás. "Do you think that this man, El Keed, fool and gringo that he is, would be rash enough to attempt to set her free?"

"Señor," said the Rural, "he is always fool enough to keep his word. It is a promise that he has given."

"He never would do it," said the rich man, shaking his head.

"Would he, though! Would he not, though!" murmured the girl.

THE SONG OF THE WHIP

"May I tell you a story?" said Jalisca.

"Tell it then," said Don Tomás. He took out a cigarette and lighted it from the ready match which Emiliano Lopez held.

"I tell you," said the Rural, "that on a time two scoundrels came to El Keed, who is called Montana in the land of the gringos, and told him of a rich man, named Lavery, who had lost a son, kidnapped by Mexicans years before. And there was a birthmark on that son, on his back. And the child had black hair and blue eyes. So they tattoed the birthmark on the back of Montana, called by us El Keed, and he went to the house of the rich millionaire, and the mark on his back was seen, and he was accepted as the son of Lavery. But then El Keed remembered that he had seen, long before, the so-called son of Mateo Rubriz, the bandit, and that son was named Tonio, and Tonio was captured, covered with wounds, in a terrible battle, by the Rurales, of whom I was one, and led into a city to prison. And as he went through the streets, half-naked, bleeding, El Keed saw on the back of Tonio the birthmark, the true birthmark. So he knew that that was the son of Lavery. And he came south into our country. Against the will of Tonio he carried him back to his own land, and Rubriz like a mad wildcat trailing them, striking at them. And so he gave Tonio back to his real fortune and name, which is that of Richard Lavery.... I tell you this, señor, to show you that there is in El Keed a devil such that other men cannot understand him, and he does things that no other men would do. But as surely as he gave up a good name, the love of a good family, and millions of pesos in land and cattle, so surely he will come down out of the mountains to redeem the promise he has made—if you so much as lift a finger against the mother of Julio Mercado."

"Ah!" said Don Tomás.

"Let it be done!" cried Dorotea Lerraza. "Seize the peon woman. Flog her. Throw her into the house behind the barred window. And *there* see if El Keed is such a man as they say he is."

"Patience, patience, little one," said Don Tomás. "All this shall be done, and presently."

CHAPTER 6

Brother Pascual paused. He put down his staff. He lifted it again and jammed it down hard into a crevice among the rocks, splintering the heavy, strong point of the wood a little.

Still he could hear the song as it floated down the mountain pass, coming among the great rocks, drifting down from the barren hills which took the blue and the brightness of the sky.

It was an old song. He had heard it before, and it had made him shake his head because it was not entirely a moral lyric. But now his heart ached a little because he recognized the voice of the singer.

Who can translate into our hard, heavy English, the swiftly blurring words of the Mexican tongue? But to take it line by line and try to reproduce it, the verses ran somewhat as follows:

> March wind, when will you blow again
> And empurple our mountains with flowers?
> April, when will you breathe upon us
> And polish our eyes with soft light?
> May, when will your breeze be blowing,
> Blowing my lover to me in the night?

The last line is not at all like the original, because the last line of the original could hardly be written even by the hardiest author without blushes. But in Mexico people laugh at what are called, in our cold country, "the facts of life."

At any rate, Brother Pascual remained there, listening, and leaning on the huge handful of his staff, until around the bend of the trail came a girl so light-footed that she seemed about to spring from the earth.

When she saw the friar, she threw out her arms with a cry and ran to him. She laid her hands on his great, broad, heavily-muscled shoulders and leaped up and kissed him on either cheek. She was panting and laughing as she stood back from him and said: "Brother Pascual! Ah-hai! How happy I am to see you! And what a strange thing it is that with all this trudging across the mountains your stomach never grows smaller!"

She pushed a forefinger into the folds of his robe, above the belt.

"Why do you say that, Rosita?" he asked, forgetting what he had been about to say. "As a matter of fact, you see that my stomach is not so very large, but I pull my robe up, here, in order to give my legs better room for walking, and that makes a big fold of this heavy cloth. But really I am not fat."

"I can't believe that until I see," said Rosita.

"In that case——" said Brother Pascual in his simplicity. He made a gesture, but desisted in time. He said: "Ah, Rosita, you are almost a child of the devil! He is never very far away from you."

"He has such good taste," said Rosita.

"Yes," said Brother Pascual. "You are rather a pretty girl."

"You see a thousand prettier every day," said Rosita.

"No, I don't think so," said Brother Pascual. "When I walk through the mountains and think, ever, of lovely women, they all wear your face."

"What are you doing walking through the mountains and thinking of lovely women, Brother?" she asked.

He withdrew the staff from the crevice where it had bitten deep and then struck it home again, heavily, with all the weight of his huge arm.

"Do you know, Rosita," he said, "that there are times when I don't know how to talk with you?"

"Did you ever know how to talk with women—except old ones?" she asked him.

"I? Well, I'm not sure," he said.

"Why aren't you sure?" she asked.

"I never have asked," said Brother Pascual sadly. "Do I talk very badly to women?"

"You talk so that I love you," said Rosita. She tried to kiss him again. He put out a huge brown hand, as big as two, and warded her off.

"Rosita, I have to talk to *you*, my dear," said the giant.

"I am ready to listen. Shall we walk along?"

"I never can think when I'm walking," said the huge friar.

"Then what a lot of time you waste on mountains and such things," said the girl.

"I was going to talk to you about something—I forget what," he said.

"It was something about me," she said.

"Yes," he answered. "It was about your song. Yes, it was about the beautiful—I mean, it was about the bad song you were singing, Rosita, as you came through the mountains."

"I thought there was no one except the mountains—and the sheep—to hear me," she said. "I wasn't singing it for men, dear Brother."

"Why do you have to have men constantly in your thoughts?" asked the friar.

"What else is there for a girl to think about?" she asked.

"There are these mountains, and the blue, pure sky over them, and sacred life eternal above the blue, Rosita."

"I asked, what is there for a *girl* to think of?"

"Hush, Rosita. Sometimes you make me a little angry."

"But, Brother Pascual, if I sang about those beautiful, sacred things, what would be left for you?"

"I don't know," said the friar, troubled. But suddenly he lifted and stamped down his staff again.

"You are laughing at me once more, Rosita," he said.

"Not very much," said the girl.

"You are, though. But, Rosita, it is not that you anger me. It is because you sadden me still more. You should not go through the world singing about men."

"I don't go singing about men. I was singing about the wind."

"Now God forgive you, poor child," said the friar. "And God forgive me for finding you so pretty that I cannot be angry with you."

"But really I am not singing about men, but only about *a* man."

"Is that any different?"

"As different," said Rosita, "as holy wedlock—and the other thing. We don't want to talk about that."

"No, no, no!" said the friar. "Of course we don't. But—ah—Rosita, my dear—"

"Yes, Brother?"

"I was about to say—What was I about to say?"

"Something about *the* man."

"Have you found one?"

"I have."

"Does he love you?"

"A little," she said, canting her head to one side in thought.

"Is he a good man, Rosita?"

"He talks well," she said.

"Ah, Rosita," he protested, "have you been captured by some smooth young tongue?"

"He is a very brave man," she said.

"So he says," murmured the friar, shaking his head.

"And I love him so much that he has taken me all this distance into the mountains."

"I must pray for you, Rosita."

"Pray a little for yourself, too."

"I shall. I do."

"But what brought *you* so far into the mountains? *This* is not your parish or your place where men look for you."

"The poor friars, Rosita, must go wherever there are men who need help and comfort, either of the flesh or of the spirit."

"But, Brother, are you going to many men, or towards one?"

"In this case I am travelling towards one man."

"Is he a man who needs you?"

"Yes."

"Is he a great sinner?"

"There are few greater sinners, Rosita."

"When you talk to him and pray over him, will he listen?"

"Listen? I hope so."

"Has he ever listened before?"

"Rosita, what are you talking about?"

"Brother Pascual, Brother Pascual, what a dear blind idiot you are! Don't you think I know?"

"What do you know?"

"I am here on the same trail that you are travelling."

"That seems to be true, since I met you on it."

"Don't you see that I'm going towards the same man?"

"Kind Heaven!" murmured the friar.

"Not always so kind—but may it bring me to him! You are hunting for El Keed."

"Rosita, is it he whom you love?"

"Why do you say that as though it were a pain to you? You love him also."

"True. But he never will give happiness to a woman."

"He will to me—a little."

"Rosita, that way lies sin."

"Isn't there always a little sin in happiness?"

"Hush, child. Happiness in sin? Sin in happiness? Of course not!"

"What should I do?"

"Marry some good man, child."

"One who goes to bed at ten o'clock and keeps a shop?"

"Why not?" asked the friar.

"Well, Brother," she said, "would you be here among the strange mountains and the strange people for the sake of such a shopkeeper?"

"I hope so," he said.

"You hope—but would you?"

He was a very honest man. He fingered his staff and shook his head.

"This is all very strange," he said. "You begin to show me my heart—and God forgive me."

"God will love you all the more, Brother."

"Do you know, Rosita, that you seem to be teaching me, and yet I should be the teacher?"

"Walk on with me. If we talk about him we'll be teaching one another. Do you want to talk about him?"

"My heart aches to speak of him. . . . Who could call him a bad man, Rosita?"

"Who could call him a good man?" she asked. "He's a robber, of course."

"That is true. But so kind, Rosita. So gentle. So brave."

"And how many men has he killed?"

"True. That is true! He has killed men. For every one he has killed, I have said a hundred prayers—but still, he has killed men. That saddens me very much. I don't wish to think of that."

"We must think of that if we think of him."

"True," said the friar. "So sing me a song, Rosita, as we walk along towards him."

She lifted her head and sang that old Mexican song which says:

> The lizard runs into the crevice,
> The goat bounds down the mountain-face,
> The hawk drops from the sky,
> And I know that he has come, he has come,
> The ringing of his spurs soon will be near me
> And I see . . .

"Hush, Rosita," said the friar.

She was laughing, and panting for breath, because she had been dancing on the trail as she sang.

She said: "Well, when my heart is full of him, I have to sing him, I have to dance him. Hurry on! How lucky that I met you, Brother! Because you are the password that will take me into the valley."

"What do you know about the valley?" he asked.

"I know whatever men expect me not to know," said the girl, and she began to laugh again. The friar put back his shoulders, shook his head, and strode on in gloomy thought. He saw that questions and their answers never would bring him closer to Rosita.

CHAPTER 7

The man from the north was a desert rat, lean, sun-dried, wrinkled deeply about the eyes. The eyelashes had been sunfaded until they were almost blond. He stood before Rubriz, who walked impatiently up and down the room, glowering first at the messenger, and then at Julio Mercado, who stood by the window, shaking his head in trouble.

Finally Rubriz said: "You—hold your tongue. You've told me and Mercado. Don't tell another soul. Above all, don't tell El Keed."

He waved the fellow out of the room and turned to Mercado.

"If El Keed learns that your mother has been whipped—a little bit—and locked up, he will go straight as a pigeon north to the Lerraza place. He will fly into the fire. That's what it is. A fire. Nothing can come near that place without being killed. They've raised hundreds of armed men. Every trail is watched for fifty miles in every direction. They want to crucify El Keed and tear the skin off his body while there still is a little life in him.... You understand, Julio?"

"I understand," said Mercado, blinking.

"Afterwards," said Rubriz, "I'll go myself, with some of my men, and I'll manage to get her out safely. Afterwards—when things have quieted down a little. And she—why, she's a tough old woman, isn't she? She's a real little old *viejita,* isn't she? Of course she is! Very well, then. She'll endure. Jail will be a rest for her. And afterwards I'll have her out, safe and sound. You hear?"

"Yes, señor."

"And you believe?"

"Yes, señor."

"Then get out of my sight. You've brought me too much trouble. More than you're worth. . . . And if a whisper about this comes to the ears of El Keed—I'll take off your hide like a goatskin!"

They still were feasting in honor of the return of the Kid. And as long as he remained with them, or as long as the supply of beef and goats and sheep held out, there was sure to be high barbecue and great rejoicings.

That night a special luxury was produced on the table—for a noble porker was roasted on the great spit and placed whole before Rubriz. He was in his element when it came to carving such a dish. He had a broad-bladed axe with which he clove through the bones. With his hunting-knife, which had a sixteen-inch blade, he severed great cuts and slices, which were passed along the table. That table was something to be remembered. It was on account of the table that the house had been built on that site. For here lay a mighty pine tree, fallen to the ground in a storm at the end of an ancient life. It struck the imagination of Rubriz, and while some of his men set to work to build the log cabin around the fallen trunk, he and some of the others of his men, with fire and with heavy axes and adzes, began to work at the fallen monster.

First, they gouged away the top half of the tree, producing in this manner a vast slab of solid pine eight feet in diameter and weighing many tons. Then they fell to work on the under surface, which they mined away until they had made knee room and even room to stretch out the legs beneath the massive log. It was taking on the shape of a table now. At one end a specially capacious hollow was carved where Rubriz himself sat. At the other end there was an exactly similar niche which was never occupied, ordinarily. But on this night the Montana Kid was ensconced there. The ends of the log had been levelled off and made into great heart-shaped buttresses. The table was now exactly forty feet long and yet the log was so vast that it tapered only a little from one end to the other, and gave an odd aspect of tricky perspective. Around this huge board sat over twenty men, and in the center of the table were carved the initials or the full names of many others. For the huge board was a sort of Round Table with the titles of the knights inscribed.

Most the men were young in years. In the sort of life they lived, a man is a veteran after two years of riding and shooting, and if he lives five years on end he is considered one chosen out by good fortune. A good number of these lads had served with

Mateo Rubriz for more than five years, but that was because he was well known for his ability to bring his crew with small harm through mighty adventures.

All the score of those present were famous men, except for Julio Mercado, the latest recruit. There was Viljoen, celebrated for his cleverness with a knife. It was Viljoen who came down from the mountains alone against General Papantla and his thousand men. Viljoen crept through the camp and in the silence of the night men heard a slight whistling in the air; a blow was struck; a great knife buried itself in the breast of the general. And when they picked up the dead body and removed the knife, they found written on the haft of it: "Affectionate wishes to the dear general for a happy voyage. Viljoen."

When they hunted for Viljoen he was gone in the dark which had covered his coming.

Colonias was a round-faced little man with an expression as naïve and smiling as that of a country girl. He had a genius for drawing secrets out of the stoutest minds.

Paredon was a celebrated pickpocket and all-round sneakthief. It was said of Paredon that he had been able to steal the gold tassels of a bishop's cloak while he was kneeling to receive the blessing of the churchman.

Robles lived for the sake of his guns. He kept a pair of them always in fine condition and ready at his hand. He was a very quiet, good-natured man except when he was sent on a dangerous mission, and then his talents overmastered him. He was apt to kill for the pleasure of the killing.

Orozco was the man who went clear to Mexico City because he had seen in a newspaper a picture of the splendid horses of the President of the Republic. Orozco stole those horses and rode them all the way back to the north.

Behind every face at that table there was a story, and a good and long one. They were so many tigers, but the strong hand of Rubriz kept them well in check. Now he presided over his board with a happy face, sweating, shining his contentment on all who were there. And as the huge, steaming slices of pork were distributed, together with stacks of admirable tortillas, and red-hot frijoles cooked in three different ways, and crusted whole-wheat bread, and marvellous new corn, roasted, incredibly delicate, and sweet to the center of the cob. As all these things were being passed around the table together with a river of red wine, the door of the great room opened and the mighty form of Brother Pascual appeared on the threshold.

The whole table stood up with a roar. Rubriz, leaping on to his chair, ran barefooted down the center of the table towards the door. From the table he bounded to the floor and there caught both hands of the big, smiling friar. The men were shouting, lifting their wine cups as they came crowding around the new guest.

Montana did not hurry. He waited until there was a dense mass of men around big Brother Pascual, each thrusting forward his wine cup and hoping to be distinguished by having his wine accepted first; then the Kid ran lightly forward, put a hand on the shoulder of a rearward member of the crowd, and vaulted lightly high into the air. He landed at the side of Brother Pascual.

There was a rousing yell at this exploit. But it was nothing to what followed. For the friar, to give token of his happiness at meeting with the Montana Kid again, gripped him in both hands and lifted him bodily high above his head. There he sustained that writhing, twisting, kicking weight while he marched straight forward to the table.

The men of Rubriz went mad with delight when they saw that celebrated fighting-man held on high, helpless, like a little child. Montana, unable to free himself, had to submit with a smile. But his face was crimson when he was replaced carefully upon his feet by the huge friar.

Here the cook appeared with a huge tankard that would hold at least a quart, and into this half a dozen cups of the red wine were emptied until it was filled with red foam to the brim.

Friar Pascual lifted the mighty cup. He raised his eyes also and exclaimed: "Lord God, look down on these evil men and see only the good that is in them. Amen!"

After that he sat down between two of the bandits, who were ready to draw knives to herd the rest of the men away from him. But the others refused to keep at a distance. They would swarm up and clap him on the back, or finger the vast muscles of his arms and tell him that he was dwindling to the meagerness of a stripling lad.

He started up from his place, suddenly, exclaiming: "Mateo! Mateo! I've almost forgotten the most important point.... But do you remember the dancing-girl, Rosita? She has come here with me because she guessed, as I guessed, that El Keed would be here with you. She guessed as soon as she heard the story about what had happened at the Lerraza hacienda. Shall she enter? Shall she come in?"

A voice said, near the door: "Who talks about letting a girl come into the fellowship? Who talks about having a woman here?"

All eyes turned towards the speaker, and there they saw the handsome face and the tall, lithe body of Richard Lavery. He was laughing as he added: "And what sort of guard is kept over the valley when a man can ride into it in the wake of a fat friar, and never receive a single challenge?"

From half the throats of the bandits the shout arose, "Tonio!" in memory of the long years when the kidnapped lad had been raised among the robbers as the true son of Mateo Rubriz. But then they fell into a sudden, rather alarming silence. For it was only known that "Tonio" at last had been stolen away from the band through the agency of the Montana Kid. What the relations were now between "father" and son no man could tell.

They looked towards Rubriz as the lad advanced, and there was much to study in the face of the chief. He had put a foot on his chair as though he would run to the welcome of "Tonio" Lavery even as he had run to the friar, but on second thought he put the foot back on the floor and drew himself up proudly, waiting. He was breathing hard. His red cap had been knocked to one side of his head. With an air partly savagely defiant, half in startled expectancy, he remained staring as Richard Lavery came slowly over the floor. He himself was in an equal doubt, it was apparent. He grew pale. His head lifted haughtily. When he was a pace or two from Rubriz he came to halt. Not a breath was drawn in the big room until "Tonio," giving way to the old impulse, suddenly threw open his arms and caught Rubriz in a great embrace. The bandit, in return, crushed him to breathlessness. He began to laugh and shout with such joy that the tears ran down his ugly face.

"Let all men bear witness to this!" thundered Rubriz. "Friendship is greater than the love of women and the love of God. Here, when El Keed appears, the others throng to him. I was alone with my rascals one day, and the next I am surrounded by true hearts! ... My God! I could give my blood more freely than I ever cut throats in my life...."

The thundering voice of the friar broke in again: "But the girl, Mateo! The girl! What about Rosita?"

"I'll go out to see her," said Montana, frowning. "She should have had better sense—"

THE SONG OF THE WHIP   45

Here that terrible warrior of the knife, Viljoen, leaped up with an Indian yell.

"Bring her in with her eyes blindfolded," he cried. "If she knows El Keed by the touch of her hands in the darkness, she is his; otherwise she belongs to the man she chooses—"

Here there was a babel of blood-curdling battle yells.

"Call to her, Brother!" directed Rubriz.

"No!" shouted Montana.

But his voice was entirely drowned by the uproar made by the others.

Rubriz, laughing heartily, clapped his hand on the shoulder of the Kid.

"Be quiet. Be content," he said. "Or do you love this girl enough to marry her?"

"I don't know," said Montana.

"If you don't know, you don't care. At any rate, leave everything to me. All shall be as you wish."

The friar, reaching the door, was shouting loudly. Half a dozen of the men of Rubriz followed him. Running past him, they made their capture in the dark. The shrill, sharp outcry of the girl made the Kid leap. Rubriz caught him with the hands of a giant.

"Hush! Hush!" he said. "If a girl is fool enough to come to this part of the world, she must play a new game in a new way. My men are not servants of the law, they are makers of it... But you shall see. No harm will come to her."

At this moment they had brought her through the door of the hall. A big bandana knotted about her head effectively masked her.

She cried out: "El Keed—is he here?"

And twenty throats howled: "Yes!"

Rubriz held Montana on one side; young "Tonio" Lavery held him on the other.

Richard Lavery was saying: "Be still, old fellow. These wild devils, when they take an idea into their heads, will put it through. Rubriz can hardly stop them except by craft. You have to submit. No harm will come to her. You and Rubriz and I will see to that."

They were explaining, at the end of the hall, the terms under which she was brought into the place. Viljoen wound up by yelling: "She will choose me, brothers! My blood tells me that she will choose me. But all of you be still. Not a whisper. Each man take his place at the table. Now, Rosita, ask your hands to be true friends. Ask them to have eyes. But remember that there is not a man in the place who's not in love with you—"

Another tremendous shout of affirmation drowned his voice.

Rosita, being led to the table, touched the first man—a scar-faced youth of twenty years and thirty battles. Over his features she ran the tips of her fingers and went on.

He said: "If I could kill Oñate again, I would do it, and twenty times over, because he signed his name on my face with his knife. When you open your eyes, sweetheart, look at me again; you'll find that I'm worth as much as El Keed, seven days in the week, in spite of this face of mine."

She passed on, running her hands delicately over the face of man after man; and she threw herself enough into the moment to begin to sing that famous old Mexican song which runs like this:

> He is not swifter than the puma;
> His right hand is less strong than the grizzly's paw;
> He is not so tall as a tall pine tree;
> The mountain lakes are bluer than his eyes,
> But among all men, he alone is mine!

There are many verses to that old song, always ending with the same last line. Rosita kept on singing, while she went from man to man until she was two-thirds of the way around the table. In the meantime the men whom she had touched and passed over were joining in the singing of the song with the silver-bright thread of her soprano running lightly above their deeper voices. Those who waited kept the beating of the measure, silently, their eyes burning as they watched the progress of the girl.

She had reached the place where "Tonio" Lavery sat—and there she paused.

Montana, seated beside his friend, saw her hands linger over that handsome face. He saw the lips of Lavery part to whisper a word that would correct her in case she were about to make a mistake. But the word was not uttered. In spite of the uproar of the singing, Montana could be sure that Dick Lavery had not spoken.

Suddenly the singing ceased, as though a signal had been given. All could see that she was on the verge of making a choice. And the Kid saw a slight shudder of excitement pass over the body of Lavery.

And still the word of warning was not spoken.

THE SONG OF THE WHIP

He could remember the old saying, that all is fair in love and in war. And as a matter of fact, Rosita, even blindfolded, was beautiful enough to make the heart of a man leap, and the grace of her hands alone was like music in the eyes of the men of Rubriz.

"Tonio" had grown pale. He stared up into the girl's face as she leaned over him, hesitant, her head close to his.

She lifted a hand.

"My masters," she said, "if I go on, can I come back to this man?"

There was a shout of protest.

Rubriz, enjoying the game, laughed: "Make one choice! Only one choice!"

"Ah-hai!" cried Rosita, suddenly. "If my heart and my eyes are not in my hands, God forgive me. *This* must be he!"

And to make her choice more definite, she slipped suddenly into the lap of "Tonio" Lavery.

Then, while the yell lifted the roof, she snatched the blindfold from her eyes and saw what she had done.

She tried to leap up. Other hands held her down until "Tonio" waved them away. Then he helped the girl to her feet. "Here!" he said. "This is the man . . . and I—well, I must be the unlucky one."

He laughed, but his face was white. And Montana saw the whiteness. Rosita, catching the back of Montana's chair, closed her eyes and dropped her head against his shoulders as he rose.

"You see," she said, "that I had almost reached the right place? . . . But these hands of mine are worth nothing. I would throw them away and take the paws of an ape instead. How could they have thought another man was you? . . . Forgive me!"

Rubriz was thundering: "She has to pay for her man. He cannot be given to her. Toss her up on the table. Where are the guitars? Music! Music! And she shall dance for us!"

They tossed Rosita into the air. Half a dozen guitars began to clang and tremble. Hands beat and feet stamped to make the rhythm. And Rosita went spinning up and down the center of the great table with feet that winked in and out of the eyes of the beholders. She danced with feet and body and arms and laughter, and always returning in her dance, she made her point in the bow and the special smile that gave thanks to handsome "Tonio" Lavery.

The Kid, watching her, nodding and laughing with apparent pleasure, really was seeing one thing only—and that was the staring, entranced face of Dick Lavery.

The dance ended in a great shouting.

A chair was placed for the girl between Montana and Lavery. She sat on the edge of it, panting, hardly touching the great platter of food that was put before her.

"Was it all right? Was it good? Are you pleased with me?" she asked.

Montana smiled at her... but still there was Lavery just beyond her, pretending not to notice that she was at the table—but a little white, a little strained, talking with too careless an abandon of many things until someone asked him what way he had ridden.

"Close to the hacienda of the Lerrazas," he answered. "I wanted to know what they had to say, still, about the coming of El Keed."

"Hai, muchacho!" cried Rubriz. "Do you forget that in Mexico you are still known as a *bandido?* Do you forget that they have ropes, in this country, to hang every man that ever rode with Mateo Rubriz?"

"Well, I found them still talking," said Lavery, "and Lerraza in such a rage that he and Don Emiliano have taken the poor old mother of Mercado, flogged her, and thrown her behind bars...."

"Be quiet!" exclaimed Rubriz.

He held up one hand. The whole table was silent, staring not at Mercado, the new recruit, but at the Montana Kid.

He rose slowly from his chair.

"Did you know about this, Mateo?" he asked coldly. "Did you know about it and keep it from me?"

"How should I know about it?" asked Rubriz. "I am not a—"

"Mercado!" called Montana.

The peon leaped to his feet.

"We ride to-night," said Montana, and turned on his heel from the table.

CHAPTER 8

In every Mexican town there is a café or something that takes the place of a café. In the town of Lerrazas there was a hovel, a broad-spreading shade tree with little round tables placed under it, and a supply of pulque together with fire-hot brandy. In the hut a fire kept the pot of frijoles simmering, and together with the drinks there could be supplied, always, a certain amount of food. The great Lerraza himself, the celebrated Don Tomás in person, rode out on this day with his daughter Dorotea on the one hand and Don Emiliano on the other, and when he came to the café in the failing light of the evening he paused to look on from the back of his horse at the scene of merriment.

The next day one of the important events in the history of the Lerrazas was to be performed, for the daughter of the house was to be betrothed, solemnly, to Emiliano Lopez. There was to be a huge entertainment at the great house, and from miles around the people had poured into the village, preparing to come to the free eating and drinking at the hacienda. Don Tomás was pleased by the signs of festival which he saw in his town—where he owned every mud brick, and every soul that lived inside the whitewashed walls. It was proper and fitting that his peons should laugh and sing and dance like fools to celebrate the festivities of the morrow. It seemed to Don Tomás that for the lower orders there is nothing so fitting as an opportunity to see the sports and the pastimes of the higher classes.

He was rather touched that, on account of his family, all the peons should not be making merry in the village. He reined in his horse, therefore, and looked down at the gathering under the tree. And behind him his bodyguard of a dozen chosen fighting-men drew in their reins, also, and there was a jingling of bridle chains and a light clanking of spurs. The horses fretted a little, stretching out their heads against the bits, and stamping. But these small noises did not attract the attention of the crowd under the tree. Their eyes were riveted on a dancing-girl who spun barefooted on the naked ground.

"You see, Dorotea," said Don Tomás, "that the people already are honoring you; all this dancing and music and laughter is in honor of your betrothal to-morrow."

At this she lifted her fine head and looked curiously at her father.

"Do you think so?" she said. "Don't you see, father, that all the men under that tree are simply dizzy about that pretty dancing-girl?"

"About her?" asked Lerraza, scowling. "Why, what is she? Tut, tut! Merely a little ragamuffin picking up a few pesos a week by dancing her feet raw on the bare ground."

"My dear," said Dorotea, "if you dressed her in chiffon, she would do for the stage in Mexico City—or Paris, for that matter. She's an artist. *What* in the world is she doing in Lerrazas town?"

"I'll ask her," said Don Emiliano.

She had come to the end of her dance, and there was a wild uproar of applause.

One of the peons, a giant of strength, was so inspired that he had to dance in his turn, and the only way he knew of making the beauty his partner was by picking her up in the chair into which she had sunk and so whirling and wheeling and prancing with the girl still in the chair and elevated above his head.

Two or three excited guitars furnished the music. And when the peon finally staggered to a halt, exhausted, and the girl had sprung down to the ground, laughing, Don Emiliano called out loudly.

The dancing-girl came at once through the opening lane of the peons, who fell back with a start from the imposing array of the gentry. She made curtsies to all three.

"What brought you to Lerrazas?" asked Dorotea.

"I heard that the beautiful señorita was to be betrothed, and I hoped that I might have a chance to see her," said the girl and bowed until her head almost touched the ground.

"Stuff!" said Dorotea. "What is your name?"

"Rosita, if the name pleases you, señorita."

"Do these fellows give you much money when you dance for them, Rosita?" asked the other girl.

"They give me a great many bits of copper," said Rosita. "And that is enough for me."

"Do you know that you ought to have silver and gold?" asked Dorotea.

"Señorita, that is a thing to dream of but never to see."

"Do you know something, Rosita? I think you've had those pretty hands of yours overflowing with gold and silver long before this."

"I? Ah, señorita! If that were so, why would I be here in rags?"

"That's what I'd like to know," said Dorotea. "Come closer to me."

Rosita, bowing again, came close to the shoulder of Dorotea's horse, and the girl leaned from the saddle and ran her hand over the face of the dancer.

She murmured: "How many fine creams have you used to make that skin so velvety, Rosita? And what did you pay for that French perfume? There's just an echo of it left but I think I recognize it. I've used it myself, and I've had gifts of it and valued the presents. . . . Tell me, Rosita, who you are and what you are doing here?"

Rosita murmured, in a voice equally low: "Señorita, you see everything and know everything. And you can tell what a poor girl will do for the sake of the man she loves?"

"Is it someone who makes you wander like a poor little beggar around the world? Is it someone who takes away the money you earn?" asked Dorotea curiously.

"No, señorita. It is a proud devil of a man who will hardly look at me."

"What sort of a man, Rosita?"

"One with blue-eyes, señorita."

"Is he here in Lerrazas?"

"I hoped to find him here."

"What is his name?"

"He has several names, and only the kind saints can tell which one he will be using."

"Do you mean that he's an outlawed man?"

"Alas, señorita!"

"I think I knew when I saw you," said Dorotea, "that you were too pretty to be happy altogether. . . . Tell me—will you come to the house of my father to-morrow, and dance for the guests?"

"Señorita, if it would give you pleasure. . . ."

"What are you two talking about?" asked Don Tomás.

"Give her some money," said Dorotea. "She is coming to dance for our guests to-morrow at the house, and she'll need some money to buy proper clothes."

"Can she find them here in the village?" asked Don Emiliano.

"Money can find anything in a Mexican town. You'll see!" said Dorotea.

Don Tomás, reaching into his wallet, took out a whole handful of coins and showered them into the cupped hands of Rosita, and then the trio rode on, while the sweet, soprano voice of Rosita called out blessings after them.

"What did she tell you?" asked Don Emiliano.

"Oh," said Dorotea, "she told me two or three little secrets that men ought not to know."

Afterwards, in a dry draw behind the town, in a little hollow further sheltered by a thick growth of shrubbery and filled with bright moonshine, Rosita sat on the bank and waited until she heard a sharp whistle down the gorge. She answered it with two shrill notes, and out of the distance, presently, she heard the thrumming hoofs of two horses.

They came up at the full gallop, were halted and two big young men jumped down to the ground. Montana threw the reins of his horse to "Tonio" Lavery and went to the girl.

"What have you found, Rosita?" he asked.

"Bah!" said the girl. "I come away for three whole days, I sweat and leap and prance and sing myself hoarse; I let the greasy peons hold my hand; and I smile at them and pretend their garlic breaths are sweet as May flowers—and then you come and say: 'What have you found?' I have found three days of wretchedness, if you want to know."

"Beautiful Rosita," said Montana, "adored of my heart, pearl of virtue, moon of my darkened life, radiance of—"

"Stop it!" commanded the girl.

"As a matter of fact," said Montana, "I'm too busy to be polite."

"Ah-hai!" cried Rosita. "Polite? Polite? . . . Are you the witness to that, Tonio? This is the man who swears on holidays that he is my lover; but I forgot that this is only an ordinary day of the week."

"He's cold-blooded, Rosita," said Tonio. "If I were you, I'd leave him. No girl can keep in his eye for more than ten days. But here is Tonio who has a heart ever faithful. . . ."

"Be quiet, Dick," said Montana. "Sit down here and talk to me, Rosita. . . . When did you start whining like a spoiled baby? That's not the old Rosita that I used to know. . . . And where's the friar? Where's my Brother Pascal?"

THE SONG OF THE WHIP

"Stuck in a bramble bush, somewhere—tangled up in a cactus, for all I know or care."

"Where's Rubriz? Where's Mercado? They both should be here."

"I don't know. I'm not their keeper."

"You have a devil in you to-night."

"You don't deserve anything better," said the girl. "You're only a gringo lover, after all. What do I expect from you except a cold heart and contempt and—"

Montana yawned. "Don't be a bore, Rosita," he said. "This Mexican snapdragon stuff isn't worth a damn. One of these days you'll stick a knife in somebody when you get into one of your tempers, and then I'll have a devil of a time getting you out of the hoosegow."

"You won't care," said the girl. "You'll have forgotten me. You'll be away with another woman."

"She's not like this except when she has an audience," said Montana. "She's a good, steady, wholesome girl, born to be a housewife and darn stockings and socks, and stew frijoles, and make tortillas, but when there's a stranger around she has to be what the stranger expects a Mexican girl to be. Now, Rosita, have you found out anything worth knowing?"

"Ai-hai!" sighed Rosita. "When you talk like this, I see my whole sad life spread out before me. And I know that I was born for unhappiness. . . . Here is what I've learned. Here's the plan of the entire house of Lerraza."

"I have that already," said Montana. "What else?"

"The names of the people in the rooms."

"Where's Mercado's mother?"

"She's kept in the old rooms that serve as a jail for the lawbreakers on the hacienda."

Montana had spread out the sheet of paper, frowning at it in the dimness of the moonlight.

"Which room is hers?"

"Here—under the others. In a cellar room."

"The dog of a Lerraza!" said Montana. "To put a poor old soul in such a place!"

"You see, Tonio," said the girl, "for other women he has pity, even for old ones."

"Leave him, Rosita. You and I were made for one another. Every day I'll make a poem for you and set it to music, and sing it, too."

"He has a damned, cracked voice on the high notes," said

Montana. "Your ears would ache, listening to him . . . they've put her down here in the cellar? What sort of a lock is on the door?"

"They've put in new American locks on all the doors."

"The devil!" groaned Montana.

"You gringos have one good thing—your jails," said Rosita. "How many jails have you been in?"

"One for every finger on your sweet hands, Rosita . . . A cellar room, with a Yale lock on the door, and—how many guards?"

"The house is filled with armed men."

"Crowds always are blind," said Montana. "Only a fool will trust to numbers. In an army, each man trusts to the next fellow and nothing ever is done. . . . Rosita, you're better than diamonds."

"By the way, I'm asked to dance at the great house to-morrow and Don Tomás has given me money to buy new clothes."

"Don Tomás? What the devil are you doing with Don Tomás?"

"Why should I tell you where and when I meet the men who admire me?"

"Well, let it go, then."

"You see, Tonio? There is not even a spark of jealousy in him! *Ay de mi!* This is what it means to be in love with a gringo!"

CHAPTER 9

Afterwards, young Dick Lavery sat for a time with Rosita: out of the distance a whistled signal had taken big Montana away at a gallop, and Rosita put her head in her hands and swayed slowly from side to side.

He looked at her for a long time. If there had been only her hands to see, she would have been beautiful.

"If you weep because of him now, you will have to spend a great many tears about him later on," said Tonio.

She lifted her head suddenly, and he saw that her face was dry.

"If I were one of your gringo girls," she said, "I could be weeping. The sorrow would run out of me then and I could sleep, and in the morning already I would have half forgotten. But the old Mexican agony is in me, Tonio. And there are no tears in that. It is hot and dry as our summers. You are gringo yourself, and that is why you can't understand."

"I was raised in Mexico," said Lavery. "You know that Rubriz made me almost as Mexican as himself. All those years I was taught to hate the gringos and their ways—and I can't unlearn in a few months what I was taught my life long. I know what you mean by dry eyes and your heart burning."

"Do you know?" mourned the girl. "But you're young and rich and handsome, Tonio, and no girl would dare to make your heart ache."

"There is one who does, Rosita."

She did not seem to hear.

"But it is only his way," she said, musing. "He thinks I'm only laughing and pretending when I talk as I did to-night. He doesn't know that I'm almost serious."

"Shall I tell you something? There's nothing in the world that he cares about except a horse to carry him into trouble and a gun to fight his way out again."

"Ai-hai! I sometimes think so!"

"I know it. He was to marry my sister, Rosita. She'll have half my father's money. And she's a beauty, besides. But she couldn't hold Montana. Three times the day for the wedding was fixed, and three times something happened and Montana was not there. So it was given up. I think he was sorry—for a while. But he can't be sorry for long. As long as his hands are busy, his heart will take care of itself well enough."

She sprang up and struck her hands against her face.

"I'm going to forget him, Tonio!" she cried. "See how he galloped away with a wave of the hand! Does he think that I'm made of iron and dry mesquite wood? May God teach me to love some other man! Tonio, tell me a kind lie—tell me that *you* love me, and teach me to forget him!"

He caught her hands.

"I do, Rosita!" he exclaimed.

"Ah-hai! Hush, hush! You are trembling," said the girl. "Is it true then? In the name of the kind God, Tonio, never let a whisper of it come to his ears. Because if he thought that I had made trouble between him and you—ah, then he would hate me indeed, and my heart would be broken!"

And Tonio said nothing.

Afterwards, when he was alone, he tried to think, but nothing came into his mind except the voice of Rosita and the way the moonlight had brightened on her hands, in her eyes. That dry, bitter, intense longing of which she had spoken came over him. It was true that he had lived too much of his life in Mexico to escape being a Mexican. The thing was like a poison in his blood. He could not be rid of it.

And then his mind began to work, swiftly, thrusting towards a definite and terrible conclusion.

It was later, when a house mozo at the Lerraza hacienda came to Don Tomás with word that a masked man waited outside the house and asked to speak with him.

"This is a very good thing!" said Tomás Lerraza. "A masked bandit rides up to my house and invites me outside so that he can pistol me at his leisure. Send word to my guards and have them capture him and drag him in here! *Then* I shall speak with him."

"Señor," said the mozo, "he has a horse that looks like a thoroughbred. It would run very fast. Perhaps it would not be overtaken. And this stranger, señor, speaks like a true gentleman.

You will think so, the moment you hear his voice."

"I shall go," said Don Emiliano, suddenly, and got up from his chair, where he had been listening to Dorotea at the piano. It was a wrecked tin-can of a piano, as the bad weather is apt to make them in that dry climate, warping the wood between the humid spells of rain.

"I'll follow to the garden wall and listen," said Dorotea.

That was what she did, while Don Emiliano rode dauntlessly out and found before him a tall man on a tall horse that looked like the finest of thoroughbreds. It had been in the mind of Don Emiliano that he might attack the stranger single-handed and bring him away into the house for a closer examination, such as Don Tomás had suggested. But when he saw the rider Lopez changed his mind. The long booster which contained the rifle, the crossbelt of ammunition worn across the chest, the two long revolvers, gave the stranger the look of a professional fighting-man. Lopez felt that discretion was the quality needed now.

A mask, or rather, a hood, covered the entire head and face of the stranger. His voice, however, was that of a young man, and he spoke Spanish like an educated gentleman.

He said: "You are not Don Tomás."

"I am Emiliano Lopez."

"You will do then. I've come to bring you a warning. Sometime to-morrow, either during the day or in the night, El Keed will appear in the house of Lerraza. Be on your guard!"

"Why does the fool come?" demanded Don Emiliano, sharply.

"Because of the old woman, the mother of Mercado."

"Do you mean," cried Lopez, "that he'll try to rush the house with brigands for the sake of one withered old hag of a peon woman?"

"He has given his word to her son. He will not fail to come."

"A thousand thanks for the warning. We shall be on our guard. Who are you?"

"If I could tell you my name, I would not wear a mask."

"How many men will he bring with him?"

"Not a crowd. Two or three, at the most. But each of them will be a fighting tiger."

"We shall be on the watch!"

"Remember that when his skin is darkened, he can go barefoot like a peon, and there is nothing to call him gringo except his blue eyes."

"We shall watch, always, for blue-eyed men."

"God give you strong hands."

Don Emiliano watched the stranger turn and ride away. Then he went slowly back toward the big mansion, and found Dorotea watching for him.

"I heard," she said. "And what a pity it is, Emiliano, that there should be traitors in the world."

"Traitors?" he echoed, emptily.

"Traitors, of course. That rider was a traitor. Depend on it that the money of El Keed bought the horse he was riding. He is one of El Keed's trusted fighters. Ai-hai! If I were a man I would rather have my tongue torn out of my throat than to betray a hero!"

"What are you speaking about, Dorotea? Hero? El Keed is a devil and a red-handed devil."

"I am going to talk with that old Maria Mercado," said the girl, and went straightway down to the cellar room where the old hag was imprisoned. She was allowed to come in at once, by the guard.

And what a guard it was! Four men, armed to the teeth, watched over the safe keeping of Maria Mercado night and day, three outside the door of her cell and one inside it.

She was an ugly old witch. She looked like one of those dried old goats that pasture on the naked hillsides and seem to live on the hard rocks rather than on real pasture. She sat cross-legged, knitting with rapid old hands in the dim light of a lamp. When she saw Dorotea, she jumped up, surprisingly light and young in her movements.

"God bless the señorita and bring her happiness," said Maria.

"Why do you pray for us? We have not been good to you," said Dorotea.

"It's a thing that we peons learn to do," said the old hag. "It's better to pray for the masters than to be beaten by them."

"I'm sorry you were whipped, Maria," said the girl.

"It didn't hurt me a great deal," said Maria. "Old hide is tough hide, you know. And then I had no pride to be hurt at all."

"Why have you no pride, Maria?"

"Because I have no hope," said the old woman. "The saying is: No pride with no hope."

"I'm sorry that you've been brought here," said the girl. "I would be glad to have you set free. But I've come to tell you a strange thing."

"Tell me, señorita. And God be kind to you twice over."

"Men are coming here to try to set you free from my father."

"They are fools," said Maria. "I've been a slave to him so long that I wouldn't know how to be the slave of another man."

"Not a slave, Maria. Only a peon."

"Slaves are better off than peons. Masters take care of slaves because they have to pay big money for them, many pesos. But for peons there is no charge at all."

"Maria, tell me—do you know who it is that will try to rescue you?"

"There is only one man in the world who would dare," said Maria.

"Who is that?"

"The gringo—El Keed."

"Does he know you? Is he fond of you, Maria?"

"I hate all gringos," said the old woman. "I would rather die in a dark cell than be rescued out of it by him."

"Do you mean that you would not go with him?"

"Not if kicking and screaming could stop him," said Maria Mercado.

"What? Stop the man that saved your son from such trouble?"

"Saved him from a whipping that already was finished, and made him a wretched outlaw? Is that saving my foolish Julio?"

The girl nodded her head while she peered at the crone.

"This is what it means to have the blood run cold!" she murmured. "Now I, old mother, would have other things to say to such a man as that! And I think that if he comes you will find your own mind younger than you think."

"Of course," said Maria Mercado, "the chicken never can tell whether it will fly or run until the hawk is over its head."

CHAPTER 10

The Kid sat on his horse at the side of Rubriz and Tonio Lavery. Julio Mercado remained a little in the background.

"You see now, Mateo," said the Kid, "why a crowd of your fighting-men and a bull-rush would not do the trick?"

Rubriz nodded. From the top of the hill, they could look down over the entire hacienda and see it mapped and charted in dotted lines of lights. The inner patio and the outer patio were particularly brilliant, for in these places, converted into rooms with the ground covered with matting, the main reception was going on. In there, the ladies and the gentry for many leagues around had been gathered. They were now listening to music at the end of the day in the inner patio, but they would pass from this place into the outer patio for the dinner which was being set out at the long tables. And there the betrothal would be announced with all due formality. But besides this inner core of guests of honor, there were outer lines of stirring people. For every family invited to the feast had come like a feudal lord surrounded by armed retainers. Literally, there were hundreds of riders, all armed to the teeth, all fighting-men by training and by instinct. They were enjoying great barbecue feasts on four sides of the house, but as a matter of fact their extended numbers made outer lines which hardly could be rushed by hostile forces. Kegs of drinks had been rolled out. Whole oxen were roasted, to say nothing of swine, chickens boiled in twenty-gallon vats, kids roasted on twenty big spits, and everything else that the heart of Mexico could desire.

The outer patio had been the first place of entertainment, in the afternoon, and potted trees borne into the place by swarms of peons, had furnished the shade during that hot time of the day. Now as the tables were laid, the trees were borne out, gradually by one stream of peons, and smaller potted plants and boughs of fragrant evergreens were carried in by a counter flood of workers.

THE SONG OF THE WHIP

And as the sound of music whirled up through the air to the listening ears of the four watchers, they could see in the inner patio the whirling, colorful figure of the dancer.

"Ah-hai! That Rosita!" said Rubriz. "If you marry her, *amigo*, you will become a true Mexican and stay with us forever."

"That is to say," said Tonio Lavery, "for a fortnight—or until his throat is cut, or the law hangs him, or a rifle bullet cuts him down, eh?"

"She's a treasure," said Montana. "The last word from her is that four men are guarding old Maria day and night."

"Then one man can do nothing to set her free," said Rubriz.

"Certainly not," said Montana.

"Then why are you dressed like a peon—as though you intended to get down there into the whirl of things?" asked Rubriz.

At this moment Montana was lighting a cigarette, and the flare of the match flame showed his face embrowned and dark with walnut stain. He smiled as he flicked out the match and drew in a breath of smoke.

Then he gestured toward his outfit, which consisted of white cotton trousers and a white shirt deeply opened at the throat and *huaraches* on his feet, with a broad-brimmed straw hat on his head—one of those straw sombreros that make all lower-class Mexico look alike.

"I'm going down there, but only to look about and listen," said Montana.

"What good will that do you?" demanded Rubriz, sharply. "What can you manage down there alone?"

"At least," said Montana, "I can be near things for a few minutes."

"I know what you mean," said Rubriz. "When I was your age I was the same way. God, how like we are to one another, in spite of your straight legs and my crooked ones!... But I know that you have to be near enough to the devil to feel the heat of his breath. Well, if you go down, be careful, *amigo!* The peons have eyes sharper than cats, and they might find you out."

"The peons will not lift a hand against him, even if they know," said Mercado, suddenly.

"Hello!" said Rubriz. "How do you know that?"

"I say what I know. I cannot tell how I know it," said the peon.

"I hope he's right," commented Montana. "And in case I find all the doors open and angels guarding the way—in case I come out with Maria Mercado—you'll be waiting up here to cover the retreat, Mateo?"

"You don't have such craziness in your mind?" demanded Rubriz.

"Certainly not," said Montana.

"But I'll be here, waiting," said Rubriz, "till the mountains are worn down smaller than molehills. *Adios, amigo!*"

Montana walked down the hill, leading his horse, which he tethered at a group of big rocks which sprouted like frozen vegetation out of the soil close to the hacienda.

Rubriz, looking after him, could not help exclaiming: "There, but for the weight of conscience, goes the greatest natural robber under heaven. *Valgame Dios!* What a bandido he would make! What a king for our mountains, above the law! But he cannot take except from an enemy—and a rich one. And how can the entire land be furnished with rich enemies to be robbed? . . . Tell me, Mercado! Was there ever another man such as El Keed?"

"No, señor," said the peon, fervently.

"Tell me, Tonio," said the outlaw. "Was there ever such a man?"

But Tonio did not answer. He was staring, rapt, at the illumined house of the Lerrazas.

Smoking his cigarette, big Montana walked straight on towards the lights of the outer lines of the barbecue. When he was close enough to see the details of the group, he paused and stared, fascinated; for there were a dozen men gathered around a great pot out of which chickens and strips of fat boiled bacon were being fished, and eaten with immense lumps of black bread.

A horse stopped behind Montana. A voice said: "What are you?"

"One who comes to look, señor."

"Look from farther off, dirt!" said the voice, and the lash of a quirt scaled the shoulders of Montana.

He had both a knife and a gun inside his shirt, but he turned and fled, dodging like a frightened rabbit, until he found himself on the main road to the hacienda.

There he paused, panting. A cart was coming up the road with a great jouncing and jostling, and as it went by he saw the long shaking plumes of evergreen branches, and smelled the mountain fragrance.

"Up, up, fools, and hurry us on!" the driver was crying as he flogged his mules. "We are late! We are late!"

Montana jumped on to the tail of the cart and slipped far in among the evergreens. There he crouched, making himself small. He heard the wheels thunder over the hollow of a small bridge. Then voices shouted and the cart stopped.

The driver stood up, yelling: "I am Miguel Oñate! I am Miguel Oñate! The señor ordered these branches from me with his own lips two days ago. No man dare to stop me! No man dare to stop me!"

"You flat-faced fool!" said a voice. "Nobody gives a damn whether you are stopped or dead or not. But we have to search every load."

"For what? For what?" shouted Miguel Oñate.

"For El Keed!" said the voice.

Oñate began to laugh.

"Ah, my God!" he cried. "Suppose that I were to have El Keed in my cart, would not my mules be running away for their lives?"

He laughed, and the voice rejoined: "No, mules and fools and peons all love El Keed because he's kind to the harmless.... Look into the load, *amigo*."

Someone climbed up on the tail of the cart. He had a great *machete* with blade almost two feet long, and this he thrust straight into the evergreen. Something cold kissed the face of Montana. It was the back of the blade. If it had been the sharp edge—

"Drive on, Oñate!"

The cart rumbled on. It approached many voices. And Montana slipped out of it and dropped to the ground.

He saw the cart drive on towards the outer patio of the hacienda. White-clad peons surrounded it. Many hands lifted out the contents and piled the boughs on the ground.

And Montana, looking back toward the lights of the line which he had penetrated, realized that it might even be easier to go on than to retreat. He walked straight up to the group.

One of the Lerraza guards in person was overlooking this portion of the work.

He said, "This is the last load. Pick it up and into the house with it, lads! Straight into the outer patio, and then turn about and get out of the way. There are other things for you to do!"

The peons began to pick up the evergreens, and Montana, mingling with them, picked up and shouldered a whole young tree.

"That's too much for one man," said another peon, and promptly seized on the tapering smaller end of it.

The two of them joined the long line that labored under burdens towards the lighted gate of the patio.

As they passed through into the light, they were directed this way or that by a sweating majordomo. And according to their direction, they delivered the burdens to the swarm of house mozos who put the greenery in place. The great outer patio was being transformed into a fragrant bower, in the midst of which the tables appeared, their white cloths silver under the moonlight and the flare of the lamps.

Montana, as he put down his end of the burden and stepped back into the group, heard a voice gasp: "El Keed!"

"What's that?" snapped the voice of an armed guard.

Montana, as he turned, saw half a dozen brown, broad faces staring at him. Then someone kicked a foot behind the knees of the peon who had breathed out the dangerous name. The fellow went down with a bump.

"What's that?" demanded the guard again, bursting into the group.

But a whining voice said: "Nothing, señor. This fool of a Juan Pedro stepped on my sore foot, that is all."

"That is all," muttered several others. But they were glancing askance at Montana. He would never forget the glistening whites of their eyes.

"Well," said the guard, "get out of this then! All of you, away. Do you think your garlic and your sweat makes the kind of perfume that the gentry are accustomed to smelling? Out with you. We need you no more in here!"

They began to stream away.

A voice gasped at the ear of Montana: "Pardon, brother. But when I saw you the name slid out between my teeth. This way—with me—we will cover you—"

But at the side, Montana saw two men rolling a big-potted plant up the two steps at the side of the patio and on to the veranda. He slipped to join them as he saw them sweating and struggling with too great a weight. His strength added to theirs soon had rolled the heavy burden back up the steps and so against the wall.

"There!" said one of the two, straightening and mopping his forehead. "You were just in time to keep my back from breaking, *amigo*. Now, if we take these rolls of extra matting out of the way, we'll be through. Jesús! How beautiful all the silver looks on the tables! And for every piece of silver, in the centuries, there's been the life of a peon laid down—"

Montana picked up a big roll of grass matting closely woven, a weight enough to have given labor to two men. But he managed to shoulder it, and walked straight through the open door.

He found a big room ablaze with lights, and off this, to the side, a dimmer corridor. Into the corridor he passed with the roll of matting.

A house servant in a natty white uniform went by him.

"What place for this?" asked Montana.

"Eat it, like the donkey you are," said the servant, and passed on.

The corridor turned a corner. A savor of cookery, rich with spices, pungent with peppers, came to the nostrils of Montana. On the right, laid over the backs of chairs, were a number of the clean white jackets worn by the house servants. He laid down the roll of matting, picked up one of the jackets, and tried to slip into it. It was much too small. A second was a shade too tight, also, but it would do.

"Out of the way! Out of the way!" called a voice.

Two men went by him, each carrying a huge silver tray filled with tinkling glassware. Montana had left his broad-brimmed straw sombrero in a corner.

He straightened and looked about him, and out of the distance, to his right, he heard a sudden outburst of clapping, and then a dull murmuring of voices that repeated a name obscure at first, and then familiar. They were cheering Rosita and asking for another dance. He smiled, and as he smiled he was able to place himself accurately in the mazes of the labyrinthine house.

CHAPTER 11

The next turn of the corridor brought him to the kitchen. It was a huge room with a fume of steam and smoke inside and hurrying figures rushing about through the steam. One wall was cut away, leaving a series of arches, and through these the cooks pushed the loaded trays as they were prepared.

A majordomo stood at hand with a long rod with which he tapped on the shoulder the mozos who kept coming up the hall on the run to bear fresh burdens. The rod was instantly on the shoulder of big Montana.

"Take that tray—that one, fool—up into the quarters of the serving maids—mind that the soup doesn't spill from the bowl. ... No, not that way! Into the quarters of the—ah, God! What can a man do with half-wits to work under him?"

For the Kid had turned the corner in the wrong direction. He knew what he was doing, however, and when he came to a big vaulted door he pushed it open and went down a flight of steps into the humid dampness of cellar air.

On the level below he found three armed men walking up and down, surrounding themselves with clouds of cigarette smoke. They were three of the most villainous of the guards of Lerraza.

"Come up, *amigos,*" called Montana. "Here is some supper for you. Soup—chicken—bread that's almost white—tortillas—a flask of wine...."

"How can we leave our posts, jackass?" demanded one of the guards.

"You are told to do so," said Montana. "But that's as you please. There's a room just above, and as you eat, out the window you can look into the inner patio and see all the fine people...."

One of the soldiers seized the tray, sniffed at the odors of the cookery and then bore it off with a shout.

"We've never been served food like this before!" he called. "Come on, José! Come on, boys!"

He went shouting up the stairs, with the other two hurrying behind him for fear he might take the best titbits as the first to help himself.

Montana turned sharply back.

According to the story he had heard, there was one more guard, stationed inside the room itself to watch over Maria Mercado. He went to the door of the room with a revolver in his hand and tapped. When he had no answer to a first and then to a second summons, he tried the knob. It turned readily. He opened the door and stepped into a little chamber where the air was oily and foul from the burning of a lamp whose wick had been turned well down.

In the corner there was a pallet with a rumpled blanket on top of it, but there was no sight of Maria Mercado, there was no sight of a guard of any sort.

The door, which apparently was weighted to close by itself, now shut suddenly behind him with a strong slam. It made him leap about, badly startled. A bell had commenced to ring, somewhere. All that he could hear, or rather feel, was the stir of the strong vibration, in the distance.

It told him what had happened. The old trap was merely a bait, and the first man entered the chamber where Maria Mercado was supposed to be was well hooked and caught. He gripped the knob of the door and pulled hard.

There was no use in that. The door had locked automatically and the lock itself was a massive affair of steel. Bullets from a revolver would not smash it.

There was no use in smashing it, anyway, because outside the cellar room he could hear a descending uproar. The footfalls were a distinct vibration coming downstairs; the voices of men seemed to roll like the growling of dogs out of the ground on which he stood; and far away he heard women's cries, like the squealing of mice.

There was a three-legged stool in a corner of the room. He sat down on that and made a cigarette and lighted it. It was not the heat of the room that made his face wet. The back of his hand was covered with little beads of water that began to run together in tiny trickles. He looked at this curiously. It was hard to breathe. His diaphragm had turned into a hard, cold board and every breath was painful.

A hand beat on the door.

"Who's in there? Who are you?" shouted a voice.

He looked around him carefully. The walls of the room were solid rock. The only apertures were the door, now locked, and a trap-door in the ceiling, red with rust, and undoubtedly locked also.

He made sure of that by putting the stool under the trap and reaching up. His fingertips touched the trapdoor and he pressed hard against it. It did not give. There was merely a slight jar of metal against metal.

"Do you hear?" yelled the voice at the door. "We have you like a dirty rat in a trap. If we open the door, will you come out with your hands over your head?"

"Who speaks?" said Montana.

"Ah-hai! He is there!" shouted two or three voices.

"I speak," said a growling voice. "I, Benito Jalisca. Who are you?"

"You call me in your own tongue El Keed," said Montana.

A wild cry of joy answered him.

"Do you know me, señor?" asked the voice of Jalisca.

"I haven't that pleasure," said Montana. "Who are you, old fellow?"

"Do you remember the two Rurales—one tall with a dead man's face, one short, with crooked legs?"

"I remember you, *amigo*, like the palm of my hand. How are you? And how is my old friend your father, and your revered mother?"

"Oh, gringo dog!" cried Jalisca. "How long I have waited for this. Know that it is I who planned the trap and who removed the old woman from it only this morning so that there would be more space to hold you, señor!"

"I'm very comfortable," said Montana. "You have a good brain, Jalisca. When I get out of this place I'll pay you more compliments than you'll be able to bear."

Another voice joined the parley. It was Emiliano Lopez who was saying: "Who is it? Has someone really been caught?"

And Montana called out: "Ah, Don Emiliano! Are we to meet again? How are you, my friend? And how is your back? Are the weals healed on your skin? But the scars will stay there for a long time, *amigo*."

"It is he!" cried Lopez. "Ah, Jalisca, you have a brain that I admire. I shall find a way of getting you out of the Rurales. You must be my man for the rest of your life."

"Señor," said Jalisca, "El Keed split the heart of my dearest

THE SONG OF THE WHIP

friend with a bullet out of his cursed gun. If I see him lying dead, at last, I don't care what comes of the rest of my life. It can be yours. It can be any man's."

"Open the door!" commanded Lopez.

"If we open the door, said Jalisca, "he will spring out among us. And why should we give the wildcat a chance to claw two or three more men to death?"

"What else can we do, Benito Jalisca?"

"We can blow in the door with a stick of dynamite. You see how strongly everything is built and the walls are of rock. Nothing will fall in the house except a few bits of plaster, and the force of the explosion will kill El Keed—or better than that, it will stun him, and put him helpless in our hands."

"You are right again, Jalisca. Now I see clearly that you must be my man. Get the dynamite at once.... Stand back, some of you. Give us room.... We don't need fifty men.... Ah, Don Tomás! Welcome, señor. The trick of this Jalisca has worked and the devil himself is in the trap!"

Montana rose, stepped on the glowing butt of his cigarette, and then laid his long-bladed knife on the ground. He stamped on it, and the steel sprang into a shiver of long broken pieces.

"What is that?" demanded Señor Lerraza.

"Nothing," said the Rurale. "Nothing—unless he has killed himself."

"I am in perfect health, Jalisca," said Montana. "I salute you, Señor Lerraza."

"It is the gringo, is it?" said Don Tomás. "Listen to me!... How did you manage to come through my house to this place? What devil guided you?"

"I carry a receipt for invisibility about with me," said Montana. "Presently I shall pour myself through the keyhole of this door, and when I go past you, all you will know of me will be a cold wind in your face.... Afterwards, you'll feel the same chill in the black of your Mexican heart, my friend."

"Bring the dynamite," commanded Don Emiliano. "Why should we talk with him?"

Here a girl's voice said, clearly: "Because it's worth while hearing every syllable that a brave man speaks."

"So, Dorotea?" exclaimed Lerraza. "Begone to your room, if you please. Let the guest be taken back into the patios. Tell them that soon we'll be able to show them the bare face of a gringo murderer. That will please them. For your own part, get quickly to your room. I'll feel safer about you if I know you're there—until this *yanqui* is dead, my child."

"Why should you kill him?" asked Dorotea. "At least, why should he be killed without my having a chance to see it happen? You take me to the bullfights. Why shouldn't I see a gringo baited and killed?"

"You see what spirit is in the girl, Emiliano," said the father. "You will have to rule her with a high hand. However, Dorotea, do as I tell you. Go to your room!"

Montana had selected among the shards of the broken steel a fragment long and slender. He now stepped up on the three-legged stool again and began to probe with the bit of steel into the mouth of the lock of the trap-door. Bits of red iron dust dropped down into his face, into his eyes. He closed his eyes and went on with his probing. It was only the sense of touch that could teach him to read the puzzle of that old lock and pick it open.

He seemed to stand in a cyclonic swirl of voices, sounding above him, beneath him, and all around.

Still the thick rust held the lock.

He climbed down from the stool, blew out the lamp, and poured some of the kerosene on to his handkerchief. This he sopped over the face of the lock when he had located it again in the darkness. And that was not so easy as he had thought it would be. In the darkness, there was a continual tendency to lose balance and fall from the stool. He fell to work again with the shard of steel. Now he felt the point enter more easily, grating softly against the core of clean, strong metal. Again and again he sloshed the kerosene over the lock.

And so, at last, he felt something give, a little, a very little, and then stick again in place.

He had moved the bolt. For the first time he dared to let hope fly up like a strong bird in his heart.

Outside, he could hear the voice of Jalisca saying: "Give it to me. Someone bring me some soft clay. Yes, or some black mud out of the corral. Quickly, quickly! Yes, this fuse will be long enough.... *Valgame Dios!* It will not be long before we see his face, living or dead, Señor Lerraza!"

"You are worth more than your weight in gold, Jalisca," said old Don Tomás. "How often have the Lerrazas and their friends needed to wipe away a disgrace? And this time you have helped us to manage the thing ... Will he wait for the dynamite or will he kill himself?"

"Señor," said the Rural, "such a man will still hope for a chance to die fighting. He will hope that even dynamite will miss him, in some strange manner. Ah, here is the mud. Now we will have him, living or dead, in half a minute—"

With the last of the kerosene Montana bathed the lock above his head. Drops of the oil and rust dropped down on his face. A bit of it fell into his open mouth and set him spitting.

But now, suddenly, with a little noise like the squeak of a frightened rat, the bolt gave. He pushed, and the trapdoor lifted a little, only a little. It was a good fifty or sixty pounds of heavy weight. He could not thrust it wide open from such a distance, but hooking the fingers of his left hand over the ledge of the upper floor, he raised himself and began to push upwards with his right hand. So the weight of his own body and the weight of the door, as he heaved, came entirely on his left shoulder and pulled the tendons hard as wood.

That was when he heard the voice of Jalisca calling: "Stand back, now. Only the devil can tell exactly what dynamite will do. ... Back, everyone. I have lighted the fuse. Look out for yourselves!"

There was a scattering sound of footfalls. In the midst of the noise, Montana was pushing the trapdoor wide, then swinging himself up with both aching arms into the void exposed above him. He reached the floor, and rolled over on it as the blast went off beneath him.

A gush of wind drove out past his face. He felt the breath pressed out of his body. Something dropped from above and rapped his back sharply. Beneath him he could hear things still falling.

CHAPTER 12

He got to his feet with the strange feeling that he had been asleep for a long time. The trapdoor he lifted, lowered in place, and then put the weight of his foot on it. He heard the lock snap home.

Then he turned into the darkness about him and lighted a match.

Beneath, Jalisca's voice was saying: "It is my place to go first—if he is not stunned or dead—it is my privilege to have the fighting in my hands. . . . Keep back and—"

Then came a wild cry: "Gone! Gone! He is gone! God of miracles! He is not here!"

The light of the match showed Montana the door at the side of the little cellar room. It was locked, he thought, when he first handled the knob, but then he discovered that the door was simply lodged with moisture. It could not have been open for a long time, and now a strong tug brought it wide. Before him appeared a little, steep flight of steps with a door at the top. He went up them rapidly.

And far beneath him the voices were shouting: "Has he turned himself into thin air?"

Then: "Scatter Scatter! This is not the age of miracles! He is somewhere in the house!"

Footfalls began to race everywhere. Some of them seemed, to the excited brain of Montana, to be rushing straight up the steps behind him. Every nerve in him started shuddering.

He reached the door. It was not locked, but opened readily. And he stepped into a brightly lighted corridor. The darkness he had just left now seemed like the face of a friend. These lights were pointing their rays at him like so many terrible fingers.

He kicked off the huaraches. Bare feet would be the safest for him, now, the most silent on the tiles.

He ran to the left. A sudden noise of running feet stopped him. He turned to the right and rounded a corner of the hallway. A

THE SONG OF THE WHIP

flood of footfalls streamed toward him from that direction, also. Immediately to the left was a door. He pulled it open and leaped into a lamplit room. The moon also entered it through a big casement on the farther side, and seated in the shaft of the moonlight was Dorotea Lerraza. She was looking straight at him. Her voice was perfectly calm when she said: "Here's the window that will let you out, señor!"

He ran to it, leaped up on the sill, and looked down. Before him, he saw half a hundred men streaming in from the barbecue, drawn by the alarm. There were guns glimmering everywhere.

He jumped back to the floor of the bedroom.

"I wondered," said the girl. "I though perhaps a desperate man might cut his way even through such a crowd as that."

He stared at her. Then the knob of her door turned. Montana sank, gun in hand, by the side of the big bed. The voice of Lerraza himself was panting from the threshold: "Dorotea! Dorotea! The strangest thing in my life has happened. The devil of a gringo has turned into thin air—by miracle! We blasted open the door of the cellar room. There was force enough to have killed twenty men, if that many had been inside, but El Keed was gone. He is somewhere in the house. Dios! Dios! What a thing! What a marvel! I'll stay here and keep two armed men with me to make sure—"

"They'll need you to lead the search," said Dorotea. "Just leave two good men outside my door—and I'll keep it locked. Nothing can happen to me."

"You are not afraid, Dorotea?"

"Why should I be? Such a man as El Keed would not harm a woman."

"What are you saying, Dorotea? Do you think that women are safe in the hands of the gringo dogs? Your honor, your life—he would take them with a laugh. He would cut the fingers from your hands to take off the rings more easily. . . . *Yanqui* is another word for beast and brute. . . ."

"Well," said the girl, quietly, "if you leave two men outside the door, I'll feel safe enough. . . . Be careful of yourself, Father. Don't show yourself too freely. Such a dangerous man might wish only to murder you before he died. . . . Adios! Be careful!"

The door closed, the bolt clicked softly home, and the girl turned to find Montana lighting a cigarette. He stood in the shadow by the window, the glow of the cigarette pulsing dimly on his face.

"Señorita Dorotea," said Montana, "the moment I saw your face I knew that I was as safe as though I were in the hands of a sister."

She said nothing. She opened a box and took out a cigarette. Montana lighted it. She drew slowly on the cigarette. Her eyes were calmly occupied with the hand, the face of Montana, with the rusty red of the oil drops dripped over it. Then she stepped back and blew a cloud of smoke into the shaft of moonlight that entered through the window.

"This *is* a night of miracles," said Dorotea. "How could I guess that I was so romantic? . . . Señor, in that room you will find soap and water and a towel."

He went into the dressing-room and washed himself clean. He found a comb and put his black hair in order. His blue eyes glittered at him out of a mirror like bits of burning steel.

It was a charming little French mirror, with scrolls of fine golden wire laid over the glass in a graceful pattern. The comb he had used was carved ivory, yellow with time.

Then he went back into the bedroom.

"They make a great noise about you, señor," said the girl, sitting by the window again, smoking. "Do you hear all the voices? All the horses galloping? And there—there—"

A roar of gunshots sounded, not far away from the house.

"They are killing my ghost," said Montana.

He took a chair opposite her and sank into it.

"This is peace—this is rest—this is delightful," said Montana. "Señorita Dorotea, I am almost sorry that I interrupted the announcement."

"But not quite sorry, señor?"

"Not quite, because it was for that purpose that I came—"

"Ah, for that? No, no—you came for the poor little mother of that Mercado."

"For her, also. She was the excuse, señorita."

"And what was the real reason?"

"When I saw this Don Emiliano, I knew that it would be a misfortune for you to marry him."

"Señor?"

"A fellow," said Montana, "who will have a poor devil like Mercado flogged. Do you know why he had him flogged?"

"Because he was a rebellious rat, señor."

"No, because he sang 'The Song of the Whip.'"

"What song is that?"

THE SONG OF THE WHIP

"Shall I sing it for you?"
"If you please."
Softly Montana sang:

> "I am weary of slaves;
> Their hides are too tough;
> Many blows have thickened their skins;
> I must cut deep, very deep
> To open the peon's heart
> And let out the screaming.
> But I could make music flow
> From bodies more tender—"

Montana leaned closer. He smiled as he sang, his eyes fixed deep upon her own.

> "A song of howling, a shriek
> From delicate lips I could draw
> Give me no more the tough back of a peon,
> A Juan or José, a Pedro or Leon,
> But give me a lord from a lordly terraza,
> A Diaz, Angeles, or a Lerraza."

"Valgame!" breathed the girl. "It is almost as though you meant it!"

"For listening to that song, not for singing it, my poor Mercado was flogged until he could not stand."

"Was he a friend of yours? Had he been your servant ever?"

"I heard him from across the little river. And when they flogged him I heard him sing the song in spite of the whip lashes, until he fainted. By that I knew that he was a man, and Don Emiliano, who did the flogging—"

"What was Don Emiliano?"

"Unworthy of you, my dear."

"Ah?" said the Lady Dorotea. "Did you know me?"

"Of course I knew you."

"Had you ever laid eyes on me?"

"No, señorita."

"Had you ever so much as heard my voice?"

"No, Dorotea."

"Then how could you say that you knew me? Had you seen a picture?"

"My dear, listen to me—that which is beautiful is loved by every man. I had heard your name spoken. I had seen men look up when they talked of you."

"Do you mean that they tried to make a saint of me?"

"No. But we look up when we remember beautiful things. For mountains, and sunrise, and starlight, and Dorotea, men look up."

She began to laugh a little.

"And because of that you knew that I was not for Don Emiliano?"

He laughed in his turn.

"You see that I had to come down here to the hacienda and stop the affair, at the very last moment."

"Shall I even try to believe that?" she asked.

"It would be worth believing," said Montana.

"I think it would," she said. "I think you even half believe it yourself."

"Every moment that I sit here I believe it more and more," he said.

"You have a new way of talking," said the girl. "So I shall believe that you sit here with an aching heart, señor?"

"Not aching," said Montana. "But a cold thrill of joy is in it, as if wings had lifted it into the chill of the upper spaces. Do you know what I mean when I say that?"

"No. No, señor."

"Valgame Dios! Have you never been in love?"

"I never have had that cold breathed into my heart, if that is love."

"Now I understand," said Montana. "That is why you are still and distant and calm."

She stood up, looked him over calmly, and went to the door, in which she turned the key, while still she stared back at him over her shoulder.

She was saying: "Señor, you must think that I'm a cheap little fool. Or have you had a great success with Mexican girls, covering your gringo heart with Mexican language and trying to pretend to be a brilliant, stormy, Spanish lover? . . . How many times have you talked to other girls about a heart lifted as on wings—and the chill of the upper spaces . . . and all the rest of it?"

"It does sound pretty silly, now that you look it in the face," said he.

"What should I do about it, do you think?" asked the girl.

"I don't know. There are two or three devils in that pretty head of yours. I don't know which of them is in control just now."

"It would be worth something to you if you could guess," said Dorotea.

She leaned against the wall beside the door, her hands behind her back, and looked him over with a leisurely insolence, smiling.

"I am guessing enough to make sure what I *ought* to do," said the Kid.

"What is that, señor?"

"I ought to split your wishbone with a half-inch slug of lead, beautiful. Before you throw me to the dogs."

"But you don't do it?"

"You see that I'm a romantic fool," said the Kid.

"Bah!" she sneered, suddenly, "Bah!... Only a gringo dog! ... Now out the window with you and into the fire...."

She jerked the door open and screamed. "Help! Help! The gringo!"

CHAPTER 13

The two guards who had been assigned to posts outside the door of the room of Dorotea were veterans of the finest type in the service of Don Tomás. They answered her scream with a sort of snarling shout, and lurched for the doorway, each with a pair of guns in his hands.

It would have been hard to find two more efficient fellows, even in the ranks of the Rurales themselves. Tadeo had been a cattle thief of eminence and had a great following until he was caught on the end of a lariat and given his choice of death or lifelong service in the personal Lerraza guard. At that crisis, Tadeo hesitated, almost preferring death to the loss of some freedom; almost preferring starvation in the mountains to the flashy uniform of the guards. But after making his choice he became devoted to the service because there was even more murder in it than in the life of a robber.

Matthias, on the other hand, was one who had grown up in the dust and dark alleys of a town, developing natural talents for the use of a knife. Finally he had cut a throat too long before midnight and had found himself in jail before morning. From the jail he had been recruited for the Lerraza service when it was discovered that with a Colt revolver he could shoot the heart out of a silver peso at ten paces. He was one of those rarities, a real, two-handed fighting-man. And now he reached the threshold of the room first.

A wave of shadow greeted him as the Kid smashed the lamp with a first shot. But there was still the moonlight, and Matthias, as he ran, poured a double stream of bullets and thunder towards the shadowy figure beside the window. Unfortunately, the figure did not stand still. A glance through the window had shown the Kid that the ground outside the building still was filled with the moving throng of armed men. He did not, as Dorotea had sug-

THE SONG OF THE WHIP

gested, leap out the window into the "fire." Instead, he whirled and ran towards the door, not in a straight line but dodging like a snipe.

His first bullet crashed the lamp to the floor. His second struck the long, lantern jaw of Matthias, tilted his head back, and passed through the brain.

His third shot hit the exact center of Tadeo's cat-like, fighting smile. And before Tadeo's falling body struck the ground the Kid had reached the threshold of the room.

In the flow of her white garments, lovely as a Greek sculpture, Dorotea had not stirred from her place by the wall. Her hands were empty, but there seemed to be no fear in her. She clapped those soft hands together and cried out: *"Bravo, torero!"*

The Kid, pausing on the threshold glanced left and right. The hall was, so far as he could see, empty. But footfalls were rushing upon him from the left, from the right.

He stepped back, closed the door, locked it, and threw the key through the window.

An agile pair of figures had appeared at that window, shouting, trying to clamber in.

"I'll only frighten them away, Dorotea," said the Kid, and he clipped the thigh of one of them with a quick shot.

The man screamed and fell. His outcry seemed to strike down the other also. Nothing but the pure white of the moonlight streamed through the window now.

The Kid glanced again at the girl. She was gliding towards the fallen body of Matthias.

"Excuse me," said the Kid, "but the tiles are slippery now—and you might fall."

He took her arm just as she was bending towards a revolver which had fallen from the hand of Matthias and lay now glistening on the edge of the pool of moonlight.

The fallen gun he picked up but put away inside his coat with a gesture. There were two other revolvers to retrieve. He found them in the shadows. Four guns were an overweight, but they might be dangerously employed if one of them came into the fastidious fingers of Dorotea.

He began to shift some of the cartridges to reload his own favorite six-shooter.

As though he had lighted a cigarette with a match burning blue with sulphur flame, there was a slight pungency in the air, stinging his throat and heavy in the lungs. That was the smell of the gunpowder. It was a familiar strangeness.

Someone was pounding at the door of the room. The voice of the great Lerraza himself was shouting: "Dorotea! Dorotea! Open! In the name of God, what has happened?"

After he had stopped that swift gesture of hers towards a weapon. Dorotea had not moved. She said to the Kid, calmly: "May I answer?"

"My dear, you may do as you please," said Montana, and split the panel of the door with a forty-five caliber bullet.

The pounding ceased. There was only the shouting voice of Lerraza.

Dorotea had not answered it.

Lerraza thundered: "Tadeo! Matthias. Where are you?"

'Señor—" called the Kid.

"Ah, my God!" cried Don Tomás. "It is the gringo... Dorotea? Are you living? Can you answer?"

The girl said nothing. The Kid stared at her fixedly. She was waiting there in the middle of the floor, moveless, her head thrown back a little, expectant.

Montana went close to the door.

"I have covered the lips of Dorotea just for the moment. I did not wish to have too much squealing to deafen my ears."

Someone came pounding up the hallway. The gasping voice of Emiliano Lopez was out there, shouting: "Señor! Señor Lerraza! What has happened?"

And the groaning voice of Lerraza answered: "He has murdered my girl!"

The Kid turned towards the girl.

"She said: "Emiliano! Do you hear?"

"I hear you!... Be silent, the rest of you!... Ah, Dorotea!"

"Tadeo and Matthias are dead," she answered. "But I haven't been hurt. And if—"

The Kid raised a finger. She was still again.

"She lives!" Don Tomás groaned. "There still is a God! There still is a God!"

"But the gringo is there with her!" cried Lopez.

A hand struck three times on the door.

"I hear you, *amigo*," said Montana.

"Silence the howling outside the house," shouted Don Tomás. "I'm deafened, and my brain reels.... Señor, will you listen honorably to honorable terms?"

"Honorable?" said the Kid.

He began to laugh, a full-flowing, mellow-toned laughter. Dorotea slipped into a deep, overstuffed chair and sat there with her head bowed.

"Honorable—yes!" cried Don Tomás. "For your honor and mine, and the sacred name of my daughter, señor."

"True," said Montana. "There's the sacred name of your daughter, too."

And he laughed again. Dorotea lifted her head to listen. She began to stare at the face of Tadeo which was upturned in the moonlight. The bullet had made a horror of it. One arm of Tadeo was outflung and lay across the back of Matthias.

"When I speak of honor," said Don Tomás, "I mean the word. The honor of all of us. And I mean to make the most favorable terms, señor. Everything that you can wish. . . . An immediate free opportunity to leave the house is the first of them."

"And my hands are to be empty?" asked Montana.

"No," gasped Don Tomás, as though relief were making it possible for him to breathe deeply, now that he was in conference with Montana. "Your hands shall be as full as you please. . . . In my daughter's room there are enough jewels to make you a very wealthy man. They are yours."

"Certainly they are," said the Kid. "And how shall I be sure that when I try to leave there will not be a bullet through the back?"

"That I will swear by the Mother of Heaven, and by the sacred honor of the Lerrazas!"

"The sacred honor of the Lerrazas?" said the Kid. He laughed again, lingering over his amusement.

"Name any oath to me and I shall take it, señor. I shall clear the crowd from the place. From the window you can see with your own eyes that the way will be free for you. . . . Emiliano, go at once and send everyone from about the house. Send them away . . . and a curse on the blind dogs that let him come through the lines to the house!"

Emiliano hurried away with steps that clanked loudly through the corridor. Montana, stepping close to the door, could hear the faint creaking of leather as the men stirred uneasily in their places. He could hear, he thought, their breathing, and through these small sounds came the groaning, trembling voice of Don Tomás.

"You see that I shall do everything, señor. But in the name of God's mercy leave the room of my daughter quickly."

"I need a little time for thinking," said the Kid.

"Whatever more you wish shall be given to you. There is a certain sum of money in the house. It will be brought here and passed under the door to you. You shall have your hands filled, señor."

"You might say it's my professional duty not to leave with them empty," said the Kid.

"Señor, I understand perfectly. I see you are a gentleman. And for the past...for certain hasty and harsh words...I ask ten thousand pardons. I shall know you better hereafter."

"Much better," said the Kid.

He turned from the door and added, over his shoulder: "In a short time I'll be able to give you an answer."

"But what occasion is there for thought? Why do you need time, señor?...You can hear the people being driven away!"

Don Emiliano, in fact, was executing the commission in the most thorough way. He had mounted a dozen of the guards and they were whipping the crowd from the premises with their quirts. As for the gentry, these were being escorted to their horses or carriages. Wheels began to rumble over the little bridge.

The Kid went to the girl where she sat with bowed head. He put the heel of his hand against her forehead and pushed back her head until it rested against the cushioned back of the chair.

"Shall I go at once, or do you think I ought to stay here and think it over?" he asked.

Her great, dark eyes considered him carefully. They moved as she studied him, feature by feature.

"Señor! Señor!" cried Don Tomás.

"I have to have time to look things over," said the Kid. "There are the jewels to examine, you know. Give me a few moments of quiet, Don Tomás. You know that as a connoisseur I mustn't fill my hands with things that are not worth taking."

CHAPTER 14

Montana went to the table and opened the jewel-casket. He lifted his hand with a great pearl necklace dripping from it. He turned and regarded the girl. She was lying back in the chair as before, but she had removed her necklace, her bracelet, her rings, and all that glittering brightness now filled a hand which lay listlessly along the soft arm of the chair.

He dropped the necklace back into the casket. The little pearls clinked in a soft shower against one another.

In the hall men were waiting. The only sound was the clicking heels of Don Tomás as he strode back and forth. The Kid opened the cigarette-box, took out two of them, and returned to the chair. He sat on an arm of it and placed a cigarette between the unresisting lips of Dorotea.

"Will you smoke?" asked the Kid.

She said nothing. Her eyes, wandering past him, were fixed unwinkingly on the shadowy ceiling. The moonlight, slanting farther into the chamber, had reached the silver of her slippers.

The Kid lighted a match and held it. The radiance poured from his hands over her face. If she so much as breathed the flame would ignite the cigarette; but she did not breathe. The match stung his finger-tips.

He took the cigarette from her mouth, lighted it, inhaled a deep breath, and replaced it between her lips.

She began to smoke, lifting her hand to the cigarette and withdrawing it. Her lips did not purse. The smoke drifted but in a thin, fragrant stream.

"Do you need more time for thinking, Dorotea?" he asked.

"*Si, señor*," said the girl.

He looked about the room as far as the face of Tadeo. Then he went to the bed and ran his hand over the drape which covered it. The cloth was encrusted with arabesquings of heavy gold thread.

He pulled the cover clear, crossed the floor, and dropped the richness of the cloth over the two dead men, over the pooled blood on the floor. After that he returned and sat down on the arm of the chair again.

"Thank you, señor," said the girl.

"Dorotea!" cried the frantic voice of Don Tomás.

"I am here, Father!" she answered.

"Señor! Señor! ... In the name of God..." shouted Don Tomás.

"You interrupt me, Don Tomás," said the Kid. "I've found a flawed emerald and a spoiled ruby already."

"They shall be replaced, but for the sake of—"

"I must have quiet when I study, Don Tomás."

A groan answered him. The footfalls began to pass up and down the hall again.

"Those two fellows on the floor," said the Kid, "are two more weights on my conscience, Dorotea."

"*Si, señor,*" murmured the girl, always with those sightless eyes fixed on the ceiling.

"I owe them to you, Dorotea."

"*Si, señor,*" she said.

"And so?" said the Kid.

She lifted the handful of jewels. She raised her hand so listlessly that the weight of the gems seemed to overburden it.

He took her cigarette, tapped the ash from it, and replaced it between her fingers. She took another breath of smoke.

"There is the old woman, the *viejita*," said Montana. "Where is she kept?"

The girl made no answer. He touched her cheek so that her face turned towards him. Montana laughed, silently.

He selected from the handful of jewels a big dark ruby ring, lifted her left hand, and slid the ring over the smooth, soft joints of a finger. She lifted her hand and turned it, looking at the jewel like a child at a toy. The heavy bracelet he clasped around her wrist. She seemed to see that also with new eyes. Then the length of the necklace he dropped over her head and looped it three times around.

"Do you keep nothing, señor?" she asked.

"You know, Dorotea," said the Kid, "up in gringo land even the worst robbers only take from a woman what she's willing to give."

He slid another ring back into place. Her eyes were still blankly staring at the ceiling but her fingers closed softly over his hand.

"How far away are you looking?" he asked.

She smiled slowly and was silent.

"But," said the Kid, "there is an old woman, the old mother of my friend. Where is she kept?"

"Is it she that you want?" asked Dorotea.

He leaned closer. Her eyes had left the ceiling and were moving slowly, with a half sleepy curiosity, over his face.

At last he said: "Yes. I came for her."

"Well—" said the girl.

He rose from the arm of the chair and he blew a stream of smoke upwards.

"She's kept in the south wing of the old stable," said the girl.

"Where is that?"

"You can see it—the one with the cross over the entrance."

"How many guards are with her?"

"Only enough to amuse you, señor."

"Can you tell me a safe way to go to her?"

She stood up and went to the wall near the window. Behind the curtain her hand worked a moment and then a section of the wall swung out with an oiled silence.

The Kid looked into the dark mouth of the passage that was revealed.

"It leads to the back of the house and underground. It comes up in the middle of a patch of shrubbery. It is a passageway that the first builders cut in the ground."

"Ladies had to have a touch of liberty in those old days," said the Kid.

She smiled at him.

"Shall I take you through to the farther end?" she asked.

"Is the way out easy to find?"

"Perfectly. There's a projecting knob. Lift up on it and the section of the wall will start swinging.... I'll show you the way."

"My dear, I don't want to compromise you," said the Kid.

Her smile came again, lingering and slow.

"This is better than wings and moonlight and chilly heights, señor," she said.

"It's more expensive, at least," said the Kid.

"True!" said the girl. "But here—you forget all the jewels in the casket."

"I forget nothing," said the Kid.

"Shall I be sure of that?"

"Yes," said Montana.

"I give you a memento, señor," said Dorotea.

She took one of the rings from her fingers, chose his left hand, and slipped the ring on to the little finger. She touched the ring with her lips when it was in place.

CHAPTER 15

When he stepped into the mouth of the passage, the wall section behind him closed at once.

Fear struck him heavily, over the heart.

And then the voice of the girl was crying out: "Father—do you hear?"

The Kid bared his teeth. The match he lighted showed him no handle that might work the secret door.

The sweet, high voice of Dorotea was crying: "Only have a little patience, Father. In a few minutes he swears that he will leave—"

The Kid turned. He took a great breath and then strode on down the passage. It dipped down an incline, abruptly without steps to help the feet make the descent. The walls were hewn in living rock. The match-light glinted far away on the chisel strokes of the Indian miners who had dug that channel.

It was long. It turned to the right, made an elbow bend, and then slanted up. At the end of that passage he found, by the light of a fresh match, a flat wall of masonry with a projecting knob. When he lifted there was only a slight delay before the weight began to turn out of his hands.

A gap opened, and he stepped out into a circular patch of brush all silvered by the white of the noon. Through the bushes he could see the whole sweep of the buildings of the great estate, and the thing that amazed him was the silence. Every soul had been frightened from the Lerraza place. Only, near the corner of the farthest patio wall remained a group of horses saddled and bridled, and a few men beside them, the outpost of the Lerraza guards. But it was not necessary to go close to them in order to reach the old stable. The Kid skirted the rear of it, beyond the dungheaps and moved more softly when he came to the sound of voices.

He heard a man calling: "Ah-hai! Where are you?"

And from within the stable a harsh, guttural voice, hardly feminine in its intonation, answered: "Here am I!"

"Be still!" broke in another. "Be quiet, Maria. If you yell out like that, we'll have El Keed on our backs.... This way, Oñate! What the devil do you want?"

"I've come to bring news. There's no need to watch over this little *viejita* any longer. El Keed won't come to rescue her withered old bones, you can be sure."

"Have they killed him, then?"

"Killed him?"

A voice began to laugh. "Yes, and buried him in the chamber of Señorita Dorotea."

"Hai! What are you talking about?... I know the Lerrazas are mad enough to whip every man and woman and child off the place and home to the village. But not mad enough to—what do you mean?"

"Matthias and Tadeo—do you know them?"

"Do I know myself, you fool? Of course I know them."

"They are dead in the room of Dorotea. And El Keed is in there counting the jewels of the jewel-casket and telling Lerraza that one is imitation and the other is flawed...."

"Don Emiliano will go mad!"

"He has chewed off one side of his moustache.... Don Tomás strides up and down in the hall and calls on Heaven.... The house is kept as still as a ghost.... Come out here in the moonlight and see how quiet everything is."

"I can't leave Maria."

"Maria Mercado, are you fool enough to try to run away?"

"I'm not such a fool," said the old woman. "Besides, how can I reach through the wooden wall and unlock the back door of the stall?"

The Kid, leaning beside that door, nodded to himself.

"I think she's safe enough."

"We know where El Keed is at present. He won't leave until he's driven his bargain with Don Tomás. My God! I'd give a year of life to listen to that bargaining! A Lerraza in his own house trying to ransom his daughter, his heir. What would you think of that, Oñate?"

Their voices grew dim on the farther side of the barn, and the Kid turned the key in the lock of the rear door of the stall. As he drew it open, softly, the moonlight entered and showed him a withered little old woman with a dried-up face like a monkey's.

She sat cross-legged on some straw in a corner of the stall; a long-legged Spanish mule was tethered on the farther side. Even in the semi-darkness she was knitting; and still her fingers flew and the needles clicked softly as she looked up with round, bright eyes at the Kid.

The voices of the two guards were dim beyond the stable.

"Ah, mother," said Montana, "are you ready to take a trip?"

She whispered in answer: "It is not the night air that I'm afraid of. But go away quietly and save your skin."

He dropped on his heels beside her.

"What shall I say to Julio Mercado if I come away without you?" he asked.

"Are you El Keed?" murmured the old woman. "Jesús! How big the young men are!"

"Will you come with me, mother? Or must I put a hand over your mouth and throw you over my shoulder?"

"You would have your hand bitten to the bone, señor," she answered.

"Look, Maria! I have ridden a long distance to come to you."

"Then ride a long distance to go away again."

"This is a poor way to talk."

"If I talk louder, those fellows outside would hear me," she answered.

Still her needles flashed in the moonlight and clicked constantly. The Kid sat down and lighted a cigarette.

"Do you think you can stay here, like a stupid fellow?" asked old Maria.

"Maria, I am staying until you will come away with me.... Look—there is the mule ready, and the saddle, there, hanging from the wall."

He got up, drew the saddle over the back of the mule, and pulled up the cinches. He fitted the bridle over the long, tender, furry ears.

"Do you know what you are doing?" Maria asked Montana.

"I'm saddling the mule for you, mother."

"The mule that belongs to the overseer, Antonio!... Ah-hai! He would polish his teeth with some fine curses if he could see that!"

"What do you care about Antonio? Have you forgotten your son?"

"Because a bad penny has been thrown away, should a good penny be thrown after it?" she asked.

"Julio is not bad."

"Not until he ran away with a bandido."

"Does that make him a devil?"

"It makes him a fool, which is worse.... Señor were you really in the chamber of Señorita Dorotea?"

"I was, mother."

"What a thing to believe!"

"And what a place to be!" said the Kid. He laughed a little, silently and she looked up at the flash of his eyes.

"How can I believe such a thing? How did you part?"

"Honorably—as friends," said the Kid.

"How? As friends?"

"Do you see?"

He held out his hand with the ring pressed tight on the little finger.

The knitting-needles no longer flashed and clicked. Maria Mercado bent to stare at the jewel, and as she did so her old head began to nod. She whispered: "It is true! It is true! Lord keep our sinful souls! Lord have mercy upon us! It is the ring! I have seen it with my own eyes. I have seen the shine of it on her own lovely hand!"

"Stand up, Maria. It is time to go."

She seemed to be stunned. All resistance was gone from her. She rose at once to her feet and the Kid led the mule out into the moonshine. Very dim were the voices of the guards on the farther side of the barn.

Maria Mercado let the kid help her up to the saddle. She was laughing, noiselessly, convulsed with mirth.

"These are the hands that touched the Lady Dorotea!" she kept whispering through that laughter. "Now they serve Lady Maria! When did a Mercado receive such honor?... If they have the hanging of my poor old neck, they are welcome to it. There is not enough juice of life left in me to fill a teaspoon. But I have a hero to be my squire.... I could sing a ballad...."

She kept on laughing.

Montana, stepping back into the stall, picked up the big black-wrapped bundle which had been on the straw beside Maria Mercado. He carried it out and lashed it behind the saddle. Then he took the reins and led the mule forward, stepping slowly just in front of the tall animal, so that it would be forced to move with caution and make no noise.

She began to talk in a louder voice.

THE SONG OF THE WHIP

"Is it true that they trapped you in my old cellar room?"

"I was there, Maria."

"Did you smell the cellar damp?"

"I smelled it. Even a rat would have shuddered in such a place."

"*I* did not shudder."

"You are brave, Maria. Now tell me—is it true that they flogged you like a beast?"

"No, not like a beast, because they did not strip away my clothes. That was a great mercy. I thanked them for that."

"But they flogged you, Maria?"

"Only a little. Hardly enough to warm my back. Not a thing to remember for a single day."

They were passing into the lower land beyond the barn.

"I think you don't hate the Lerrazas in spite of what they've done to you," said the Kid.

"Why should I hate them?"

"Why?" asked the Kid, glancing back in astonishment over his shoulder.

"Because they flogged me? Tush! They flogged all my people before me for four hundred years, and so why should I be unhappy? There always have been Lerrazas in this land and there always have been Mercados—until my fool of a boy brings the line to an end."

"Do you know what he will have?" asked the Kid. "He will have plenty of money, the prettiest wife in the mountains, and fourteen sons. Then what will you think of that?"

"I think he's a liar and a thief," said Maria Mercado.

"No, but a brave man willing to fight for his own."

"What did he have that was his own? The land he walked on belonged to the Lerrazas. The house he lived in was a Lerraza house. It was a Lerraza that gave me to his father as a wife. With Lerraza money I clothed and fed my Julio. And now he has run away from them, like a fool running away from his own soul."

"Was he to be beaten like a dog?"

"If a Lerraza will make a dog of a man, the man must be a dog. Afterwards, if he is good, he will be patted again."

"Mother, this is a strange way to talk. Is there none of the good, pure Indian blood in you?"

"I don't know what blood there is in me," said the woman. "Some say, long ago, that there was even a bit of Lerraza blood given to my family, a precious strain. But they were born to own, and other people were born to be owned. That is the will of God."

"And beaten to death?"

"If a man steps on a sharp rock, he may throw away his shoe if the sole of it should be thin. But my Julio was not beaten to death. He was simply beaten into good sense."

"I saw his blood run down his back, down to his heels. And still he sang 'The Song of the Whip'."

"He should have been flogged again until the white of his bones showed through the flesh. But Don Emiliano is too tender-hearted. He is no Lerraza. That is why there is so much trouble in the world. That is why the world is filled with people who growl like bad dogs—because there are not enough Lerrazas.... Tell me, did Señorita Dorotea give you that ring or did you take it?"

She put it on my finger, mother."

"Our Lady of Guadalupe! Think of that! That is why you walk tall, with a light step. If a lady of the Lerrazas touches a man, his blood is changed forever.... Ah-hai! The house is wakening! Do you hear the shouting? What an old fool I am to let myself be carried away from the Lerraza land! Here! Here! Come to me, *amigos!* El Keed! He is here!"

CHAPTER 16

From the house of the Lerrazas had broken out a sudden distant clamor and men could be seen running, small, distant objects, out of the gate of the patio towards the waiting horses. It was at this moment that Maria Mercado suddenly lifted her voice in a scream that cut the moonlight with a knife. The Kid leaped on to the back of the mule behind the saddle. With Maria's own hood he stifled her mouth; the other hand managed the reins, and his spurs drove the mule into a swift gallop. There was the blood of a racing mare in the hybrid. He stretched himself over the ground like a running horse. The Kid, cursing softly, saw a score of men tumbling into the saddles of the horses near the Lerraza house.

He could understand perfectly what had happened. As the mule plunged into the shallow waters of the stream and splashed across to the farther side, there was time enough to think of the end of the scene. Lady Dorotea, true to her word, had given him enough time to put a safe distance between himself and the house before she opened the door of her room to her father and Don Emiliano. And now the uproar, the search, would follow. No need of searching, when the screeching of this old hag had guided the hunters like a flaming torch.

As the mule mounted the farther bank of the stream, he looked back and saw the Lerraza guards coming like a splendid cavalry charge, each a picked rider, each on a well-chosen horse. And Montana groaned as he turned the mule aslant towards the hiding-place where he had left El Capitán. Now he could see the head of the stallion above the brush. He was out of the saddle and on to the back of the tall horse in a moment.

Maria Mercado sat well in place, gripping the reins with both hands, laughing, crying out: "If I'm worth stealing, I'll be worth the theft. Ride, ride, señor! I'll go for the mountains as fast as the mule can scamper. They'll pay no attention to me when there's game like El Keed to follow—"

He gripped the rope of the mule, nevertheless, and then he lifted his head and set his teeth in despair. For down the slope of the hill that faced him like a wall swept a stream of riders—half a dozen wild horsemen, leaning far over the necks of their mustangs.

They cut him off. They caught him between their charge and the forces of the Lerrazas.

He dropped the reins and drew two guns. That was when he heard the strong, high-pitched shout: "El Keed! El Keed!"

He knew the bull-throated roar of Rubriz, the ringing tenor voice of Tonio, the harsh yell of Julio Mercado. That other thin, sweet sound that came like a song through the yelling of the men was from the throat of Rosita.

He shouted a joyous answer and urged the stallion into an easy canter. The mule galloped most gallantly forward.

About them whirled the banditry. He saw Julio Mercado half out of his saddle as he leaned and embraced his mother; and the voice of Maria Mercado was shouting: "Give me a knife and I'll help in the fighting. Ah-hai! I feel the heart of a man grow big in me. A gun! A gun! Julio! Give me a weapon, and let me charge with you."

They were sweeping on at a fine speed, not directly up the steep of the slope, but slanting across it to make the grade more easy. Off to the side, well across the river and spurring desperately in pursuit, came the men of Lerraza. They had commenced to shoot. Tonio and Mateo Rubriz answered, firing from carbines as they galloped. A Lerraza horse went down, the rider plunging headlong as the poor beast tipped forward. And Maria Mercado began to yell with pure Indian joy.

Sunrise found the party far up in the hills—Julio Mercado and his old mother who had ridden like a monkey through the night, and Rosita with the Kid and Tonio, and Viljoen the knife-fighter, long and narrow as a blade.

Half the party had separated among the narrow maze of ravines and gorges during the night. Now the rest were halted on a high plateau among a scrub of small pine trees, with a drip of water over the edge of the great rock. High above them, on a pinnacle of rock, Orozco, the famous horse thief who had stolen the charges of the president himself, kept watch on all the round edge of the horizon. Below, they bivouacked, easing the horses of the saddles, lying about on the pine needles, and smoking while Maria Mercado's swift, hunched figure went here and there rapidly, building the fire, preparing the breakfast of chocolate. The shepherd who had furnished them with the milk of his she-goats sat at a distance, leaning on his crooked stick, grinning continually. He looked like a brown-faced goat himself. And happiness was in him to see all these free, fierce, wild men who lived above the law.

Flame rolled in a broad river up out of the eastern sky. But young Dick Lavery—"Tonio" to all that band—did not need the brilliance of the sunrise. He sat with his chin on the back of his knuckles, staring at the ground and trying to purge his brain of the picture of Rosita. But that picture would not grow dim. If he closed his eyes, her face was redrawn against the dark of his brain. There was no light in his mind except the flashing of her eyes. He could not hear the musical run of the water, but only the sound of her voice.

For she sat beside the Kid, whose head and shoulders lolled comfortably back against the trunk of a pine tree. The sense of his bigness in those shoulders put the teeth of Tonio on edge. He kept looking down at his own hand, fine-fingered, swift—a very sure instrument.

The Kid was munching some dried goat's meat that Julio Mercado had brought to him. Julio Mercado, also, had brought to the Kid a canteen of cold mountain water mingled with a strong part of brandy. And now Julio Mercado sat on his heels and smoked a true cornucopia-shaped Mexican cigarette, and grinned with a greasy-faced content as though, in watching his benefactor eat, he were filling his own belly. As for the mother who had been restored to him, he had not as much as looked at her after that first embrace. All his mind was poured out toward Montana.

And it seemed to Tonio that the shining face of the peon was a damnable thing.

He could have endured that, but he could not endure the chatter of Rosita and the monosyllables of the Kid as he answered her.

"*Querido mio!* We have climbed out of the night. We have washed ourselves clean of it, like mud. . . . Kiss me, *querido*."

The Kid paused in his eating to indicate, with a slow finger, the men who were around them. Orozco saw the by-play and laughed. The horse thief stood up, stretched himself, and faced the others.

"There is a walled room behind me; El Keed and Rosita are inside it," he said. "You too, Tonio, look the other way."

Tonio looked the other way, but still the voice of the girl plucked at his heart-strings and sent a wildly sorrowful music through his soul.

"I was dancing. I was whirling and laughing and leaping like a silly frog when the yelling began, and then a shout that scattered all the fine people, as though they were dead leaves. 'El Keed! El Keed!' Ah, my God! how my heart leapt up on a column of fire! I tried to scream, but my heart filled my throat. A fool took my hand. He told me that he would protect me. I could have dissolved in laughter. Protect *me* from El Keed? I wanted to say: 'Idiot, to me he is no danger. He would come to me like a falling star out of the sky!' That is what I wanted to say. Would it have been true, *vida?*"

"Yes," said the Kid, his mouth full of the dry meat.

"Drink, and when your mouth is clean, speak to me," said Rosita.

He shook his head and refused the canteen she had put to his lips.

"Bah!" said Rosita. "The meat tastes better to you than Rosita. Is that true?"

"Yes," said the Kid.

"Hai! Is it true? Is it true?"

Tonio, in an agony, had glanced aside, and he saw her with a fierce face holding his hand, pressing up one of the fingers.

"Yes," said the Kid.

"What is this on your finger?"

He had finished eating. He took a long draught from the canteen and called Mercado to drink the rest of it.

And Mercado thanked him for the leavings; and Rosita was rolling a cigarette that her lord might smoke. Now she was lighting the match. Now she was smiling as her master inhaled the first long breath.

"But the ring, *querido?* Where did you find it? I never saw it before on your finger. Let me see it now."

"Go away, Rosita. I want to sleep."

"Little ... obstinate ... devil!" said Rosita.

She caught the hand and stared at the ring.

"Hai!" she cried. "Was it true, then? Was it true?"

"Yes," said the Kid.

"You say 'yes' before I ask the question. But was it true? Did you escape the room of Dorotea?"

"Yes," said the Kid.

He closed his eyes. He continued to smoke, deep breaths. His

THE SONG OF THE WHIP 97

whole body relaxed. His face relaxed, also. He yawned. A horrible detestation sprang through the flesh of Tonio.

The girl was peering anxiously into that almost sleeping face, but she made her voice bright as a smile when she said: "She is lovely, that Dorotea."

"Yes," said the Kid.

"I never saw a more beautiful face," said Rosita.

"No," said the Kid.

Rosita shook a fist under his unconscious nose.

"And she is kind, too. Think of a Lerraza being kind!"

"Ay," said the Kid.

"So kind," said Rosita, in a changed voice, "that she has given you her own seal ring."

She was trembling. The earrings flashed and shuddered with light.

Montana had lifted his hand, spread the fingers and regarded the ring with sleepy indifference.

"True," he said, and closed his eyes again.

The mouth of Tonio twitched. A hungry satisfaction grew in him as he watched the face of Rosita turn savage. But, before she could speak again a voice drifted down to them, far and thin as the scream of a hawk. It was that fellow Orozco, high on the rocky pinnacle, signaling and waving towards the south.

Were the men of Lerraza coming again?

They would receive a sufficient welcome from these fine riflemen if they tried to work their way up the rocky gorge.

Tonio stood up and saw, far beneath, climbing rapidly with his horse, a single rider who now took off his peaked sombrero and waved it.

"Robles!" said Viljoen. "But why does he come alone? Where are the rest? Where is Rubriz?"

"They've gone to the other place and will wait for us there," said Tonio. "The chief is getting fat and hates to climb the steep places."

"If you're never fatter than he is, you'll be better than a mountain goat," answered Viljoen sharply.

Tonio drew in his breath. He had been long away from the band and they had almost forgotten him. This Viljoen, perhaps, would be the one of whom he should make an example.

Robles, spurring his horse, came up to the edge of the plateau. The hat which he had taken from his head he allowed to fall to the ground.

That was strange. The sombrero of a Mexican is more priceless to him than a shield to a Greek warrior. But Robles came on with his hands folded over the bow of his saddle.

Then Tonio saw the blood that stained the whole side of Robles's body. Viljoen had run forward. He was helping the wounded man to the ground.

In a frightened silence the others thronged near. Only the Kid was lying half senseless with growing sleep when Robles said, gasping out the words: "Dead! All dead! . . . And Rubriz . . . dead!"

CHAPTER 17

The name of Rubriz sank into the brain of the Kid, roused him from sleep, started him rubbing his eyes, while Rosita tried to hush him like a child, saying: "It's finished, vida. There's nothing that you can do. It's ended—poor Mateo!—he had to die one day...."

Montana leaped past her.

Robles sat on a rock with his hand at his wounded breast, shaking his head; blood was overrunning his hand slowly. Montana took him by the long hair and shoved back his head.

"What do you say of Rubriz?" he demanded.

"Dead!" said Robles. "Dead..."

"You lie!" said the Kid. "You ran like a yellow dog and left Rubriz behind you, but he cut his way through them. All the Lerrazas in the world and all their hired men never could put him down. Robles, speak the truth! You did not see Rubriz shot down?"

Robles still shook his head, his dull eyed wandering over the face of Montana, as though he never had seen before those big, handsome, brown features.

"Dead," he said. "Dead. Señor! Rubriz will never lead us again!"

Montana stood up. He pulled the Mexican sombrero from his head not as any tribute of grief to the dead, but as one stunned. The fresh morning breeze cut into his face. And the Mexicans studied him curiously. As for their own grief, they had lost a priceless leader; but this tall gringo had been the friend of Rubriz. The story of that long battle which had cemented their friendship was still epic through all the mountains; you could hear the shepherds singing the tale of it as they walked the high plateau. And afterwards they had loved one another well enough to risk death, over and over.

Now the men of Rubriz saw the gringo jaw thrusting out as

though to meet a blow. He changed color a little. And that was all.

He was saying: "Take off your shirt, Robles."

And Robles answered: "There is no use. I am gone, señor. The life has leaked out with my blood."

Montana grasped the shirt of Robles at the shoulders and drew it up strongly, over his head. The arms of Robles fell limp out of the sleeves. He sat naked to the waist. The goatherd, who had crept nearer, shuddered and crossed himself. He was seeing the price of the freedom which he adored.

He saw Montana pick up the wounded man and lay him on his back, then sit cross-legged beside him. A bullet had struck the breast bone of Robles, fractured it, and slashed to the side, breaking ribs, opening a long cut out of which the blood had been pouring.

"Maria!" called the Kid.

She came and peered at the wound.

"You need the priest, not me," she said.

"Get out needle and thread from your bundle," said the Kid, "then sew up the lips of the wound so tight that the life can't get out.... Bring me some brandy.... Lend me that saddle and blanket to put under his head.... Do you hear me, Robles? This gunshot wound is only a scratch."

"It has scratched me to the heart, señor."

"Not a bit. If there's courage in you, you'll still live.... Here, take the brandy. Are you ready, Maria? Begin, then. Send the needle deep. Hold up the lips of the wound, so.... Take more brandy, Robles. Ay, there's courage in you!"

Robles, as the needle plunged again and again into his flesh, set his teeth hard. He turned green-grey, Sweat trickled down his face in spite of the coolness of the morning.

"Think of something else," said Montana. "If you keep your teeth set so hard, you'll set your brain aching. Talk a little. Tell me of Rubriz, will you?"

"In the dark," said Robles. "We rode through the dark..:. There was the moon, somewhere, over us... but it was dark where we were... in a valley. The wind was whining somewhere.... The horses kept the walls of the ravine echoing.... Why did we forget that there was that gorge cutting in from the west? The noise we made covered everything; it was thunder in our ears.... Then I saw them coming with a rush, boiling like a current of water out of the mouth of the western draw.... The moon shone on them for an instant before they entered the shadow of the valley. I saw Benito Jalisca, the Rural, leading the men of Lerraza. I saw big Don Emiliano.... Then the bullets came in a storm. My God! They all had repeating-rifles. There was no light for good shooting, but they fired fast. There were twenty of them and four of us.... They swept us all down in the first volley. It was like a mule-kick in my breast. I fell off the damned mustang.... I got up, my head was spinning.... I saw Rubriz jumping up from his dead horse; I heard his voice roaring like a great waterfall.... Ah-hai, it is hard to remember! But he was down again.... I saw Benito Jalisca run in at him and as Rubriz rose a second time, Jalisca beat him down—"

"Jalisca—beat him—down!" said Montana, his head thrusting forward as he drank in the words. "Benito Jalisca.... Go on, friend."

"And a horse ran by me with the reins hanging. I caught the reins. I was jerked off my feet and dragged. Dragged into the shadow of the big rocks. The horse stopped. I got into the saddle. They shot at me, but only a little, as I rode away.... They were all insane, screaming for the death of Rubriz."

"Like buzzards, eh?" said Montana.

Maria had finished her work. Montana held up the head of the wounded man and poured a great gulp of brandy down his throat.

"So—so—so!" gasped Robles.

"Viljoen!" called the Kid.

The thin knife-blade of a man was instantly before him, kneeling, staring at Robles, staring at Montana in turn.

"Viljoen, where will you go now?" asked the Kid.

"As far from this place as Mexico has room to let me run," said Viljoen. "When the hen is dead, the hawks soon have the chicks. We have lost our leader, señor."

"You have me," said the Kid.

"You?" cried Viljoen. "Will you lead us, señor?"

"Will you follow me, Viljoen?"

"As far as the edge of hell, and then down into it."

"Paredon, will you follow me?" asked the Kid.

"Señor, how could I be fool enough to refuse you?"

"Send the word to the rest, wherever you can find them. And hold them here—here with Robles. Viljoen, you are the nurse over him. You—and Maria—and Rosita—you will nurse him, all three of you. Send Orozco to spread the news that this is the rallying-place for all the men who followed Rubriz."

"And you?" asked Rosita.

He looked at her with unseeing eyes. "I have something to do, first," he said.

"I know what it is," said the girl. "You are going to go hunting Jalisca; you are going to throw yourself away. What a fool you are, querido! Do you suppose that Jalisca is not waiting for you? If Jalisca baited a trap for you with old Maria, don't you suppose he knows you will come for the sake of Mateo Rubriz? Don't you know that Jalisca is licking his lips and waiting?"

"Bring me my horse, Julio," said the Kid.

Mercado brought El Capitán, the tall horse stepping with a long, flowing stride.

"If you go, I'll follow!" cried Rosita, springing towards her little blood-colored mare.

"Viljoen, catch her," said the Kid.

Viljoen ran at her like a greyhound. She turned at him with a scream of anger, a knife in her hand. Viljoen caught her by the wrists. The knife dropped.

"Pardon, señorita," said Viljoen. "But he commands me."

"You molting buzzard—you mangy son of a blind coyote!" screamed Rosita. "Will you let me go?"

"In the name of God, señorita, you heard him give me commands."

"Keed! He is killing me! He is breaking my wrists!" cried the girl.

The kid was dusting his sombrero, turning the curled brim of it swiftly through his fingers. Now he settled it on his head and shook out the fringe of the brilliant scarf that belted him around.

"Patience, Rosita," he said. "I'll be back for you one of these days.... Watch her, Viljoen. If she gets away from the camp, I'll have words to speak to you.... Adios, all of you.... Adios, Rosita!"

Rosita, in a screaming passion, began to try to bite the hands of Viljoen. He shouted to her. They began to struggle together.

Mercado was running at the side of the horse of the Kid, crying: "Let me go with you, señor, or I shall die of grief!"

"Come if you can catch me, then," said the Kid. "If you can follow El Capitán and the trail, you're welcome."

And he sent the long-legged horse swiftly down the valley.

CHAPTER 18

Don Emiliano took his ease.

It was true that the formal announcement of his betrothal—almost as binding as marriage itself—had not taken place. It was true, also, that Don Tomás had been more than a little upset by the coming and the going of El Keed. But against all of this, Don Emiliano could consider that he had come to a lucky day. He had taken a person who was, perhaps, Mateo Rubriz!

Benito Jalisca had planned the stroke and guided it, but, nevertheless, Emiliano Lopez had been present, leading the horsemen of the Lerraza estates; and no one could remove that glory from him. A thrilling happiness was rising in the soul of Don Emiliano. When he looked at the tossing, silver head of the patio fountain, rising out of the slant, black paint of the shadow and springing into the moonlight, it seemed to Lopez that the fountain was a symbol of his own happy, upward-aspiring soul. The small song of the water chiming in the fountain-bowl was too small a music.

He looked to the side, and there he saw Dorotea dim in the shadow, though she was all in white. There was little air stirring in the patio. The fountain made a sound of coolness, but the evening was hot. The hanging-lamps that burned under the arched colonnade that bordered the patio had been turned low. Four guitars were kept at a mere tremble somewhere in the distance, four excellent voices sang no more loudly than the chiming of the fountain. All sounds of work inside the house were hushed. When the family took its ease in the patio, it would have been worth the skin of the servant who was unlucky enough to let a copper cooking-pan fall in the kitchen, or permitted a door to slip through his fingers and slam. To the frightened ears of the domestics of Lerraza, it seemed that the lowing of the cattle, mournful and far away, was an insult to the lord of the manor.

Don Emiliano's eyes took heed of the stars in their places, of beautiful Dorotea, and of the striding of Don Tomás as he moved back and forth through the patio, never pausing except when he turned. He spoke as he walked:

"A mystery! A brigand—a gringo . . . and yet to leave the jewels behind him. Do you hear me, Dorotea?"

"I hear you, Father."

"Then why don't you speak? . . . There were the necklaces, the rings, the bracelets, and the pendants . . . only those you were wearing would have made him rich. . . ."

"I offered them to him in my hand. . . ."

"Rather than have the brute tear them from you. Naturally. And then. . . ."

But Dorotea laughed a little and said nothing. Don Tomás took a stand, his spike of a beard jutting forward.

"And then?" he demanded, his voice raised.

"And then he put them back on me—the rings he slipped back on my fingers—the earrings he reset in my ears—"

"Dorotea!" exclaimed Don Emiliano, and all his self-content vanished.

"He has a very delicate touch," said the girl. "The bracelet he clasped around my arm as though he were—a jeweller! . . . And the necklace he looped around my neck and made sure that the biggest stone hung at the bottom of the loop. No one could have been more careful."

"What else?" exclaimed Don Tomás.

"What else? . . . Well, he lighted my cigarette."

"Damnation!" cried Don Tomás. "Dorotea!"

She stood up.

"Where are you going?" demanded her father.

"To my room," she said.

"I desire you to remain here."

"That is impossible," said Dorotea, "when you are in such a passion."

"But what am I to understand?"

"Yes," said Don Emiliano, leaning forward. "What are we to understand?"

"That El Keed uses no oaths. Only the most careful Spanish—the most poetic Spanish, Emiliano."

"But his leaving—and the jewels remaining behind him!" cried Don Tomás. "Do you want to drive me mad, Dorotea? Do you want to drive me mad?"

"What could he do?" asked the girl. "He had come for Maria

Mercado—and you see that he took her."

"A thousand devils!", groaned the Lerraza. "Maria Mercado? What has she to do with a fortune in jewelry?"

"He could not have the jewels and Maria. He had to make a bargain with me. And I showed him the entrance to the secret passage, naturally."

"And then what kept him from gagging you—the gringo beast!—and carrying away the whole casket?" demanded Don Emiliano.

"What kept him from that?" asked the girl. "You forget the song that even the peons know—the word of El Keed is better than gold. Besides, he is not a beast."

Don Emiliano laughed a little with an uncertain voice.

"I think you lost your heart to him, Dorotea," he said.

"Emiliano," broke in Don Tomás, "sometimes you talk like a fool."

"I beg your pardon, Don Tomás."

"Well, let it be—but at any rate he is gone, and the old peasant woman with him. . . . When I think of how he might have filled his hands and what he took, instead—a mule-load of old hag!" muttered Don Tomás.

"That was what he would do for a friend," said the girl.

"What friend?" demanded the Lerraza.

"Julio Mercado."

"He is not a friend. He is only a grovelling peon."

"Then perhaps El Keed carried Maria Mercado away for love."

"Bah!" snorted her father.

"Either to please himself or to please Julio Mercado," said the girl. "Or is El Keed a man who will do something for nothing?"

"He is a gringo dog, and money is the gringo's god," said Don Emiliano.

A footfall crossed beneath the arches of the patio. The voice of Benito Jalisca said: "The man is ready, Señor Lerraza."

"What man?" demanded the hacendado.

"Rubriz, señor."

"Rubriz? You are sure it is Rubriz?"

"I am almost sure, señor."

"Can he walk?"

"He is recovered enough to run from here to the mountains. That is a reason why I think he is Rubriz."

"Bring him here then."

Jalisca bowed and retired.

'You may go to your room now, Dorotea," said Lerraza.

"I prefer to stay and see him," said the girl.

"Why do you wish to stay? He is a beast—a bandido."

"He's a hero of the songs the peons sing."

"What songs?"

"Twenty. And above all the song of Rubriz and El Keed."

"Is there a song about them?"

"All through the mountains the peons and the goat-herds and the charros sing that song. You know some of it, perhaps? You know the part that goes:

> "Beware, Rubriz! Wise bear of the mountains, beware!
> He comes like a mountain lion,
> His feet are shod with the soft of the night,
> His eyes are yellow in the darkness.
>
> "Who is that beside you? Your son?
> Look, it is the gringo! It is El Keed!
> He has leaped from the night;
> He is away again, carrying your son.
>
> "All the horses, all the horses, all the horses
> Galloping swifter than thunder rolls,
> Ah, Rubriz, why do your bullets turn aslant?
> Do they love the man you follow?
>
> "Do they love him for the blue of his eye
> Or for the strength of his shoulders,
> Or for the speed of his great hands?
> Or do they love the red heart of courage in him?..."

"That's enough!" exclaimed Don Tomás. "Dorotea, where have you been hearing stuff about bandits and gringos?"

"If you open your ears wide, you'll hear the songs everywhere."

"The gruntings and the mumblings of wretched peons! But I thought that El Keed and Rubriz were blood-brothers?"

"So they are. But that was after the great fighting. Each of them saw that the other had blood of the right color—red blood, rather than blue, my father."

"What do you mean by that? What are you saying, Dorotea?"

"Nothing. I only tell you what the songs say. For instance:

THE SONG OF THE WHIP

"He is coming—El Keed—he is coming!
I have seen him on the mountain;
The wind of night tells of him;
The coyotes whimper and are still;
The great wolves howl up from the valley;
And my heart rises up like a wild stallion;
My heart sings as I . . ."

"Enough!" broke in the Lerraza again. "Dorotea, I forbid you to learn these snatches of stupid doggerel, these songs, common as the dust—"

"I'll have to learn to close my ears then," said the girl.

"Ah, here is the man!" cried Don Emiliano, and sprang up from his chair.

There entered, first of all, half a dozen of the chosen life guards of Lerraza, armed to the teeth, with double crossed bandoleros and cartridges over their shoulders, like soldiers, rifles in hand, and revolvers hanging low down on their thighs, ready to the hand. This double file of men turned inwards, and through the lighted door behind them came another pair who thrust forward a man of less than middle height, huge-shouldered, waddling somewhat like a bear in his gait, a picture of enormous power.

His wrists were held by double chains; his feet dragged a heavy lead ball behind them. Behind him moved half a dozen more of the guards, and Benito Jalisca among them.

"Now you have seen the monster, go, Dorotea!" advised Don Emiliano. "It's better for you to look at crawling tarantulas than at that animal."

"Tell me, Emiliano," said the girl, "how the friend of El Keed could be an animal and a monster?"

"Will you stay then?" exclaimed Don Emiliano.

"Certainly," said Dorotea.

CHAPTER 19

Don Tomás sat enthroned. It was a moment before he could speak, for the huge-shouldered captive had thrown himself on his knees before the chair of the hacendado, and the Lerraza heart fed on the spectacle for a moment. He noted the thick bandage around the head of the prisoner, and the bruises and cuts on the huge, naked arms. The man was bare-footed, and his feet were large enough to have supported the weight of two normal men.

"You are Rubriz, fellow?" asked Don Tomás.

"I am his man, señor, and God and Your Excellency forgive me."

The prisoner remained with his head bowed.

Don Tomás said to Jalisca, with a frown: "I'd heard that Rubriz was a fellow who would not bow down before the devil himself."

"It is part of his trick, señor," said the Rural. "The man is as clever as a fox. The more humble he is, the more he knows that we shall be baffled. It is only a trick and nothing else."

"I think you're right," said Don Tomás. "But what makes you feel that this is the true Rubriz?"

"By his look. There are hardly two men like him in the world."

"Have you seen his face before?"

"No, señor—except at a distance."

"He is a powerful beast," said the Lerraza.

"So was Rubriz," said the Rural.

"How was he taken?"

"A rifle bullet ploughed a furrow in his thick skull and knocked him down. We were charging. He sprang up, and the shoulder of a horse knocked him over like a thrown stone. Still, he was up again in an instant. I broke the stock of a rifle over his head, beating him down for the last time."

"And without breaking his head for him?"

"Señor, in a few seconds he was again struggling. A dozen of us fought to put ropes on him and make him a prisoner."

"Why not have put a knife or a bullet through him, and so an end of all the questions?"

"Señor, if this is Rubriz, he knows many things. There are a few amends that he can make to the law."

"Amends of what sort?"

"May I speak close to your ear?"

"As you please," said Don Tomás.

But he shrank a little from the lips of a common Rural, when Benito Jalisca murmured at his ear: "Señor, you have seen that El Keed would come right into the mouth of death for the sake of an old peon woman?"

"What of that?" demanded the hacendado.

"What will he do, then, for the blood-brother like Rubriz?"

"All men have a certain sense, Jalisca," said Don Tomás. "Not even a witless gringo like El Keed would dare to come out of the mountain again for a year and a day, after what he went through in my house."

"Señor, I beg you to believe me. I told you that I knew him before, and still I know him."

"And he will come?"

"Certainly he will come if this is Rubriz."

"How shall you prove it?"

"I have an old peon who is being brought up from the village. The man once was carried away by the gang of Rubriz. He would know the man. Here, this is the fellow!"

Don Emiliano took his stand close to the chair of Dorotea. He said: "Now we shall see. But that is Rubriz, I swear."

"Why should you swear, Emiliano?" asked the girl.

"How does a man know that he has caught a great fish? By the weight on the line! That is how I know. It is Rubriz! Do you see, as he kneels there, how his huge slab of a mouth twists and twitches? Do you see his great shoulder shrug? Now he stands up, and he keeps his head bowed, but he looks strong enough to bear the weight of the sky, does he not?"

"You know, Emiliano," said the girl, "such a man might be a thing for all of us who are Mexicans to be proud of."

"Proud? Are you mad, Dorotea? . . . Yes, proud as we are of a wild stallion."

"As in the song, Emiliano," said the girl.

He looked quickly down into her face and saw that she was laughing.

After all, a Lerraza, even a female of the race, had a right to be different from other people. So, at the time, he said no more.

They had brought in a little old man all twisted and weakened by time. Usually the years dry up people in a straight stick in Mexico, but in this case the wood had warped and the man was bent.

He was led straight up to the huge captive.

Benito Jalisca said: "There is the man. Who is it, father?"

The old man stared at Rubriz.

"That is a strong man," he said.

"I know it's a strong man, you fool," said Jalisca. "But is it Rubriz?"

"That?" said the old Mexican. "Rubriz? No, no, señor. That is not Rubriz! Rubriz? Indeed, no!"

Jalisca, the Rural, cried out in a passion: "The brains of the man have dried up! He's a half-wit—or else he's afraid to identify the great bandit!"

Don Tomás said: "Afraid? Come here, old man. Listen to me. You know that I am a father to all of you."

"Si, señor," said the old fellow, bowing.

"Where I stretch out my hand over you, there is no need for any one of you to be afraid of anything under heaven."

"Si, señor."

"Now open your eyes and tell me truly—is not that the bandit whose band carried you away not so very long ago?"

"No, señor. I never have seen this man before."

"Enough!" said Don Tomás.

The old man was waved away. Jalisca made a movement to kick him as he went.

"You see, you are wrong," said Don Tomás, to the Rural. "There would have been a thing to be remembered even by the Lerraza, if we could have caught and put an end to such a famous man as the Rubriz. But you merely are wasting our time!"

The Rural came close to him.

He murmured: "Let me try him once more. This old man was afraid to use his eyes. He did not look any higher than the feet of Rubriz. But that hulk that stands there, cowering, if he were to think that he was about to die, you would see him change. He would laugh at death if it were to come belching at him from the mouths of the rifles."

"Shall we threaten to shoot him to death?" asked Don Tomás.

"That is what I would do. Let me tell some of my men to

shoot—but just over his head. Then you would see him change and stand like a strong tree."

Don Tomás turned his head and regarded the Rural for a moment.

"You have a good brain in your head," he said. "It might be that I could find an excellent place for you among my servants, Jelisca. Would you serve me?"

"Señor, I would be as happy as a saint to serve you. I know that you make all men rich. But my life runs like a river towards the sea. It runs towards El Keed, señor. Until he is hanged at the end of a rope, or shot to pieces by the guns, I cannot rest, señor."

"Well," said Don Tomás, carelessly, "let us see you try."

He raised his voice and added, carelessly: "Talk no more to me, Jalisca. Whether this is Rubriz or not, the man was caught among the bandits. He must die. And let it be now. Stand him against the wall and let him be shot to death."

Jalisca drew in a breath of satisfaction. He turned and cried out orders. And at once some of his men took the prisoner and marched him to the wall at the other end of the plaza.

At this the prisoner burst into a loud wailing.

"Señor, you will not murder me?" he shouted. "Let me have a saint! Don't send me to hell with my sins tied forever on my shoulders! Have mercy! A priest! A priest!"

"Who are you to talk about mercy, you murdering dog?" demanded Jalisca. "Stand there at the wall.... Stand fast.... Face the firing-squad."

Here the clear voice of Dorotea called out: "Friend, if you have a last request, make it of me."

The prisoner threw back his head in astonishment. Don Tomás cried out a word of anger.

And the prisoner exclaimed: "Señorita, promise me one prayer to your own saint, and that will be better to me than the shriving priest."

"I promise it," said the girl.

"Get ready!" called Jalisca.

Six of the guard of Lerraza raised thier rifles to the ready.

"Take aim!"

The guns lifted to the shoulder and steadied.

"Fire!" called Jalisca.

But before that word left his lips the prisoner had pitched forward on the ground with a howl of terror and lay writhing and kicking at the earth in an agony.

The guns roared. Flecks of white were knocked off the stone face of the wall.

Jalisca snarled like an angry dog. He went to the captive and kicked him in the ribs."

"Get up!" he commanded.

"I am a dead man, señor!" groaned the other. "I am shot through and through—"

"Get up, dog!"

A fresh kick, aimed with all Jalisca's force, lifted the prisoner to his feet. There he stood, staggering a little.

Don Tomás said, dryly: "Wrong again, Jalisca!"

"It may seem that I am wrong," said Jalisca, "but after all I have the feeling that I am right. This is all acting. Let me keep him in the prison for a little time, señor, and then you will see."

"Let him have a taste of the whip," said Don Emiliano, "and then take him away. Am I right, Don Tomás?"

"Yes, the whip," said Don Tomás. "It's never wasted on the low rascals."

Two men held the hands of the captive. A third ripped the shirt from his back and then stepped back, drawing the long lash through his fingers before he laid it on.

He cracked the whip each time as it landed on the flesh. The skin was slashed through as though by knife strokes. The marks stood out one after the other, like black paint in the moonlight. Some of the paint began to run and blur the marks together, but at first they were in an ordered row, one beneath the other.

"There is skill!" said Dorotea. "What a man! What a hand! What an artist's hand!"

She clapped her hands together. Don Emiliano smiled fondly down on her.

"But I have seen ladies who would have been sickened and who would have grown faint at such a sight," he declared.

"They were not Lerrazas," said the girl.

The captive had been groaning from the first stroke of the whip. Now he began to howl. His contortions were so powerful that two men were by no means sufficient in strength to hold him. He began to thrust them back and forth with his mighty arms. Two others came to assist. They dug their heels and held back with all their might. In spite of that, the captive pulled them all into a confused heap about him, while he shrieked out in a terrible voice for mercy.

Don Tomás began to laugh.

"That is enough! That is enough!" he called. "My men have to sweat too much to hold that mountain bear. He has enough of the whip to give him the taste in his mouth the rest of his days. Take him away, Jalisca, and guard him. Let me know before the day he is executed."

"It shall be done, señor," said Jalisca.

He seemed troubled.

"After all," said Don Tomás, to encourage the Rural, "he seems *strong* enough to be Rubriz!"

"He is!" groaned Jalisca. "And he *is* Rubriz, I still swear, in spite of the grovelling and all the howling. I shall send at once for the warden of the prison and ask him to come to the jail and identify the fellow as Rubriz.... May I keep him here in your house for the rest of the night?"

"Welcome, welcome, Jalisca," said Don Tomás. "I recommend a little vinegar and salt rubbed well into the whip wounds. That is the thing that keeps them groaning until the morning."

It was an hour later that Dorotea Lerraza left her room and went straight to the cattle-barn in which the prisoner was kept.

She found him lying on his face, groaning, his arms above his head, with the manacles secured by a strong stake which had been driven through them into the ground. Two of the guards, and Jalisca himself, were watching over the prisoner.

The girl said: "Is that enough of you? What? Only three? And El Keed might jump into the midst of you at any moment? Do you think that three of you would be enough, then, to guard the prisoner and take care of El Keed?"

Jalisca bowed to her. He said: "Señorita, God keep me from boasting, but I wait for the day when I alone, I, Benito Jalisca, may have the joy of facing El Keed, even without help!"

"Ah, you are a very brave man," said the girl.

She stood over the prisoner.

"I must do something for this poor devil," she said. "I haven't done a good deed as yet this month, and you know that the priests say that only good deeds will get us into heaven."

She laughed a little as she said this, and the guards and the Rural laughed heartily with her. It was plain that she had a true Mexican sense of humor.

Now she, the great lady, was kneeling at the side of the wounded man. It was, really, a moving spectacle. The lantern light gleamed over the whiplash cuts, coated as with red varnish by the undried blood.

Jalisca raised his hand and withdrew with his companions to the end of the shed.

The girl began to rub, gently, a soft salve in the wounds of the captive.

"Rubriz," she said, "tell me what I can do to give you a chance to escape."

"Nothing," he whispered, between groans, "unless you can cut the chains with a breath."

"Does the salve ease you, Rubriz?"

"It eases my flesh. Who are you, lady?"

"I am a friend of El Keed's."

"He will come and scatter the dogs! He'll tear their ribs out of their flesh, they can be sure.... Do you work here in the house of Lerraza?"

"I am the daughter of the house, Rubriz."

He shuddered through his entire length.

"Is it so?" he muttered. "No, no! You are not Lady Dorotea?"

She still was rubbing the salve into the wounds. Then she took soft lint and with it packed the wounds.

"Is that better, Rubriz?" she whispered.

"God reward you," said the bandit. "But what told you my name?"

"When you threw yourself on your knees before my father, first you gave him one look, and I saw the look, Rubriz. I understood!"

"God bless you, lady. And God keep me from murder if I live beyond this. God keep me from remembering that I have forced my throat to howl for mercy, like a dog, and to fall down and grovel like a swine!"

"What is he saying?" asked Jalisca, curiously, lifting his voice.

"He says that he is about to die and begs for a priest. He says that he is not Rubriz, and begs that he should not be tortured any more. He is ready to die."

She stood up with her light, careless laughter.

"What a shame it is that God should permit such cowardly dogs to breathe the brave Mexican air!" said Dorotea.

CHAPTER 20

The telegram to Colonel Cuyas was succinct, forceful, clear. It said: "I think I have Rubriz. Will you come to identify him? If I bring him to you, there is the chance that he may be rescued by his friends on the way. Here he is safely held."

Colonel Cuyas remembered then that he needed a breath of vacation and wired back that he was coming as fast as the train could take him.

The colonel needed a bit of vacation because he attended so strictly to his duties. He was a colonel not by grace of courtesy but because he had been a good fighting-man, and when he was offered a reward, instead of asking to be made a general he asked for the post his heart yearned towards—to become the warden of the penitentiary.

He wanted to become the warden because once he had been a prisoner. Those whitewashed walls were to him as high as heaven, and he wanted to be the master of them.

Besides, he knew everything that never had come to official ears. He knew the systems of communication by which the prisoners rapped out messages to one another, plotted escapes in mass, or at least comforted one another through the use of words so sacred to lonely men.

He knew just how to apply the whip. He knew, furthermore, that if a dozen floggings are ordered for a man it is better not to give them all at the same time of day. A brave fellow may harden his spirit against the appointed hour, but if he is dragged from his cell in the morning, at noon, at midnight, at the whim of the warden, fear begins to haunt him, fear begins to gnaw at the marrow of his bones.

And fear is the keenest of all swords, as the colonel well knew.

He understood, also, that it is folly to spend on the diet of the prisoners all the money that the state appropriates for that purpose.

Beans and stale bread are enough to keep life inside the skin. They do not need to be seasoned.

The colonel put the money thus saved into his pocket. He bought a house. He proved that he was a worthy official and an honor to his occupation.

There were no more attempts to escape after he became the warden. A deadly silence settled like a poisonous mist over the prison. Even the guards walked softly. The decoys and stool pigeons did their best to gain information, but soon they found that there was little information to be gained. Men refused to trust one another. Even the friends of years of standing now looked askance at one another. It seemed that the warden was the devil and could read any man's mind.

There was silence, therefore, except when some unfortunate began to scream with madness in one of the solitary cells. That would happen about three in the morning, as a rule, when all flesh grows weaker and devils fill the night.

Perhaps it was for that reason that the colonel made his round in the dog watch. He used to come to a halt and grin, and inhale his breath when he heard the music begin. He said that it was like the howling of well-trained wolves.

So Colonel Cuyas was the lord of the high walls of the prison, amassing wealth, and absolute master of every soul under his command. The state was contented. The people looked up with awe to his face of iron, his eye of fire. His reputation grew from year to year, immensely.

And yet, at the bottom, there was one great rock on which his fame was established—the fact that, long before, he had been a prisoner in the hands of the great and terrible Rubriz and had escaped through his own unaided efforts.

That story had been printed many times. But still people would talk about it. It was fitting now that because of Rubriz—or a prisoner rumored to be like the great robber—the colonel was about to have a bit of vacation.

He took two aides and went aboard the train.

There were three coaches. He cleared the people from one of them and took possession of it. There he could extend his elbows, loll, and feel the distance, the cool distance, that existed between him and the common herd. He had been of the peonage himself, but he had risen. For God marks the wise men and wills that they should mount high before the eyes of their fellows. So the colonel used to tell himself every morning when he slipped into his uniform

THE SONG OF THE WHIP

coat with all its metal weight of medals across the chest. So he told himself now, as he rested his hand on the hilt of his sword.

He made the journey in much comfort of body and of mind, therefore, and so the train, as it neared his destination, slowed to climb a sharp grade, and there an outcry came from one of the guards. A ragged fellow had caught the train and was now on board it, the news was reported to the colonel.

He laughed and had the vagrant brought before him.

It was a tall man, his skin very dark, his hair long and black, and his eyes blue—a singular thing in Mexico.

His clothes were rags. His feet were bare. When the colonel stared at him he bowed almost to the floor of the car, and then he pointed to those bare feet.

"I thought that the iron feet of the train would not feel the cinders of the track bed as much as these feet of mine, my colonel!" he said.

The colonel did not laugh. He never laughed. But he grinned a little.

"Do you know me, fellow?" he asked.

"Colonel Cuyas—even the blind men know him," said the other.

"How do they know him?" asked the colonel, his grin disappearing.

"Every time they take a wrong step they think of the colonel," said the ragged man.

The grin of the colonel returned.

"This fellow has a certain wit," he said to his aides.

He waved his hand towards the guard.

"How did you happen to catch this rascal?" he asked.

"It was only chance," said the guard. The train still was going up the grade like a racing horse. I saw the man jump out from behind some brush. He ran like a great cat. I laughed. I was sure that he could not catch the guard rail. If he caught it, I was sure that his grip would be broken, he would fall. Perhaps the wheels would slice him up. But no! Like a mountain lion, he jumped! He caught the guard rail. His weight streamed out in the wind of the train's speed like a great rag. And a moment later he was on board. I was so surprised that I had barely enough presence of mind to put a gun under his chin. And there he is!... But he is no common man, whatever he may seem to you, señor!"

"No?" demanded the colonel. "What are you, friend!"

"I, señor, am a poor juggler."

"Let me see what you can do."

"Give me something to fill my hand, señor. This little art of mine shall be used for your pleasure, señor."

"Give him a knife, Leon. And you, give him a gun. Let me see what he can do with them."

The ragged fellow stood straight as a whip stalk, smiling, and his teeth were white, his eyes bluer than blue steel. He began to spin the revolver into the air, and then the knife. Always they were spinning, flashing, descending. He took a second knife, and then a broad sombrero. Even to watch the hat alone was a miracle, to see it soaring, as though with its own wit to guide its wings; and then to see it circle and drop back on the head, which it seemed to chase, only to be sent spinning upwards again.

The colonel began to sweat with pleasure.

He leaned forward, and grinned till his yellow teeth showed behind his moustache.

And now the juggler was making the knives, as they spun, seem to walk across one shoulder and down his arm, and so to leap again into the air as though of their own volition, untouched by the hand—or so it seemed.

"Good, very good!" cried the colonel.

The juggler collected himself, bowed, and restored the hat to the seat from which it had been taken, the knife to one waiting hand, another knife to the second aide.

"How many times have you used those quick fingers of yours for stealing?" asked the colonel.

"Señor," said one of the aides, "we are near the station."

"Go ahead and clear a place for me on the platform," said the colonel.

The aides stood up hastily and made forward, reeling a little with the sway of the car.

"And how many times, my fine fellow," went on the colonel, "have those hands been thieves?"

The blue-eyed man smiled.

"Ah, señor," he said, "when one has two hands, and each of them so quick, and each with a mind of its own, how can one tell what both of them are doing, night and day?"

The colonel almost laughed.

"Well, give me back the revolver," he said.

"Let the revolver give you something of its own accord," said the tall fellow.

"What the devil do you mean?" asked Colonel Cuyas.

"Señor," said the other, "you are the brave Colonel Cuyas. You have a second gun there under your hand. And I am a man you often have wanted to meet. I am El Keed."

The colonel stood up, automatically, his legs lifting him unbidden.

"You are about to die, señor," said the Kid. "Will you make the first move for the sake of your life?"

The train was slowing as it approached the station. The brakes were jammed on with a sudden extra pressure, groaning loudly, and this fresh shock staggered the Kid.

The colonel saw his opportunity and seized it with a lightning hand. He snatched out his revolver to fire, and saw, as the Kid staggered, a wink of flashing steel that pointed a sudden finger at him. That flash of steel turned into a thin flash of fire. A thunderbolt struck Colonel Cuyas through the brain. He fell forward. His body struck the arm of the opposite seat. Then it collapsed, face upwards, on the floor.

The explosion of that gun made the two aides at the end of the car whirl about. One of them had a chance to fire a shot at the darting figure which was disappearing through the opposite door of the car.

But the bullet missed. There were no hands ready to grasp at the fugitive because the colonel, unluckily, had emptied that car of all but himself and his immediate train.

The thing was very unlucky. And from the rear of the train it was only a step to reach some of the piles of tarred tiles stacked near the lines. And after that came the brush.

The two aides ran screaming in pursuit. Their beautiful long swords kept tripping them. No one else knew what to do. And Colonel Cuyas lay still, his eyes open, regardless of the blood that had run into them from the wound.

It was what the newspapers that evening called it—a colossal outrage.

The name of El Keed was mentioned in connection with it. And in fact, who else could have been the brutal perpetrator? Who else could have shot such a man as Colonel Cuyas with his own gun?

CHAPTER 21

They took the prisoner out in the sun and tied him down on his back. He lay there for ten hours, unable to turn his head, the fiery sun scalding his face. It was a leathery skin that he had, but the flesh under the brows, under the lower lip burned, scalded, puffed up horribly.

All the while two men took turns in the broiling sun, asking: "Are you Mateo Rubriz? Are you Rubriz? Why don't you confess? Why don't you admit it, and then the whole thing will be finished? We'll never let you up until you confess!"

But the prisoner would not confess. He would shout and yell and wail and protest and kick vainly against his bonds, but he would not confess.

So they took him out of the sun and stood him in well water that came just to his chin.

If he so much as relaxed the bend of his knees, the water covered nose and mouth. He had to remain almost tiptoe for hours of exquisite agony.

The Rural, Benito Jalisca, overlooked these proceedings in the big jail. He wanted to make sure of his man before he sent his to the penitentiary of which the great Colonel Cuyas had been the late head.

But though Benito Jalisca in person sat on the lip of the well and watched the sufferer beneath him stagger, till his head ducked under water time after time, only to save himself between weariness and drowning by another instinctive effort, Jalisca could not extort a confession from the wide mouth and the thick lips of the sufferer.

There was something else to do. Jalisca had the brains to think of it. He pinned the captive down on the ground, not in the jail, but close to it, where a nest of great red ants had been discovered.

THE SONG OF THE WHIP

They were huge fellows that gleamed in the sun. When there was a disturbance at the mouth of the hole where they had made their nest, they came bubbling up in red waves.

Jalisca went to look at them. He dropped a handful of gravel down the mouth of the hole. The red waves rose. The gravel was swept out, each ponderous chunk of stone grasped in a single pair of mandibles. The red waves poured out to the place at hand where Jalisca had fastened a living mouse by the tail to a little peg in the ground.

The red waves covered the mouse. It began to scream. Benito Jalisca cupped a hand behind his ear and listened, bending far over, to the tiny voice of the mouse.

The voice ceased. The ants kept swarming. Jalisca, with wonderful patience, bent over the spot until the waves of red ceased to bubble out of the anthole and over the place of execution. There remained a neat, a delicate little skeleton of glistening white, the skeleton of the mouse that was.

Jalisca was, in his heart, half an artist. He as delighted by the delicacy of that piece of exquisite ivory carving. He picked it up and carried it away in the palm of his hand, and he showed it to everyone, laughing. All the flesh had been carved away.

Afterwards, he had the captive brought out and pegged to the ground so that he could use nothing but his lungs, and even these inside a corseting of ropes. Then Jalisca drew a line of molasses from the hole of the red ants and ran the line to the head of the captive. The face of the prisoner he smeared with the sweet.

Then he stood by and said: "They are coming, *amigo*. All the little red ants. They've eaten a mouse for me, but that only gives them an appetite for meat. You should see them coming, like a big broad pen drawing a red mark of ink across the paper. That's the way they look. But they'll feel differently.

"They are going to climb on your face. They'll start eating the tender places first. They have sense enough for that. The lips and the eyes are the tender places. . . . But if you want to stop the thing, yell out the truth—yell out that you're Mateo Rubriz and we'll give you a different way of dying."

That moment the stream of the ants reached the face of the captive and swarmed over it.

Jalisca, excited, delighted, saw the mouth of the man jerk open. But before he could shout the ants had swarmed into his open mouth. He began to spit them out—mixed with blood. He could not even scream!

The whole face of the captive had become a living skin of working red.

Then Jalisca, regretfully, swabbed clean vinegar over the face of the prisoner and so removed the swarm. He cut the cords and let them take the captive away to the jail.

And still Jalisca stood in thought. Suppose he had waited a little longer, waited until the eyes were gone....

However, he shrugged his shoulder.

Something stabbed the back of his hand with pain. He looked down, startled, and saw one of the great red ants, which had managed to swarm up his clothes. Instead of flicking it away, Jalisca lifted his hand so that he could see the creature delivering its attack. It stood up, burying its horrible mandibles in his flesh. The pain was like the continued stinging of a hornet. A drop of blood stood out from the skin.

Then the Rural took the creature by the back and pulled it away. It had hold of the flesh by such a strong hold that the skin drew out in a small bag before the wriggling ant came clear.

Jalisca watched the blood run in a thin red pencil-stroke down the back of his hand. Then he laughed.

Instead of crushing the ant, he carried it carefully over to the anthole and dropped it safely back into the nest.

Going away, he stamped, to shake any of the little pests from his boots, where they might have clambered. Still he laughed a little. He was deciding that nature is very wonderful.

When he got back to the jail word was carried to him that the good Bishop Emiliano was, himself, in the town, and with him was that huge, lumbering friar, the giant among men, Brother Pascual. Jalisca went, himself, in haste, and found the bishop not in the church, not in one of the houses of the rich, but in the hut of a peon where he was saying prayers and giving his blessing to a bedridden old woman.

Jalisca waited until the bishop left that dark hovel. Outside, in the street, swarmed a mob of eager peons, men, women, children, all eager with their requests for miracles. The bishop stood with the sun making a dazzle of his bone-white face, so filled with pain, so filled with mercy. He was tired. The flesh was weary enough to fall from his bones, but still he was smiling. Huge Brother Pascual extended his vast arms and swept the crowd gently back from the bishop.

That was when Jalisca slipped in and knelt. As he received the blessing of the bishop, the Rural was saying: "In the jail here we

THE SONG OF THE WHIP

have the man I am sure is Mateo Rubriz. It is known to us all that you have seen him. If you will come to lay eyes on him—"

"What manner of man is he?" asked the bishop.

"Not tall, but a vast pair of shoulders, and a brutal face, and a waddling step. He looks stronger, even, than Brother Pascual here."

"Brother Pascual is a man who has seen Mateo Rubriz more clearly than I have," said the bishop, after a moment of pause. "Put the man in a line with others, and see if Brother Pascual can pick him out."

Jalisca went off in haste towards the jail. Brother Pascual remained with his great arms dangling at his sides and his eyes fixed helplessly on the face of the bishop.

"What shall I do?" he begged.

"Do," said the good man, "what your Father in Heaven bids you to do."

The bishop walked on, and still Brother Pascal stared hopelessly after him, as though he hoped that he might be able to receive a message from the mere back of the bishop's gown.

Then Pascual went to the jail, taking small, feeble steps at first, and then greater and greater ones. At last, as he walked, he was stamping the blunt end of his staff fiercely into the ground.

So he came into the jail yard, where a dozen men were lined up. They were men of all kinds. One of them was a huge, squat, mighty figure whose face was now a mottled red, the lips of the mouth swollen, the eyes strangely disfigured, blinking.

The friar strode down the line of those unfortunates. Then he stepped back and stared at them again.

"Well," said Jalisca eagerly, "have you seen him? Have you seen Rubriz?"

Friar Pascual lifted a big brown hand towards the sky, turned on his heel, and walked to the entrance of the jail again.

Jalisca followed him there. He leaned against the side of the gate and made a cigarette.

"Well, Brother," said the Rural, "this is bad luck for me. I was sure that that was Rubriz. . . . As it is, he's merely one of the band. We'll have him shot in the morning, at sunrise; and there's an end of one of the greatest hopes I'll ever have of being famous in Mexico!"

"Shot?" said Brother Pascual. "Shot at sunrise?"

He went away, slowly, his sandals dragging in the dust and his head down.

CHAPTER 22

A shoemaker heard the news first.

He had a lot of little nails in his mouth, squirting them out one by one into his fingers, and banging them home with rapid taps of his long-headed hammer. The rhythm of that hammer-beat grew ragged, uncertain, as he listened.

When the man left his shop, the shoemaker spat out the rest of the nails. They rattled unregarded across the floor. He jerked over his worn leather apron, rose, closed the door of his shop, ran out the back way, and climbed on the back of an old mule that stood in the back yard.

He beat the mule into a trot, then into a gallop, until he came beyond the verge of the village to a place where a peon was working with a great-bladed hoe in a corner of the land of the Lerrazas. There was no one near them, but the shoemaker bent far form his saddle and whispered the tidings in the ear of the peon.

The latter groaned, swept the sky and the earth with a desolate, frightened eye, and then began to run as fast as he could, up the hill and over it.

In the hollow beyond he came to a man with two lean horses that tugged at a plough, working it carefully among the tender stems of a young vineyard. That man heard the few words, and shouted with angry surprise, and straightway upharnessed one of the horses.

He left the other to go where it could, or remain anchored by the plough. The peon, on the first horse, galloped it furiously up the valley.

He came to a fence of barbed wire. The horse could not jump it. The way to the next gate was long. So the peon took a stone and beat the wires from two of the posts. Then he stepped on the

THE SONG OF THE WHIP

sagging wires and led the horse safely across.

For the breaking of a fence the Lerrazas had been known to hang a man, or do worse by him than mere death. But the peon mounted and rode on. So he came, at last, with his staggering, sweating horse, to the place of a little free farmer, one with a parcel of corn land, a few blades of grass, a melonpatch, and a great deal of time on his free hands.

He had, also, a fine four-year-old mustang, the pride of his life. The mustang was never far from him. It stood now close to the side of its master, who fanned away the flies that tried to settle on the silken hide.

To him the peon gasped out the tale. And the man with the horse rose, said nothing, but pulled the straw sombrero firmly down over his head. Afterwards he ran into the hut and picked up his saddle. The chickens which were scratching about on the floor of the house, in the vain hope of finding a few edible morsels, scattered cackling out of his way. His wife looked up with a cry from the patting of wet, cool tortillas on a flat stone. But the free farmer gave her no answer. He clapped the saddle on the back of his mustang and went flying off towards the highlands, never looking once behind him.

Far up there in the highlands on many an obscure trail where mountain goats were far more at home than even the deft-footed mountain horses, there had been movement all that day.

For men appeared at various points who had about them certain points in common.

Nearly all of them were ragged fellows, and nearly all had about them some vestiges of a former glory, such as a fine sombrero, or foolishly elegant pair of boots, or trousers from which half of the silver conchos had been broken away.

Some of them rode active little mountain mules; some of them rode mountain mustangs, fierce as wildcats; some of them, however, had blooded horses under saddles no matter how battered.

But one and all had three things in common—a fine rifle, a good pair of revolvers, and a hunting-knife of the finest steel. Moreover, in spite of the windings of the mountain trials, all of them were heading in one direction.

Their weavings through the mountains were somewhat like the driftings of the buzzards in the air when they begin to blow towards the mysterious tidings of food to be found on the earth, far below, beyond the ken of any eyes.

126   THE SONG OF THE WHIP

After a time, in twos and threes they commenced to encounter one another.

Sometimes they stared at one another for a long moment, with eyes as bright as polished black stones. But nearly always one or both would break into laughter.

Then they always would say to one another: "What, again, brother?" And, still laughing, they would strike their hands together.

What they said to one another within those groups, as they rode on towards their destination, would have made a hundred stories, long, incredible enough in most cases. But there were only the wind and careless ears to hear their conversations, and the records of their experiences during recent months. At last they came to a focus. And the focus was a sprawling little camp where the Montana Kid shook dice with the most venturesome during the day and sat up half the night to sing songs to Rosita, accompanying himself on an old guitar.

Some forty men of the mountains had pooled about him in the course of a short time. Each, as he came in, with his group, would ask: "Who has called? Rubriz?"

And the answer always was: "El Keed!"

"So!" the recruits would reply. "To me that is equal."

It was the greatest compliment that any gringo ever received south of the Rio Grande.

On this afternoon the Kid was tuning his guitar when Rosita said to him: "Do you see Tonio sitting with his chin on his fist?"

"Hey, Tonio!" called the Kid.

"Don't speak to him—don't call him over, because I want to talk to you about him. You see how far he is lost in his thoughts? He did not hear you."

"I've got to cheer him up," said the Kid. "He's thinking of his home. He's a little homesick, Rosita."

"He thinks of me,' said Rosita, sitting up straight.

"Everybody thinks of you," said Montana. "Do you know that?"

He struck the strings of the guitar suddenly and broke out into the old song which the shepherds of Mexico know and love:

"Over blue fields the flocks of the Lord,
Over green fields my sheep wandering,
And all my thoughts are blowing on the wind.
Do you hear them come whistling home to you?"

Rosita did not smile. She said: "I must talk to you about Tonio."

The hoofs of a galloping horse knocked a confusion of sharp echoes from the walls of the valley; the rider veered into the camp at full speed. The chest and neck of his horse were foam-flecked. He threw his reins and sprang to the ground.

"Will you hear me?" demanded Rosita.

"Hush!" said the Kid, and stood up. "That fellow wants me."

"What if he does?" demanded Rosita angrily. "Am I no less to you than any man?"

"Everybody's less than the last news," said Montana, and walked down from the tree.

From the distance he could hear the newcomer shouting the tidings.

"Rubriz! They have him in the jail. They have stopped torturing him. He dies in the morning, at sunrise! Rubriz—the father of the poor—he will be shot at sunrise!"

The Kid walked down into the milling crowd of the listeners.

He said: "There's parched corn and dried meat over yonder. Maria Mercado will give some to all of you. Then we take saddle and away with us all."

The messenger, who sat exhausted on a rock, began to shake his head.

"There's no use in that, señor," he said. "They have guarded the jail with many men. They expect your coming, señor, and all the men of Rubriz that are ready to die for him. They are guarding the jail with many lights and long rows of soldiers. There is nothing to do, señor!"

"No?" said the Kid. "I tell you that there are more ways of getting the wine than by breaking the bottle. We won't attack the jail—and still we'll get Rubriz. Into the saddle, every man of you."

They began to shout.

The kid went up the slope to the gloomy figure of Tonio.

"Tonio, stand up," he said.

Young Dick Lavery rose with a gloomy face.

"You're going home, Tonio," said the Kid. "Mexico's no place for you, anyway."

"You're starting to fight for Rubriz," said Tonio, without enthusiasm, "and he was like a father to me all those years."

"We don't need you for the fighting," said the Kid. "All I intend to do is to raid the Lerraza ranch and act the part of Rubriz myself. If I can't raise enough devil to make people think that Rubriz himself is alive and on foot, my name's not Montana. I intend to pick up a few of the Lerraza people and hold 'em until every man-jack in the jail is turned loose. Understand? It's the sort of thing that Rubriz himself might do, and it's going to work. But you—you head for home. I won't have you with us. Remember that they have plenty of ropes in Mexico, and they're still ready to find your neck size in lariats. So long! I'll be seeing you! Good-bye, Tonio.... Shake hands with your father for me. ... Adios!"

He went off in the direction of the tall, narrow-shouldered stallion, El Capitán.

And Tonio Lavery, watching the confusion of the departure, where every man was singing or shouting or laughing, went back up the slope to the tree where Rosita, her hands loosely clasped before her, was overlooking the scene.

He stood behind her, unnoticed, for a moment. Then he said:

"Rosita, I want to talk with you. El Keed won't have me with him on the raid. He's sending me home. And this is what I want to know. Will you come with me?"

"I?" said Rosita, looking up through the branches of the tree and not at the speaker.

"To marry me, Rosita?" he persisted.

"I'll go and ask El Keed," she said.

She took a pace before he caught her arm.

"He's told you to despise me, has he?" demanded Tonio.

She turned and stared at him. She had begun to laugh, but now the laughter faded. The whole flood of riders went sweeping off down the slope and left them still staring at one another.

CHAPTER 23

Forty men all mounted on race-horses cannot travel as fast as one man on a mule. Numbers make slowness. And besides, when Tonio Lavery got on his horse he took a short-cut of the most dangerous ground, which saved him a number of miles. That was why he was able to get through to the Lerraza ranch far ahead of the Kid and the men of Rubriz.

He rode wildly, hardly caring what happened to him, and all the way the last words of Rosita stung him like wasps, to the soul.

"If I marry a gringo, I won't take one with the soul of a half-breed!"

He tasted and retasted those words all the distance to the great ranch. He was well up the road to the ranch when a rider swung out into the shadows of the evening from beneath a group of trees and challenged.

"Who goes?"

"A friend!" called Tonio.

"What name, friend?" asked the Lerraza guard, his rifle at the ready.

"A friend in need!" cried Tonio. "Go back to the house. Tell them that El Keed and forty of the men of Rubriz are coming straight for the ranch, on a raid. They're coming down the Gregorio Cañon. Block up the neck of the cañon with fighting-men. You still have time. But hurry, hurry, hurry!"

"Tell me one more thing," shouted the guard. "Is it Rubriz himself who is in the jail or is it—"

But Tonio Lavery already had swung his horse around, and the rattle of its hoofs drowned the words of the guard. The latter took one glance after the departing horseman, spat on the ground, tugged down his sombrero, and then lit out at full speed for the house.

Don Tomás heard the news and was keen as a knife to lead his fighting-men out to the battle. Don Emiliano was able to persuade him to stay at home. His words were brief:

"If we wipe out forty of the Rubriz gang, will that repay us if one bullet strikes to the life of a single Lerraza?" he said.

Don Tomás, listening, was impressed. He did not feel that he over-valued himself, but after all he was a man with a sense of money and of men. He did not ride with his fighting-guard, but he remained mounted at the patio gate and saluted his fellows with a stern look of joy on his face.

The muster had been made quickly.

There were a score of the trained, highly-paid and privileged guards. There were three score of the wild charros off the range, every one of them hardly less expert with knife and rifle than the men of the Lerraza guard. And there were some two score more of the tougher peons, fellows ready enough to jump on a mustang and go clattering off to a fight, men who had learned that it saves money to kill your rabbit with the first shot.

They made an entire little army of well over a hundred; and Lerraza felt that he could call them picked men. If ever they confronted the desperadoes of Rubriz in the narrows of the cañon, they ought to crumple the sweep of the bandits and crush them to nothing against the rocks.

Dorotea stood at her casement and watched the riders pour away into the moonlight. She watched them listlessly. And when the uproar had died away she called down to her father in the patio: "Tell me something, Father."

"Well, Dorotea?" he answered. "Well?"

"How hard is it for the soul of a gringo to get into heaven?"

Don Tomás certainly was a gentleman. Sheer instinct made him spit to clear his mouth of the dirty word.

"Gringos? If they crawled all their lives in sackcloth and ashes, they could never get higher than a top round of hell."

He looked suddenly up at her in amazement. She was laughing gently, looking far across the night.

Don Emiliano, erect in the saddle, feeling even more the soldier than he looked, rode at the head of his men, partly because that was his place and partly because he was on the best horse. When he came to the mouth of the Gregorio Cañon, he did not pause, but pushed straight on until he had reached the narrows. Here a cañon debouched to the right and to the left, but the main course of the Gregorio Valley held straight on before him with a huge tumble of talus rocks piled up against the cliffs on either side.

Don Emiliano posted fifty marksmen among the rocks. He reserved his seventy best men to wait beside their horses on either side of the valley, well screened by the rocks. Then he commanded silence, and he was obeyed. The Mexican knows night fighting by instinct. And here was a slim beauty of a moon to guide his rifle-shots. In every heart was a gentle, brooding content. And now, far away, they could hear the first murmur of the hoofbeats. They waited, grinning, handling their rifles, silent as the rocks that sheltered them.

And so it was that when Rosita raced her mustang along the high ridge far above, she looked down into the valley and could not believe her eyes. The men were still as statues, but the moonlight stroked their rifles with silver.

There was a coating of sand, up there on the top of the ridge, that silenced the hoofbeats of her horse. She had been riding hard, so hard that, following the short-cut, she had overtaken the riders of El Keed, who pursued the more leisurely pace of a large body. Now she was ready to swing down into the larger space of the Gregorio Cañon and so let the men of Rubriz pour past her, so that she could follow behind and observe what should happen, on this night of nights.

She could see, without a prophetic gift, exactly what would befall when she noted that mass of armed men beneath her. She turned her mustang and raced it straight back along the ridge towards the booming of hoofbeats, like the flooding of a great river, that continually was pouring down towards her through the night.

Well up the Gregorio Cañon, she saw from the height the coming of the forty riders, and Rosita came down to the floor of the valley like a night hawk from the sky, with the mustang braced back and sitting down on its haunches, and the pebbles and rocks bounding high in front as it skidded down the slide to the valley floor.

That tall figure on the tall horse was El Keed. When he heard her shout, he drew rein beside her and reached out and gripped her arm.

But he merely laughed as he said: "You know, Rosita, that magpies should not fly by night. What's the matter?"

"Two hundred armed men waiting down the valley," panted the girl. "*Valgame Dios!* Two hundred at least—an army! Go back! Go back!"

The forty men of Rubriz had halted their steaming horses in a dense circle around their leader. Viljoen, of the knife, said, cheerfully: "You see what your first plan was worth. What is the second plan, señor?"

"Are they waiting on horseback?" asked the Kid.

"On foot. Ready to mount. Behind those big piles of rock that—"

"I know about them."

The Kid began to whistle that famous old Indian song:

> When you kissed me, when I heard you breathing,
> An arrow sounded beside my ear,
> A winged arrow from a bow-string in the sky;
> And now and forever my heart is bleeding.

The forty men of Rubriz did not speak. They listened to the last note of the whistling.

"We can cross that bridge and go down the next valley," said the Kid.

Orozco, the famous horse-thief, answered: "The valley is deep with sand. We would have to crawl like snails."

"And they had already heard your horses coming!" cried Rosita. "There is nothing to do. Turn back and—"

The Kid said: "We could cross the ridge and go slowly down the next valley."

"Then the men of Lerraza would be behind us," said Orozco.

"The gorge cuts back into the Gregorio Ravine," said the Kid. "There is a narrow cañon that slits in between them. Are the men of Lerraza on this side of that slit, Rosita?"

"They are," said the girl. "But listen to me—Oh, I know that the devil is coming up in you! I can see it in the shine of your eyes—but in the name of God remember that—"

"Viljoen, take five men and ride them up and down here—here where you have rocks under the heels of your horses. Ride them up and down and make as much noise as you can. Shoot off a gun once or twice—and make noise, raise the echoes with the riding.... The rest of you follow me.... Viljoen, keep Rosita...."

That was how they trailed across the divide and into the next valley, where the sand, to be sure, was deep. It was so deep that it masked the noise of hoof-beats better than padded velvet. And there was only the light creaking of the saddle leather, the soft,

THE SONG OF THE WHIP

soft, deadly jingling of spurs, and the watery swishing of the sand about the hoofs of the horses.

So they came down the valley to a narrow gorge that linked it with the Gregorio Cañon.

Here the Kid went first, and on foot, with the stallion stealing behind him like a hunting cat, and so he came to the mouth of the gap and was able to look covertly around the corner of the huge rock wall.

The picture was spread there before him with perfect clearness. He saw the men of Lerraza beside their waiting horses; he saw the scattering of riflemen among the rocks all still beneath the moon. And far away up the valley rolled the distant clangor of hoof-beats, now seeming to sweep nearer, now withdrawing, as it were. No doubt the men of the Lerrazas were beginning to wonder why those distant riders made noise without coming at last upon them, but, after all, the dwellers among the mountains understand that sound from a distance is a most deceptive thing.

The Kid went back through the gap and said twenty words to his followers.

"They're around the corner looking the wrong way. Shoot in the air. Don't make 'em fight. Make 'em run."

And a moment later the whole mass of thirty wild horsemen streamed through the gap into the wider ravine of Gregorio, all screaming like devils, firing off their guns as fast as they could, and driving straight at the massed men of Lerraza.

CHAPTER 24

Courage is the possession, the special treasure, of no nation. Americans are as brave as the next nation. But they did a good deal of running at Bull Run.

Mexicans will fight like savages to the last man if the circumstances are right. But the Mexican is a fellow to attack, not to stand still. The men of Lerraza could deliver as fine a charge, as well sustained, as fiercely driven home, as any cavalry in the world. But they did not know what to do when an enemy they had been looking for in front suddenly appeared out of the ground behind them and rushed them from the rear.

While still they strained thier ears and indubitably made out the echoing gallop of horses far away, up the gorge of Gregorio, the devil struck them brutally from behind.

There was hideous unfairness about the thing.

Whatever a Mexican is on horseback, he is only a tenth part of that on foot. And the entire mob, the entire six score, were on foot, there under the moonlight.

Even then, if some of the Lerraza fighting-men had begun to fall, others would have tuned and fought back at least in knots and groups, desperate men, killing many before they went down. But as a matter of fact not a single bullet struck home. There was a roar of guns, multiplied by the towering echoes, a rush of hoofbeats, and the dismounted rearward part of the Lerraza men tried vainly to leap into the saddle.

Those who got to the backs of their mustangs found themselves in the midst of riderless, plunging, kicking, squealing horses with the enemy pouring suddenly down on them.

So they slipped to the ground again and tried to get at a little distance from the murderous whirl of that attack. They took their distance with a good deal of speed, and found that all their companions were doing the same thing.

THE SONG OF THE WHIP

Then someone shouted: "Treason! We are betrayed! Betrayed!"

Those words were a trumpet call to the terror that always is lurking in us. "Betrayed! Betrayed!" yelled the men of Lerraza out of a single roaring throat; and they began to run for their lives.

It's hard to run over a clutter of rocks carrying a long rifle. The rifles were the first to be cast aside.

Further, a six-shooter Colt is not a light encumbrance. So the revolver went, also. Men threw off jackets, sombreros, and screamed as they ran.

Some of them in their blank terror ran up the almost sheer faces of the cliffs like wildcats.

Some tore straight up the valley, blindly.

Others, and this was the largest part, turned to the left up the first draw that opened out of Gregorio Gorge.

They were not pursued. It would have been easy to ride them down, now, and slaughter the armed rascals by the score. But the men of Rubriz were in no condition to make a charge; besides, the Kid forbade it. But all those chosen cut-throats of Rubriz were helpless in the saddles, reeling to and fro drunkenly, throwing up their arms, staggering with inextinguishable laughter.

They hardly could rally themselves to pick up the fallen loot of richly adorned hats, revolvers, rifles, and tie them in bundles on the backs of the captured horses.

The charge had lasted two minutes. Not a scratch had been received. And thirty Rubriz men had made themselves masters of a hundred and twenty fine horses, to say nothing of all the poundage of excellent ammunition, all the guns, all the little trimmings that were found in the saddlebags of the routed.

When the laughter ended a little, the Kid hurried his men through the gathering of the loot.

Viljoen and the other five from up the valley had arrived, in answer to the brief thunder of the guns, and with them came Rosita. The whole crowd cheered her, for they knew that her scouting work had saved them from a disaster. They cheered the Kid also.

"Rubriz killed with bullets. El Keed kills with laughter!" they said to one another, and still they laughed so that they could hardly sit their saddles as they followed the Kid towards the Lerraza ranch.

The Kid, riding at the side of Rosita, was singing one of the old Mexican love-songs. A good part of it, in our colder speech, would seem a little indecent, but it opened somewhat like this:

Yellow wing, red wing, white wing, blue wing,
All you flyers in the upper air,
All you who swim in the blue bowl of heaven
Tell me have you seen her, have you seen my love?

If the wind is sweeter than April,
It has blown through the warm night of her hair,
If the moon blushes golden in the sky
It has looked on her, secretly it sees my love.

She was dressed, like an Indian girl, all in white doe-skin that gleamed in the moonshine; and she looked on the Kid without laughing, brooding over him a little, watching the lift of his head as he poured his song into the night.

The buildings of the great Lerraza place were still indistinguishable in the distance when a single rider came towards the men of Rubriz. Half a dozen of them, shouting, rushed their horses forward, spreading them out in a fan to enclose the stranger. But he came steadily on, regardless of their charge, and a moment later they returned beside him, shouting: "Tonio! Tonio! Tonio."

That was when Rosita plucked the sleeve of the Kid and said: "How did the Lerrazas know that you were coming tonight? How did they know that you were following the Gregorio Cañon? Tell me, *vida mia*. How did they know, unless someone of us galloped ahead to warn them? And . . . I tell you this: You were hardly gone when Tonio threw himself on his horse and rode away like a wild man. Could he have—"

"No," said the Kid. "He could not have. I'll tell you this, Rosita: When a man begins to doubt the friends who have bled for him, he'd better die by their treachery than keep on living and doubting them. Whatever Tonio does, he can't do wrong."

That was why he welcomed Tonio with a shout and gripped his hand.

"Come on with us now, Tonio," he said. "The rest is easy. And this is the way towards the Rio Grande . . . What brought you to us?"

"I heard the guns," said Tonio. "And so I came . . . It was quick work, Montana."

"I had Rosita to see things for me; and I had luck to help me. That was all. . . . Hai, Rosita! Sing me that song about the whippoorwill and the wolf, will you?"

"I am tired of singing," said the girl, and kept her eyes fixed steadily on the face of Tonio.

They had the loom of the buildings of the Lerraza place before them, at last, and at the shout of the Kid the whole body of men spurred their horses forward into a wild gallop.

The Kid, on the long-striding stallion, led the way, but Tonio was hardly half a length behind him.

Rosita was letting herself drift off to the side, out of the confusion, out of the dust; big thoughts were burdening her mind.

CHAPTER 25

Not all the men of the routed party of the Lerrazas had lost their horses. Emiliano Lopez, among the rest, had retained his, because he was sitting in the saddle to give directions and orders at the moment of the attack.

Don Emiliano had been the last to flee, and had emptied a revolver with a rather unsteady hand in the direction of the attacking force. Then, seeing that he was alone, and with the bloodcurdling battle-cry of "Rubriz! Rubriz! Rubriz!" turning his blood cold, Lopez turned the head of his horse and, groaning, drove home the spurs.

Three or four others managed to follow him, flogging their mustangs to keep up, and so he came to the Lerrazas' house with despair in his heart.

His companions, reaching the main patio, began to shout the terrible news at once.

All was lost! All was lost!

No one had gone to bed in the great house, waiting for news of the trap which had been set for El Keed in Gregorio Pass. Now the mansion swarmed with noise and doors slamming, feet racing through corridors, men and women screaming out like mad.

Old Don Tomás brought some order out of the chaos.

First, in the patio, he met Don Emiliano and straightway held out his hand.

"We can't always be victors!" said Old Tomás, sticking out his spike of beard and gripping the hand of Don Emiliano.

Don Tomás wanted to be magnificent, and in fact he was. He remembered that Louis XIV had said something like this to a defeated marshal—Marsin, wasn't it? But Don Tomás found the line a good one in time of need.

Then he raised a thundering voice and commanded all the people of the house straightway to join him in the patio, the men

THE SONG OF THE WHIP

to bring horses and saddled mules from the stables, the women to sweep together all the valuables which easily were transportable.

But what could be transported easily?

What of all the magnificent furniture, the great tapestries, the rich curtains, the filled wine-cellar? What of the wagons in the sheds, the spreading flocks and herds, the amassed stores of all sorts in the great cellars of the house?

Don Tomás thought of these things, and his heart died in him; but he saw the women come bundling out with their arms burdened, and some ease came to him again.

Furthermore, he was planning far ahead. He was executing the vengeance.

And yet it was strange. The flogging of a peon, a worthless Julio Mercado—and then the bursting of a dam. El Keed had come, ruin had piled up like a wave above the head of Don Tomás, and now he was being driven from his mansion, his chosen palace of all the 'castles' at his command.

It was only one thing lost. Much more remained. But Don Tomás ground his teeth hard together and took deep breaths.

"Emiliano, see to Dorotea," he commanded.

Emiliano was instantly at the door of the girl's room, and there he found her walking up and down, calmly, dressed in sweeping white, trailing behind her a wisp of smoke from her cigarette.

"Dorotea! Dorotea!" cried Don Emiliano. "What are you thinking of? Do you know what has happened? We have to ride for our lives! Why are you in those clothes? Can you sit on a horse when—"

"Dear Emiliano," said the girl, "what do clothes matter? My women are getting some of my things together, and I'll be with them in the patio in a moment.... Just run back and tell father that I'll be there."

The brain of Don Emiliano was whirling a little on this frightful night, and therefore he did as he was told.

And it was only a few moments later that a peon galloped a mule wildly to the house and shouted: "They are coming! They are coming! Rubriz and El Keed!"

At that, a great wave of yelling broke out in the patio, and without further delay the whole mass of people and the livestock they rode on poured out into the moonlit night and made directly for the town.

Far, far behind them they could hear the pounding hoofs of horses. The lights of the town twinkled in the distance like cold stars. And towards that haven the people of Lerraza fled at full speed.

They had covered an entire mile when Don Tomás called to Emiliano: "Why is not Dorotea beside you?"

Lopez looked desperately around him.

"She is here!" he shouted. "Somewhere—she is here—"

"Where?" roared Don Tomás. "Where is she, Emiliano, in the name of God?" He got no answer.

In fact, Dorotea, heir to all those millions of acres and pesos, was not among the fugitives.

Don Tomás, in his frenzy, would have turned the head of his horse and ridden back to the house, and they had to tear the reins out of his hands and drag him forward towards safety. He rode on, beating his hard hands against his face.

And behind them, through the night, they heard the air resounding, trembling with the battle-cry: "Rubriz! Rubriz! Rubriz!"

"The dogs—the fools thought that they had captured Rubriz! Who but Rubriz would have dared to do such things?" groaned Don Tomás to his soul.

Ordinary riding would not do. Fast-pounding hoof-beats were rushing up behind them. It was spur, spur, spur, now. Then screamings and yellings in the rear of the tumult as the advance guard of Rubriz men drew near.

But the town was near, also. Right into the main street of the town poured the rout from the hacienda. The startled people ran out to stare, and saw the lordly Don Tomás led on his horse, like a blind man, and followed by a frightened train whose horses were burdened by all the lighter movables that could be carried out of the Lerraza mansion.

Such a sight never had been seen before. It was like a stroke of disaster, a painting of the scene of the end of the world. And therefore it was not strange that more than one of the peons grinned a little, secretly, to himself.

So they came to the most stable building in the town, the jail, and through the readily opened gates they were admitted to the big central yard of the prison.

Don Tomás and Emiliano Lopez were taken, of course, to the best of the offices. There the head of the jail and the celebrated Rural, Benito Jalisca, greeted them.

The bulldog face of Jalisca was rather pale. He stood in a corner of the room, with glowering eyes fixed upon him.

He had to hear the great Don Tomás saying: "The man you

thought was Rubriz was only a brute of a mountaineer, a bandido; the real Rubriz has swept fivescore men half the way to hell tonight, and now is burning my house. So much for you—so much for the Rurals! Mexico, Mexico, is there one man of brains left inside your borders? My house is gone, and my daughter is in the hands of devils!"

CHAPTER 26

The forty men of Rubriz, like forty wolves, swept in on the house of the great Lerraza; like wolves they yelled; like hungry wolves their mouths were watering for the loot. And yet when they arrived they did not find the place empty. It was true that most of the house servants were gone; on the other hand some remained, and along with them were the great majority of the peons who worked the lands surrounding the place. These came out in throngs and ringed the house at a little distance.

They came by families, men, women, and children. The women sat down cross-legged and held children on their laps. The men walked up and down, conversing, or staring silently, hungry-eyed.

They had light, presently, to see by. For by accident one of the Rubriz searchers for spoil set alight a shed stored with firewood, and this blaze, tossing great armfuls of red into the sky, gave a crimson, wavering light to the entire scene.

These peons were entirely fearless. When they saw the bandits carrying treasure out of the house, even the big tapestries, the rugs, the pictures tied face to face with their frames, the very gilded chairs in which Lerraza near-royalty had reposed for centuries, the peons pointed the things out to one another, and chuckled. Some drew near and examined the heaps of goods piled in the patios, and fingered them, and lifted them up for one another to admire.

To these people the bandits paid not the slightest attention, except to crack a joke with them now and then; and the peons responded in kind. A good deal of this banter was of a rather pointed sort.

It was Orozco who said to a burly farm-laborer: "How long have you been a slave, brother?"

"Longer than you have been cutting throats, *amigo*," said the peon.

"I'd rather cut throats than plough ground for the black Lerrazas," said Orozco.

"Well, *amigo*," said the peon, "one day when I'm running my furrow I'll be ploughing Orozco into the soil for fertilizer. I'll be raising wine out of the bones of the great Orozco."

"If that wine will poison a Lerraza, I'll be satisfied," said Orozco.

At this all the peons laughed a little.

Yet they showed no great envy of the bandits as the latter now began to appear made glorious by portions of the spoil.

One of the Rubriz men, for instance, had taken a lace tablecloth and turned it into a sash to girdle himself. Another was using a silver bell as a saddle ornament. A third had put on the uniform coat of Don Emiliano, all covered with decorations and brilliant ribbons, for Don Emiliano had served in the army for a few years and found advancement easy, with the Lerraza backing to boost him. By degrees the men of Rubriz were warming to their work.

They had found the way to the cellars at once, of course. Whole kegs of wine they rolled into the patios and broached—red wine and white. They brought up hundreds of bottles of the older vintages, and knocked off the necks and drank of the contents. The peons who looked on were welcome to share in the drinking, but they would taste nothing unless they were actually thirsty.

The peon women, in the meantime, would say to their children: "Do you see that man? How would you like to be him? He will have his neck stretched by a rope one day.... Señor Viljoen, it is true that you will be hanged one day, eh?"

"Of course, señora. When I hang I hope that all of you—and your children—will be there to see me walk on the air. I am going to make a fine dance for you. Already I am practicing the steps."

When the first rush poured into the house, the Kid led the way with a Colt held hip-high and eyes that were looking for trouble. He went first of all, at full speed, straight for the room of Dorotea Lerraza. The door of the room was open. A lamp burned inside and showed a floor littered with a confusion of clothes, a feathered hat here, a tumble of gilded slippers there, a white-furred cloak tossed over a chair and dragging some of its elegance on the floor. The place looked as though robbers had been here and had searched for jewels, disregarding other finery almost as precious.

And in that chair near the window, which he well remembered, sat Dorotea Lerraza, her blonde hair silvered by the moonlight, watching the delicate tendril of smoke that curled upward from her cigarette.

The Kid, standing at the threshold, took off his hat before he entered. Then he shut and locked the door behind him.

Immediately a heavy shoulder crashed against the door and a voice roared: "Open! Open!"

"What do you want with me, Robles?" asked the Kid.

"Ah, señor, a thousand pardons!" said Robles. "I thought—"

His footfall, the jingling of his spurs, drew away down the hall. Whoops and shoutings filled the house. And wide murmurs surrounded it on the outside, where the peons were flocking in like a tide to see the looting of the manor.

The Kid took out a bandana and wiped the dust and the sweat from his face.

"I'm glad you came first," said Dorotea. "That was what I was afraid of. That you wouldn't be the first one here."

"That would have been bad for your voice," said the Kid. "The screaming, I mean."

"There wouldn't have been any screaming," said the girl.

She opened the jewel-casket beside her, and he saw, on top of the glitter of the gems, the sheen of a little pearl-handled pistol, one of those old-fashioned guns which are more like works of art than weapons.

He crossed the room and picked up the gun. Her hand lifted a little as though to forestall him, then dropped limply back on the arm of her chair. He turned the pistol, admired it silently, replaced it on the heap of jewels.

"Well?" he asked, including her and the entire room in his gesture of inquiry.

"My maids were packing some of my things when they heard your horses coming," she said, to explain the confusion.

"And so you stayed behind with your clothes?" he asked.

She pursed her lips to blow up a thin stream of cigarette smoke into the moonlight. "Tell me about Rubriz," she demanded, suddenly.

Above them there was a great crash, a shouting, a splintering of wood. The girl did not stir an eyelash. Montana watched her like a hungry cat.

"Why do you want to know about Rubriz," he asked. "Mateo is a man-killer and a robber. You know that."

"Is that why you're his friend and lead his men?" she asked.

"He's leading his own men tonight," lied the Kid.

She had begun to smile. Her cigarette was burning short. He took it from her fingers and threw it out the window.

"I watched him here in the patio," she said. "I saw him pretending fear before the firing-squad. I saw him force himself to yell when he was under the whip. The other people thought it couldn't be the terrible Rubriz; but I was seeing that Rubriz could be more terrible than I had imagined."

"Who is this that you're talking about?" asked the Kid, keeping his face blank.

"Ah-hai!" breathed the girl. "You lie well! You don't know about the big gorilla of a man who was struck down and captured? Ah, no, he is nothing to you! . . . Because all the ruffians shout: 'Rubriz!' as they sack my father's house, that shows that Rubriz himself must be leading them, eh?"

"Who else?" asked Montana.

"No matter for that," she told him. "The real Rubriz will be stood against a wall of the jail and shot down at sunrise."

"What has that to do with you, Dorotea? Even supposing that you're right, what has that to do with you?"

"A gringo wouldn't understand," answered the girl.

He looked at the curl of her lip for a moment and leaned suddenly over her. Before his mouth touched hers he straightened as quickly and stepped back.

"Well," he said, "suppose that you're right, even suppose that it is Rubriz whom they're holding in the jail, what is that to you?"

"Some of the children of the rich Mexicans have only French and English women to nurse them. I had a peon woman, you see. She used to tell me terrible stories about Rubriz when I was a little girl. That was long ago. But I remember all the stories. Did you ever hear the one about Señor Llano and Rubriz?"

"Yes, I've heard that. He hanged Llano by the feet over a slow fire and let him roast to death. That must have interested you a lot."

"Also he took all the Llano account-books that showed how much the peons owed to the estate. And he burned the debt-books also. That was one of the first stories that she told."

She looked away from the Kid through the window. The fuel-shed was burning, now, and throwing a red, dim, wavering luster into the white sheen of the moonlight.

"Did you like the story?" asked the Kid.

"I kept wondering why the account-books were burned. I kept asking questions about that. The burning did no good to Rubriz;

but it saved the work of hundreds of poor devils who lived like slaves."

"But, after all, you're a Lerraza."

"After all, I'm a Mexican."

"And every Mexican means more to you than any other people. Especially the gringos from Dollar Land?"

"What do *you* think of Rubriz?" she asked.

"I think he's a murdering cross between a fox and a bear. Also, he's my friend."

"Are friendships holy to you, señor?"

He sat down on his heels before her chair.

"They are not so holy as love," said Montana.

"So you are sure to love many times."

"Only once—really," said Montana.

But at this she began to laugh a little, softly. Montana stood up and smiled in turn.

"What in the name of the devil do you want?" he asked.

"I want to pay the price of the life of Rubriz,' said the girl.

"You?"

"The Lerrazas put a ridiculous price on their women," she said. "They would trade even a Rubriz for a Dorotea, if you want to drive the bargain.... And then all these jewels remain to content the Rubriz men."

He stared at her quite helplessly. It seemed to him that the walls of his mind were broken outwards and he was looking into a new conception of women.

CHAPTER 27

Rosita spoke some of her thoughts aloud, and Tonio was at hand to hear them.

"What does *that* mean?" she demanded of the empty air. "When did El Keed bow and scrape before a woman like that? *Valgame Dios!* What has happened to him?"

This was through the shouting of peons, yelling from the men of Rubriz as the Lady Dorotea was escorted into the open patio, where she mounted a fine horse, assisted by Montana.

Tonio said at the ear of the dancer: "You have your own eyes to see what's happening, Rosita. See him grinning and gaping at her? She has the bright hair and the blue eyes that the gringos prefer, hasn't she? She has a mule load of jewels and all that. What more could El Keed want?"

Rosita turned on him a pair of burning eyes. She said nothing, but he saw that she was breathing fast. And the sight was a long draught of malicious pleasure to Tonio.

The Kid made a speech. As he sat the saddle on the back of that tall blade of a horse, El Capitán, he shouted three times, and the people grew so still that the flames of the fuel-shed could be heard flapping high in the air, like the wings of a great, bright bird.

The Kid said: "Listen to me, *amigos*. When did any of you give a cheer for a Lerraza except for the fear of guns and whips?"

A groan answered him.

"But here is one of them," went on Montana, "who could have run with the rest of the tribe, yet she stayed here to be a blood ransom for a friend of the peons, a great man of the people, that same bandido, Rubriz, whom they threaten to shoot like a dog before morning, in the jail. . . . Will you open your throats and yell for her once?"

Dorotea, sitting high on her tall horse, looked down with an unmoved face on the crowd and heard them yell, and saw them swing their sombreros. And some of the gallants among the Rubriz men mounted their horses and dashed around and around her, streaming behind them or shaking in the air the long, gaily colored scarves which were usually tied round their hips by way of belts. She did not smile as she received such homage as no Lerraza ever had heard or looked on before.

Before the uproar had died down the Kid was giving his instructions.

Of the twoscore riders at his disposal, a good part were already addled with wine. He left to them the disposal of the loot of the Lerraza place and the driving of the great herds of cattle, the long, long troops of horses, back into the mountains, from which stronghold the prize could be parcelled out and distributed to dealers in contraband goods. For himself he reserved only some of the tougher heads and outstanding men among the brigands—such as Viljoen, Orozco, and that sour-faced, enduring peon, Julio Mercado. Since it was not proper that Dorotea should ride alone, at night and after moonset, surrounded by men, Rosita would accompany her clear to the streets of the town, if the bargain could be closed with the authorities. Altogether, there was a troop made up to the number of eight by including young Tonio.

That small cavalcade had drawn out of the entrance of the first big patio and was aiming towards the far, far sheen of the lights of the town, when the Kid heard a voice crying out: "That's the one! That's the one I saw! I know him!"

Two or three of the other peons were trying to hold back the fellow who made the clamor, but now he broke away from them and came charging out, crying: "El Keed! El Keed!"

Montana drew rein and turned his horse a little.

"What is it, brother?" he asked.

"Guard your back!" cried out the man, coming up at a run.

The Kid whirled in the saddle, the gun coming automatically into his hand. But there was only Tonio behind him. He relaxed again.

"There! That is the man! That is the traitor!" cried the peon. "This same night—there—in the avenue of the trees—I saw him and heard him—"

The Kid saw the hand of Tonio make half a movement towards a gun, and that flash of movement was sufficient to make a total confession. But Montana called out in a loud voice: "That's all right, *amigo*. What Tonio has done is what I commanded him to

THE SONG OF THE WHIP 149

do. We can't have birds in the net unless we use bait, can we?"

"Ah-hai!" exclaimed the peon. "That is true! Well, I am a great fool, but I thought—"

"Thank you for the thought," said the Kid. "You know, friend, that if all of you will keep your eyes open for us, and listen with your ears, we'll know everything that happens, every grain of sand that stirs in Mexico. Thank you—and *adios!*"

He turned forward and rode on. There was a little murmuring among his men. Eyes and teeth flashed as the heads turned for a moment of doubt towards Tonio, because it was plain enough, that thing which the peon had left unsaid.

And yet it seemed that Montana had willed the thing. And who can criticize the victorious commander? The whisper grew more sibilant. The murmurs were praising the Kid. The thing began to appear more clearly. If Tonio had ridden down to the Lerraza place at the command of the Kid, it had been to give warning of the approach of the men of Rubriz, so that all the armed force of the hacienda could be drawn out into the trap there in the Gregorio Cañon.

Viljoen, that famous cut-throat, began to laugh a little as his horse jogged forward.

"What a brain! What a leader! What a brain!" he was saying.

The Kid, as his way was, had broken into song. As he ended, Rosita pressed her horse close to his side.

"It's not true!" she said. "He went without orders. The traitor came to betray us, and you know it! He went before, also. Twice he has betrayed us! If he had ten lives—the dog!—I should know how to take them from him, one by one, and keep him screaming for a hundred hours!"

The Kid said: "I don't know what you're talking about, Rosita. But I'll tell you this: Try a friend three times before you doubt him."

"What do you mean?" asked the girl. "Will you keep your eyes open—and blind?"

For answer, he broke into song again, a very old and famous song that stirred the vocal cords of the entire company and set them humming in deep accompaniment. It could be translated like this:

> The canoe glides like a shadow before me.
> With its small whisper it puts out the stars.
> From the paddle light is dripping,

Blood-red light from camp fires on the shore.
The songs of the enemy make my heart colder than the lake.
But fear not, O my friend, for I am coming.
But the knives that flash at your throat
Must loose into the sky two spirits instead of one—
Two spirits, O my friend, for you and I are one!

As the chorus grew, towards the end of the singing every throat in the group of riders took up the song, and so those last three lines went ringing out across the night:

The knives that flash at your throat
Must loose into the sky two spirits instead of one—
Two spirits, O my friend, for you and I are one.

So they swung at a long-striding gallop across the plain. The lights of the town grew brighter. They swung up on a crest of low hills called El Circulo, because the hills ran in almost a perfect circle, like the rim of some old crater, and fenced in on all sides a little hollow wooded with brush. As they descended into the hollow they found there a last warm breath of the heat of the day. So they came up on the farther side and found the lights of the town not far away beneath them. Here they drew in rein.

"Who'll go in and do the talking for us?" asked the Kid. "I'd go myself, lads, but you know that they've seen my face before in that town, and they're likely to remember it. . . . Now, it may be that no matter who goes in will be received well. Old Don Tomás is probably eating out his heart with fear about you, Dorotea. He's probably willing to pay a whole flood of gold to set you free, and he'll be glad enough to send out a single prisoner to pay for you. But on the other hand, there are the Rurales in there. And if they see a Rubriz man they are apt to do their bargaining with bullets, no matter how sharp a bargain they drive. . . . Speak up, my friends. Who will go?"

"I," said Viljoen. "I'll go, señor."

"You, Viljoen? That long face of yours is as well known to them all as the taste of hot peppers. They would kill you and leave you in a thousand cutlets on the ground," said the Kid.

"I'll go, señor," said Mercado. "If there is danger to a life, my life is forfeit. My life is yours, señor."

"Why, Julio," said the Kid, "do you think that Don Tomás could endure to talk to you even if he wanted to save his daughter's life and honor? No, no! I'll have to darken my face and make the trip myself, or else—"

"No," said a strained voice. "I shall do the thing."

"The snake!" murmured Rosita, close to the Kid. "He will go, of course. And the third time he'll sting you to the heart. He'll be the death of all the men, the chosen men! Look! Look! Where are there five more men in Mexico like these?"

The moon was setting, but still there was enough light to show Montana the faces of those about him. He drew in a breath as he saw them. It was true. There were few men like them in the world—for murder or for true service to a friend. They were of the proper steel, well hammered, refined for the purest edge, tireless as buzzards, cruel as wolves, bound to one another by a force like life, like death.

Then he stared at Tonio. That son of Richard Lavery's had not come closer, but he sat his saddle farther away than the rest and looked straight back at the Kid, giving no sign, no token, of whether or not he had been moved by the mercy he had received that night.

Perhaps that was why the Kid began to sing, softly, the Indian song that runs:

> Seven souls on a dagger's point,
> Seven poor souls on the biting edge...

But after a short moment he said: "Go on then, Tonio! There's no man in the world that I'd trust sooner than you."

CHAPTER 28

Benito Jalisca was the one who saw.

That was bad luck. It could have been anyone in the town rather than the bull-dog Rural. The moment he clapped eyes on the man who jogged the mustang down the side of the street, slowly, raising a lazy, curling stream of dust behind him, Jalisca uttered a short, high-pitched howl that cried to the world: "Tonio Rubriz!" and dropping to one knee, he steadied his revolver across his left hand for a well-placed shot.

Tonio moved also. The first gesture was that whipping flash of the hand which the Kid had taught him in some of the dull, quiet afternoons back there on the ranch—in those old, old days when the Kid had been about to enter the Lavery family through holy matrimony. It was far away now, the time and the teaching, but such lessons, so taught, never are forgotten. So Tonio jerked high his fine head, and the next moment would have started a stream of lead pouring in the direction of the Rural.

Then he remembered that he had something to think of other than his own life. He had a mission to perform.

And his hand moved up above the gun, both hands up until they were high above his head.

The first bullet from the gun of Benito Jalisca fanned his cheek. The second probably would smash out his brains, but he kept his hands there high above his head, like two dim flags of truce in the night.

The horse had stopped.

There was not a second explosion from the Colt of Jalisca. Instead, he rose, slowly, careful not to unsteady his aim, and walked up on the horseman. As he walked, he was shouting. And at his shout Rurales poured out from a little café at the next corner.

THE SONG OF THE WHIP 153

They came with a rush, their bright uniforms flashing across the paths of lamplight that streamed out of open windows and doorways. And so, in a moment, they were pooled about Tonio. Even with all their numbers, they handled Tonio as though he were fire.

Sergeant Jalisca was commanding: "You hold the head of the horse, Pascual. Catch his hands when he slides down to the ground.... Juan, keep behind him, and if he so much as shrugs a shoulder, shoot, shoot, shoot. Send him to the hell where he belongs.... *Valgame Dios*, who would think that Tonio Rubriz could be caught in this manner!... What a fool you are, Tonio, to come south of the Rio Grande! You should have kept your gringo blood safe on the gringo soil. But now that we have you, you'll pay for your murders! Ah-hai! When I think how the firing-squad will smash that handsome face of yours with their bullets! I myself shall hold one of the rifles. My bullet shall bash in that sneering mouth of yours!"

Tonio, obediently, had slipped from the back of his mustang to the ground. His hands were seized and lashed instantly behind his back.

Not before that moment did he say: "Do you think that I'd come here if I were in any danger of my life, Jalisca? Would I be such a fool, *amigo*? You think that you're going to crack my bones like a hungry dog and lick the marrow out of them, but you'll take me, instead, to Señor Lerraza. Take me to him at once, Benito.... I offer him his daughter, safe, sound, untouched, in exchange for a certain prisoner in your jail."

"Hai!" shouted Jalisca. "It *is* Rubriz that's in the jail! In spite of the whining part that he's been playing, it *is* Rubriz! Blood of God, it is Rubriz that we have had in our hands all the time, and if he were dead now there would be no chance for this damned bargaining."

One of the other Rurales exclaimed: "We'll pass by the jail and leave Rubriz dead before we take Tonio on to Don Tomás."

"You talk like a fool,' said Tonio. "Do you forget what a Lerraza can do? If you put a single shadow on his chance of getting his daughter back, he'll have the uniforms stripped off the backs of all of you. You'll wind up in prison for twenty years apiece."

Benito Jalisca lifted his hand and the gun it held, as though he wanted to smash the butt of the revolver into the middle of Tonio's face. But gradually he allowed better reasoning to weight down his hand until the gun hung down by his thigh again.

One of the Rurales said: "A wise man can learn from a thief. What Tonio has said is the truth. We must take him to Don Tomás at once."

They took him there.

The rumor, the whisper of what was to happen, began to run before them. For this purpose, to see that famous young brigand who of old had been the right hand of the famous Rubriz, every inhabitant of the town flooded out into the streets. They began to pack in dense ranks around the one commodious house in the town where Don Tomás kindly had accepted lodgings, allowing the owner to move out, bag and baggage and children and wife and all, to afford better quarters for the unhappy millionaire.

There, in the big patio of the house, Don Tomás, warned by a forerunner, came striding hurriedly down. He had gone to bed early, not to sleep, but to lie staring into whirling blackness with an empty ache of the heart as he realized that he was childless, with an empty house forever.

It seemed to him, as he lay there, that the Kid had grown on his mind and life, blighting all before him, like a pestilential shadow.

And then came the first word of hope!

He leaped up, stepped into slippers, caught a linen robe about him, and strode with long steps down to the patio. Entering it, he found the Rurales with a prisoner standing among them. Beyond, was the stir and hum of a street filled with people.

Don Tomás fixed his glance on the captive. Never in his life had he seen a face more handsome, or a bearing more erect, or a step more elastic and light.

Benito Jalisca, the sergeant in charge, said, bluntly: "Señor Lerraza, this man is the foster son of the great Rubriz. This is Tonio Rubriz, who found himself another name in the gringo land. He has come to tell us that El Keed offers you your daughter again in return for one prisoner in the jail.... Señor, in the law, the disposal of that prisoner is mine and not yours. But, señor, I know the power that is in your hands.... It is Rubriz that they ask for. Mateo Rubriz.... Señor, will you give him up for the sake of a girl—"

Benito Jalisca choked as the nature of the bargain loomed more and more clearly in his mind.

Don Tomás was trembling. He said, huskily: "Is she unharmed? Have you seen her? Do you swear that she is unharmed?"

"She is as she was when you left her in such a hurry, señor," said Tonio.

The teeth of Don Tomás flashed as he felt the lash of the insult. But he had something to think about that was more important even to him than his personal reputation. And he said: "The thing is done. The brute in the jail *is* Rubriz then, after all?... Thank God that he was not stood against a wall long before this and shot down. Ah, when I think that in all Mexico there is not enough wealth to pay for the vengeance of El Keed if we had struck down Rubriz—do you realize, Jalisca, what it would mean?"

"El Keed!" murmured Jalisca, his face twisting slowly to the side. "El Keed! Like the name of the devil always in my ears! At hell's gate when I reach it, I shall hear them singing: "El Keed!" He will be before me in all places.... Señor, it is your wish that Rubriz should be set free? You will take the responsibility? You will write me a letter commanding me to set free Rubriz?"

"Exactly," said Don Tomás. "Tell me, young señor, how my daughter is. Is she terribly shaken? Is she hysterical?"

"Señor, when I last saw her she and El Keed were singing a very good song together," said Tonio.

One of the Rurales burst out with a guffaw of laughter. Jalisca turned on the man and silenced him with a glare. And Don Tomás kept staring at Tonio like a man in a dream. At last he reached an explanation that satisfied him.

"That is the true Lerraza spirit!" said Don Tomás, sticking out his fine spike of a beard. "To sing, even in the face of danger and death, dauntless in the midst of low ruffians. Ah, my brave girl!"

They made all the arrangement in detail, Tonio Lavery sitting with free hands now, and Don Tomás writing out the letter of authorization which poor Jalisca demanded.

There had been one last appeal, Jalisca speaking with a passionate earnestness:

"If we keep Rubriz for a little longer, señor, we shall have both him and El Keed. You see what the man will do? He could get a ransom of a million pesos from you for your daughter, but he gives that up for the sake of Mateo Rubriz. He would give up more. The blood in his veins, also! He would come to die with Rubriz if he could not save him. Such is their blood-brotherhood, señor. Nothing can change it. Give me a little more time—"

"And Dorotea Lerraza—what of her? Shall I leave her in the hands of murderers and villains? Is there a brain in your head or are you the fool you look?" demanded Lerraza.

Jalisca closed his eyes to keep himself from leaping with a knife at the throat which was behind that spike of a beard. Then he turned and left the room.

Tonio had smiled a little during that interview, but afterwards he made the arrangement succinctly.

He was to return to El Keed and receive from him Dorotea Lerraza. Afterwards he was to bring her towards the town. When he appeared, Mateo Rubriz, under strict guard, would be ridden out past the incoming procession. When Dorotea Lerraza was in the town, Rubriz would be in the open. There he would be surrendered to the men of El Keed, the exchange would be duly complete, and the escort which brought Dorotea to the town, Don Tomás declared, would be allowed to return safely into the night.

When these details had been decided upon, Tonio stood up and lifted his right hand. He said: "Señor, by my honor as a gentleman I swear that I shall execute, to the best of my ability, all the details of this contract."

"Very good," said Lerraza. "I shall trust you."

He would have let it go at that, but the bright, waiting eye of Tonio compelled him, in the same manner, to lift his right hand and repeat: "On my honor as a gentleman, I shall execute this agreement." After that, Tonio went freely out of the house, freely through the whispering crowd in the street, and so vaulted into the saddle.

And Benito Jalisca, watching him gallop away, bowed his head and groaned in agony.

CHAPTER 29

The red rim of the moon was down. There were only the stars, which suddenly had begun to burn brighter and lower, when the Kid gave Dorotea Lerraza into the keeping of Tonio, for the ride into the town. Rosita would go along as chaperon, so to speak.

The Kid said: "It's no good thanking you, Dorotea. But when the thing's known there will be songs about it. And songs are what Mexico never forgets. Good-bye."

He took the hand of Dorotea.

"If there ever should be a song," she said, "will you come and sing it, one day?"

"Across an ocean, if I have to,' said the Kid. Then he checked El Capitán, and watched the trio ride off. The men of Rubriz cheered them on their way with one brief shout. And then they were gone, dimly silhouetted in a hollow, rising against the stars on higher ground, and at last they had vanished.

Viljoen said: "That is a shot in the dark. We hope it strikes the heart, señor."

The Kid said nothing, for he still was straining his eyes at the vanished trail.

Tonio was quite near the edge of the town before he saw an obscure procession of half a dozen riders coming out. He shouted loudly: "Who goes? Who goes?"

And the thundering, familiar voice of Rubriz answered: "Ahhai! Tonio! Is it you?"

"It is I!" yelled Tonio. "In twenty minutes I'll be back from the town and seeing you."

A roar of happiness from Rubriz answered him and the two groups passed one another. A moment later, Tonio was passing through the dim streets of the place. He went straight on until he came into the main street, close to the house which Lerraza was occupying, and there he found the silently waiting crowd of the townsfolk. They set up a yell at the sight of Dorotea Lerraza, a shouting which followed them through the entrance to the big patio where Don Tomás himself was waiting.

He was fully dressed, in the meantime, and striding up and down in nervous impatience. When he saw the girl, he took two or three running strides towards her before he remembered that a Lerraza never showed real emotion in public. For that reason he came to a halt. The girl, slipping out of the saddle, hurried across to him and threw herself into his arms. All about the patio were standing grim-faced men. They were the Lerraza guards, now plunged into deep disgrace since their shameful rout in the Gregorio Cañon and eager to redeem themselves at the first chance. They could at least make a great noise when they saw the daughter of the great house returning to her father. But in the middle of that uproar a gesture from Lerraza caused a dozen of them to drift towards the place where Tonio and Rosita were looking on.

It was now that a sudden beating of hoofs sounded through the town, with an outburst of Indian yelling. Lerraza had no sooner heard it than he held up his hand for silence. And as the patio grew quiet, they all heard, from far away outside the town, a dull, crackling noise such as is made by a fire when it has dry food in its jaws. Those were gun-shots, a storm of them.

Tonio whirled the head of his horse suddenly towards the patio gate, but the loud voice of Lerraza shouted: "Stop him! Down with him, lads!"

And those hungry-handed guards of the Lerrazas instantly had plucked Tonio from the saddle. He went down like a fighting wildcat, but they mastered his hands quickly.

Dorotea, catching at the arm of her father, seemed about to break out into a violent protest.

But he cried out in a high exultation: "Do you hear the Rurales shouting in the street? They've brought back Rubriz. He's back in the hands of the law, where he belongs. And here is his fosterson, who'll soon be made ready to hang.... Take him away and throw him into the same cell with Rubriz. Let them lie there and groan to one another. But guard them every moment; keep half a dozen of the Rurales around them. We'll wait till the daylight before they're settled!"

Delight so overmastered Don Tomás that he began to laugh loudly.

THE SONG OF THE WHIP

"And you hear that, Dorotea? Do you hear the guns? They come no nearer; they are firing no farther away. It means that El Keed has been surrounded by fifty men; he still fights, but he cannot run. Do you understand?"

Dorotea, closing her eyes, let her head tilt slowly back. Afterwards she began to laugh in her turn.

Lerraza was delighted. As he led her into the house he was saying: "It is always this way. The stray wolves annoy the lion for a little while, but at last he turns and tears them to pieces. So—do you see?—all in one moment the tables are reversed. We were in wretchedness, defeated, and the young gringo dog could laugh in our faces; and now—you hear the rifles crackling? He may be down now; he may be dead!"

He paused, to shout over his shoulder: "Take the girl, too. Take the dancing-girl and find a place for her in a cell. She's as dangerous as the rest. . . . Ah, Benito Jalisca, what I owe to that good brain of yours for planning this double stroke!"

"You know, Father," said Dorotea, "Rosita has been a friend to me. Except for her, I would have been alone with—I don't know what."

"Was she kind to you?" asked Don Tomás.

"Like a sister."

"Sister?" echoed Don Tomás, angrily. But then he shrugged his shoulders. The moment was too perfect and he could not permit it to be spoiled by passion on his part. "You may have her then. . . . Here! Bring the dancer over here. . . . If you can handle her, you can charm snakes, Dorotea. But have her if you will. Ahhai, see the devil working in her face! Be careful, be very careful, Dorotea."

A rider came plunging through the crowd, wildly waving his hand above his head, shouting: "Señor! Señor! Señor Lerraza!"

The Lerraza called out: "I am here! What is it?"

"We have cooped El Keed in the hollow of El Circulo. We have lined the hills with men. He lies in the brush with his people. The first stroke of daylight will be the end of them!"

A long, wavering, knife-edged scream shrilled into the brain of Lerraza. He saw the dancing-girl leap half-way from the arms that were holding her; then her body pitched forward across their arms.

Dorotea Lerraza went quickly through the crowd, which was shouting with a thousand tongues. And the guards of Lerraza were the loudest. They had run like rabbits earlier in the night from that same El Keed; now they screamed for his downfall.

But Dorotea Lerraza was supporting the head of Rosita, commanding the men who carried her to step carefully with their unconscious burden.

CHAPTER 30

Viljoen was always the doubter. He and Orozco, the famous horse-thief, Colonias the confidence man and killer, and Robles the gunman par excellence, were the four who remained with the Kid, waiting for the coming of Rubriz.

And Viljoen said: "Why did you give her up—why did you send the Lerraza girl away before Rubriz is with us, señor?"

"You understand, Viljoen," said the Kid, "that if we did not trust them, they would never trust us."

"Ay, but they would have trusted you," said Viljoen. "All Mexico knows that your word is better than gold."

"Did you hear Tonio say that Lerraza had sworn by his honor as a gentleman?"

"But he made the oath to an outlaw. Do you consider that, señor?"

Here Orozco said: "Do you hear something off there to the left?"

They could make it out, dimly, a faint creaking of saddle leather and a dull treading of hoofs.

"Some muleteers heading for the mountains," said the Kid. "They often start just before dawn."

"Here come some riders from the town, I think," said Robles. "No, they've stopped. Look! Have they turned back? They have? What would that mean?"

"There on the right," said Orozco. "Hush! Are those more of your muleteers, señor?"

Robles spoke after a moment.

"On the left, on the right of us," he said. "I don't like it! Suppose that they turned and charged—they would catch us in a net! And where is Rubriz? The girl would be in the town by this time, but where is Rubriz?"

"Tonio will not take her into the town until he sees and hears Rubriz," said the Kid. But he was troubled. He let the stallion

161

range to one side and then to the other. As he stared into the darkness he heard a voice that exclaimed: "Señor! El Keed! Are you there?"

"Here!" shouted the Kid. "Are you there, Rubriz?"

"Something better than Rubriz is here. Accept it, El Keed!" cried the other voice, and instantly rifles crashed.

The whirring of the bullets maddened the Kid. In that madness he thrust his horse forward as though to charge straight at the winking line of fireflies, the little lights of the exploding rifles.

Robles caught the rein of El Capitán and turned him. "This way!" he shouted. "They have not caught us yet!" And he headed down into the hollow of El Circulo. All five of them were charging at full speed. From left and right the many rifles were roaring, but if they could gain the farther ridge of the hills, they could gallop on through the gap between the two firing lines and trust the speed of their horses to bring them to liberty.

So they swept through the crackling brush in the bottom of the hollow and poured at a racing speed up the farther slope. They were nearing the upper rim over which they might rush to safety when a calm voice sang out, and the Kid recognized the voice of Benito Jalisca.

And with that, the whole edge of the hollow blazed with gunfire. The charge was wrecked as though it had struck the face of a cliff. The Kid saw two of his riders go down beside him. El Capitán of his own volition swerved and raced back into the hollow. There the Kid threw himself to the ground and forced the horse down beside him. They were in the deepest part of the hollow, where the upswell of the sandbanks all around gave a little shelter. And into that same hollow the two remaining riders came with a rush.

There was no outlet from the dangerous place. They were securely held in a bowl of fire. All around the rim of the hills they could see the winking lights of the guns; there was no gap in that line of dotted fire.

"Orozco, is that you?" asked the Kid.

"Here, señor."

"And you, Viljoen?"

"Here, señor."

"Robles and Colonias are already in hell," said Orozco, "but they won't be far ahead of us. By the time they've blazed the trail we'll be breathing on the backs of their necks.... Señor, have you any of that brandy?"

"I have plenty of it. Are you hurt?"

"One shoulder was a little scalded by a bullet. That was all."

The Kid pulled out the heavy flash and unscrewed the top. Orozco took a pull at it, tipping it up slowly, with a dim, frosty starlight touching it here and there. A dozen bullets blasted the sand at a single instant and knocked up a stinging spray of dust. But Orozco finished his drinking, undisturbed.

The Kid, unsheathing his Winchester from the long saddle holster, took aim at one of the winking fireflies on the edge of the hollow. Behind him, he heard a heavy blow, a soggy blow, like the sound of an axe chopping into green wood.

"What was that?" he asked.

"My horse—through the head," said Viljoen calmly. "Orozco, you will have to steal me a better one."

"After the dawn comes we'll have something better than horses. We'll have wings to travel on," said Orozco. *"Valgame Dios!* How they waste their poundage of ammunition in the darkness!"

The Kid squeezed the trigger. High over the roar of the guns came a piercing scream that went out in the middle like an extinguished light.

He took a snapshot at another of the winking little fireflies and another yell answered him.

The Kid laughed.

"They've been kneeling or standing, the fools," he said. "They'll lie down now and give us a little more peace. Think of the dogs wanting to keep us awake on our last night, *amigos!*"

"Give me the brandy," said Viljoen. "Ha! I like the runlet of fire down my throat. If a man has good brandy and a rifle and something to shoot at, why should he care when he dies?"

Orozco said: "I hope you killed one of them, señor. We need all the company we can get together for our trip in the morning. And if—"

He stopped talking. It was as though he had clapped his hands together, but the Kid knew the difference of the sound. It was not the first time he had heard a bullet strike human flesh.

Orozco stood up.

"Sit down, man!" commanded the Kid. "Where are you hurt?"

"In the belly," said Orozco quietly, *"Adios, amigos!"*

"Well—*adios!*" said the Kid.

"Adios, amigo," murmured Viljoen.

Orozco went on, carrying his rifle. They lost sight of his silhouette farther up the slope.

Then a firefly began to wink half-way towards the upper rim.

Viljoen said: "He felt the life running out of him and had to start shooting from the ground. Brave Orozco!"

There was a sudden freshening of the uproar of guns. No more bullets centered on the sandpit. Apparently every rifle was concentrating on that deadly firefly that winked half-way up the slope.

It gleamed again, much closer to the top.

"See!" said Viljoen. "He gets up and crawls forward, shooting as he goes. A dozen bullets have struck him by this time.... Now he shoots no longer.... He lies dead.... Dios! Dios! When have the Rurales put out a brighter light than that?"

The Kid said nothing. He licked the dust from his lips and aimed at another gunflash, and fired. Another screech answered him.

Viljoen, shooting in the opposite direction, said: "How do you manage to hit the devils, señor?"

"I am a cat," said the Kid, "and I can see in the dark.... Aim low, Viljoen. Very low. The bullet will drive through the sand."

"They've had enough," said Viljoen. "They stop firing and wait for the morning. Well, when the morning comes we'll dance with one or two partners before we finish, eh?"

"We'll start one or two of them dancing," agreed the Kid.

"I thank God," said Viljoen, "that Orozco had some good brandy in his belly before he took his last walk."

It was not entirely because of the accurate shooting of the Kid that the firing of Jalisca's men had ceased. There was another reason, and a good one, for a strange interruption had come to the fighters. A huge figure of a man in the sweeping garment of a woman had appeared through the night, striding along with a great handful of staff to support his steps.

"Who's there?" a Rural challenged.

"I am Brother Pascual," said the giant.

"Well, Brother, you see that the road is closed in this direction. Go around on the side of the hills and you'll get away from bullets."

"Who is that groaning yonder?" asked the friar.

"That is only a certain Gisbert with a bullet under his collar bone."

"Poor man! Must he die?"

"He must die, Brother."

"Shall I talk to him?"

"If you wish.... Hai, Gisbert! Here is Brother Pascual."

THE SONG OF THE WHIP

Pascual went and knelt in the sand, sitting back on the heels of his sandals.

"Gisbert, shall I talk with you?" asked the friar.

"No, Brother Pascual. Only hold my hand. The life is going out of me now.... So. That is better. My God! How strange it is that a little thing like a bullet can let out such a great thing as the life!"

"It is strange, Gisbert."

"But I suppose it is the will of God that a few of us should die because we have trapped El Keed with lies, Brother Pascual."

"You have trapped him with lies. But let me pray for you, Gisbert."

"Pray for me afterwards. Hai! What a pain bores into me! Brother Pascual, if you are going to pray for me, be sure to keep mentioning my name to the holy saints. So many important men are dying on this day, that poor Gisbert will be overlooked, otherwise. Who will pay attention to me, when there is a soul like that of El Keed leaving the earth? But you, Brother, if you keep repeating my name—repeating my name—repeating—"

He began to struggle.

The huge friar cried out in a great voice: "Repent, Gisbert, and have trust in the mighty God, our Father.... Repent, Gisbert! And have faith! Have faith!"

In a spiritual agony almost as great as the torment of the dying man, the friar lifted Gisbert bodily, holding him high.

Gisbert grew still. He lay like a child in the enormous arms of the friar.

"So!" he whispered. "Among the stars. Who would have thought it of Gisbert? Who would have expected..."

His head fell back. The friar laid him on the ground.

"Is he dead?" asked a Rural.

"Dead," said the friar, on his knees by the body.

Then he stood up.

"We have to pay down a few lives. That's to be expected," said another man. "But the ones that remain, they'll have something to remember, afterwards. We that will have seen the dead body of El Keed. That is something for a man to remember, eh?"

The friar said: "I am going down into the hollow, if you will let me."

"But how can you go there, Brother? Half the night we'll be shooting, from time to time, just to keep them from resting too much."

"In all things it must be as my Father wills," said Pascual. "But I must go down into the hollow.... Also there is another man behind me who wishes to go."

"Who is the man?"

"Julio Mercado."

"But, the fool—does he wish to give himself up and die like a poor dog?"

"He wishes to die with his master."

"Think of that," said the Rural. "Where is Jalisca? Jalisca! Ho! Oh, Sergeant! Jalisca."

The sergeant came up. The strange request of the friar and of Julio Mercado was repeated to him.

"If Mercado goes down into the hollow, he never will come out again alive," said Jalisca. "Does he know that?"

"He knows that," said the priest.

"Well, then, are you willing to tell him that it is a good thing to do?" asked the sergeant.

"I have prayed to God very earnestly," said the friar, "and I cannot receive any certain instruction on the point. However, when I ask if a man should die at the side of his friend, it seems to me that Heaven answers: 'Yes.' So, for that reason, I have not tried to change the mind of Mercado."

"He is saving us work," said Jalisca. "Yes, as far as I'm concerned, let every outlaw in Mexico ride down there into the trap. We'll close it on them in the first light of the morning.... But you, Brother, can return from the hollow when you wish. There will be no more firing until the morning—and that is due to commence before very long. Just make sure that you are out of the hollow before the sun is well up."

"Julio! Julio Mercado!" thundered the great-throated friar.

A single horseman came slowly out of the darkness and approached them.

"Are you Mercado?" asked Jalisca. "Do you know that if you ride down into that valley you'll never come out again alive?"

"Señor," said Mercado, "I do what my heart forces me to do. If I die, that is the will of God."

"You talk like a churchman and not like the damned peon outlaw that you are," said the sergeant. "But get out of my sight, the two of you, and go where you please.... Only, I swear that El Keed has bewitched his friends if they are willing to die for him."

CHAPTER 31

Don Tomás was so exceedingly happy that he could hardly remain in his chair. He had to start up, now and then, and pace the floor.

It mattered very little to him that, on this same night, a great, ponderous, living wealth of cattle had been stolen and rolled away in a wave from his hacienda. It mattered little that the costly jewels of his daughter had been stolen, also. What was important to him was that the girl had been returned to him unharmed and that three of his enemies who had annoyed him were dying or about to die.

He could not help saying to Don Emiliano: "You see, Emiliano, that the fortune of the Lerrazas always holds in the end. True, I have lost a little money, but what of that? What is money compared with glory?"

"Glory?" said Don Emiliano, rolling his eyes a little and loosening the collar of his shirt. "Glory, Don Tomás?"

"Of course!" said Don Tomás. "What else would you call it? To be confronted by two of the most famous bandidos that ever cut throats in Mexico, and by my own force of brain and hand to check and destroy them—is not that glorious, my friend? Does that not show the people in the street that the blood of the Lerrazas is still redder, even in its old men, than is the blood of ordinary people?"

Don Emiliano nodded, but he blinked a little.

"Even the common, worthless rabble in the streets," said Don Tomás, "even the hungry dogs in the town must be saying that the Lerrazas are stronger than ever in brain and in body."

"They say, señor," said Don Emiliano carefully, "that it is a very dangerous thing to be an enemy to a Lerraza."

"They have reason to say so. The whole world must know it!" said Don Tomás.

"But they murmur a little about promises given and then—avoided, señor."

"Promises? Promises?" said Don Tomás. "By the God in Heaven, do they think that a gentleman of the old Castilian blood needs to keep his promises which had been given to a common dog of a gringo outlaw? What sort of a fool would I be to keep such promises?"

"Exactly, señor," said Don Emiliano, rubbing his chin a little, in thought. "But the common people have stupid brains."

"They have no brains at all. What do they say?"

"That if El Keed dies, there will be a red stain on the name of the Lerrazas, señor."

"By Heaven! Emiliano, I believe you think the same as the peons!"

"I, señor? Certainly not! Why should I doubt the wisdom of Don Tomás? If your mind is at rest, why should I worry?"

"Why, indeed?" said Don Tomás. "Tell Dorotea she may come to me now. I am ready to hear everything that happened to her."

Dorotea came in and rested the tips of her fingers on the table as she smiled at her father.

"Now, Dorotea," he said, "tell me everything."

"In the morning, Father," said the girl. "After I have bathed three times and begin to feel clean again."

"The dogs! Did they touch you?"

"Not with their hands, Father."

"Let it wait for the morning, then. Are you tired?"

"Frightfully tired! I hardly can keep my eyes open!"

"Ah, my poor child! But remember that they are paying now! In the morning you shall see Tonio and Rubriz die. And El Keed will be dead with the first light of the dawn.... What's the matter, Dorotea?"

"I am only yawning," said the girl. "I'm too tired to talk, Father."

"I'll have a servant take charge of the dancing-girl."

"No. She'll be out of the house very soon. She's harmless. And I think she wants to get into the merry-making. You hear it?"

For the entire town, having been so aroused, had decided to turn the night into day. There was dancing in the street, and the musical noise of guitars and mandolins trembled in the air from all sides.

"They celebrate another Lerraza victory," said Don Tomás.

"Victory?" said the girl. "Ah yes. Of course. And El Keed— are you sure he is not dead yet?"

"A very strange thing has just happened. A certain friar,

Brother Pascual, a huge fellow all beef and brawn and no brains whatever, has gone down into El Circulo to talk with El Keed and with him went—who do you think?"

"I don't know,' said the girl. "Some friend?"

"The same dog of a black-hearted peon who was the starting-point of all this trouble. That same Julio Mercado."

"Ah—I remember."

"Well, he will die with El Keed. But what a madness for him to have ridden down into the trap! An insane, poor creature."

"Or else a sort of hero," said the girl.

"Hero?" cried Don Tomás. "Peon—hero—can you put the words into the same sentence?"

"No, I was wrong, of course," said the girl.

She said good night and went back to the room that had been assigned to her.

There Rosita lay face down on the bed, her hair astray, her hands clutching at the dark tangle of it, moveless.

Dorotea went to her, picking up a glass of water and a thin paper twist from the table as she went.

"Take this, Rosita," she said. "After you've taken it you'll sleep."

"Keep your hand from me," said Rosita. "There is a curse in the touch of every Lerraza."

Dorotea moved back half a step, her face unchanged.

"You must sleep, Rosita," she said. "You know, if there is trouble to come, a person ought to be strong to face it. . . ."

"He is dead!" said Rosita. "Ah, my God! I have felt the bullets striking his body."

"He is not dead," said Dorotea. "Brother Pascual and Julio Mercado have ridden down into the hollow to join him."

Rosita leaped to her feet.

"Have they? Both of them? God bless men with manly hearts!"

"So you see, nothing will happen for a long time, and you must sleep. . . . This powder is very strong. In five minutes it will close your eyes fast. I have seen it work."

"Why do you talk to me about sleeping?" asked Rosita. "He will be dead before the sun is five minutes above the edge of the sky!"

"What a strange thing," said Dorotea, "that when the pinch comes, and the strain, then all the cheap blood comes out of a common dancing-girl!"

Rosita, stung by the whiplash of that remark, leaped suddenly to her feet, not too deep in sorrow to be made furious with rage.

Dorotea, facing her calmly, said: "Because we love the same man, I thought we must be women of the same sort."

The full implications of that remark began to strike into the brain of Rosita like repeated blows. The anger died quickly out of her eyes and left them rather wide and frightened.

"Do you—Dorotea—do you?" murmured Rosita. "It was not just amusing yourself?"

The Lerraza smiled. "Afterwards, we can hate one another," she said, "but now we can try to do something for him."

"Do something for him?" asked Rosita. "Do something? You and I? Even Rubriz and Tonio hardly could do anything for him— and they are in prison! What could you and I do?"

"Well," said Dorotea. "I don't know. Perhaps follow the example of that Pascual—and Julio Mercado."

She spoke so casually and quietly that Rosita stared at her again; and this was the moment when Don Tomás rapped once at the door of the room and then cast it wide open.

He called out: "Dorotea, are you still dressed? Can we come in? I want you to hear from my brave friend, from Benito Jalisca himself. He'll tell you the condition of the scoundrel who kidnapped you. He'll tell you what is coming to El Keed!"

"The beast—the blood-drinking beast!" whispered Rosita. But Dorotea called out: "Ah, let him come in! Of course I want to see him!"

Jalisca came into the doorway and bowed two or three times stiffly, with a jerk of the knees.

He came in, grinning with pleasure to be admitted to the chamber of a Lerraza woman, with his eyes on the floor.

His eyes were bloodshot. His face was suffused. His breathing could be heard. He was like a drunkard whose brain is giving way. When he spoke, his voice was husky. But it was only excess of triumph that was maddening him with its foretaste.

"Brave Sèrgeant Jalisca," said Dorotea, coming forward while Rosita remained, fascinated by horror, at the back of the big room. "You have been doing things that will always be famous. What a happiness to see you, señor! Sit down—take this chair—here. I'll bring you some wine because I see that the dust of the riding is still on your face."

"Good, very good, my Dorotea," said her father. "Every Lerraza must know how to honor courage, no matter in whom."

She was at the little side table, picking up a flask of wine which was kept cool in some standing water. This she poured into a big tumbler while she called over her shoulder: "Ah, but Sergeant Jalisca is more than merely brave. Think what he has done! Everything! Think of the cleverness—of pretending to give Rubriz away—and then snatching him back, and so setting me free for nothing! Think—I never heard of a cleverer thing."

Jalisca laughed aloud. He was drunk, indeed, with joy. He had been noticed by a Lerraza. He had been smiled upon, flattered, by a Lerraza woman.

"One does what one can do—now and then, with luck," he breathed. "But El Keed is in the hollow. . . . Ah—I drink to you, señorita! Deeply I drink to you."

Lerraza stood by, beaming a benediction on the hero. The smile of Dorotea brightened and her eyes were as blue as heaven.

"And in the morning,' said the Rural, "I stand Tonio and Rubriz against the prison wall and with my own hands use one of the rifles. . . . That, señorita, first. I have, as you see, the keys of the jail. All shall be kept quiet there, under lock. In the morning I see the two die. You shall be present if you will—"

"Brave Sergeant Jalisca," cried the girl again. "Of course I want to be there to see the beasts die. They will make you a captain, a colonel—"

"No, no, señorita!" said Jalisca. "That is too much."

"You shall have another taste of wine," said the girl.

"I have had enough, señorita."

"No, no! Just another taste. A colonel cannot end with a single swallow of wine. That never would do, Colonel Jalisca."

She was pouring the wine again, and as she did so she picked up two of the little papers and tipped the white powder they contained into the glass. The sediment disappeared at once, totally absorbed. Perhaps the wine had a stronger sparkle, and that was all.

"Now, Colonel," the girl was saying, "drink again. To the death of El Keed! How many songs will be made about you! How people will sing of Colonel Jalisca! You will become a general! You will lead an army!"

He drank, his eyes rolling in a frenzy of delight.

"In fact," explained Lerraza to his daughter, "it seems that there is no chance for El Keed. The thing is ended, practically. As soon as there is a little daylight—"

"I'm sleepy," said 'Colonel' Jalisca, yawning. "Pardon, señor, but if I could lie down for a mere moment—"

"My brave Jalisca! There is a room exactly across the hall," said Don Tomás. "Come with me, my friend.... Ah, three in a single night... three at one stroke, as it were! Do not think that I shall forget. Do not think that I shall allow my friends in the capital to forget you. There will be advancement. Ah, in here, Colonel!"

And he led Jalisca through the door across the hall.

CHAPTER 32

Rosita, coming softly towards Dorotea, said to her: "I think I see the beginning."

Dorotea sat down in a chair and looked straight before her with great, soft blue eyes, smiling a little, a strange concentration in her look that gave her an other-worldly expression.

"First—if we can find the keys on him. He will sleep a full two hours, I think, strong beast that he is," said Dorotea. "And that should be time enough to do something.... If only they would stop the singing and the castanets in the street, I could think of something."

A rap at the door, and Lerraza appeared again for a moment to laugh and say: "Brave, honest fellow—tired out with his heroic work. Sound asleep and snoring already...All is well. I feel young enough to sing. Good night, my dear."

The door closed.

"The keys first," said Rosita. "And we can do something else afterwards, when we have them."

"Yes, the keys first."

They opened the door on to the hall. Voices were bawling in the distance—drunken, happy voices. They stole across the hall and pushed open the opposite door. A lamp burned in the room, with the flame turned down low. Benito Jalisca lay on the big bed with one leg dragging down towards the floor. His arms were thrown wide. His jacket and shirt, pulled open at the collar for air by some last movement, showed a chest blackened with a heavy growth of hair. A strong odor of stale sweat came from him as Dorotea leaned over him. There was the reek of horse sweat, also, on his clothes.

She shrank back, a little nauseated. But Rosita stepped straight forward.

"What a throat for cutting! See how he presses back his head so that I could use the knife!" said Rosita. "But that can't be my pleasure. El Keed—would he ever forgive me if I killed Jalisca instead of leaving the brute for his hand? So... here they are—big enough to rattle like a set of castanets!"

She pulled the heavy keys out of a bulging pocket, and a moment later they were back in their own room.

Rosita carried the keys to a closet and hung them on a hook, a closet filled with the clothes of a man, for the young son of the family had used that room.

She came back and sat on the arm of Dorotea's chair.

"Suppose that we slip through the sidestreets to the outer door of the jail—" said Dorotea.

"There is no outer door. The three doors all open on the big patio of the jail," said Rosita.

"Then if we go into the patio—"

"They are singing and dancing there, and every eye will follow the Lady Dorotea."

"Will they stare at me? Yes, of course they will. They hate all Lerrazas enough, tonight, to stare at me like dogs at meat. But what a people we are, Rosita. All these townsfolk love El Keed and Rubriz. They love them both. But they use the fine night to sing and dance."

"It's a great event," said Rosita. "And therefore it has to be celebrated, of course. But, whatever is done, you cannot join in the doing, Dorotea. If you are seen, it will be as though a searchlight were drawn on us."

"Because I have this bright hair? It shall go off my head then," cried Dorotea.

She jerked open a table drawer and took out a pair of scissors, and holding out the heavy metal length of her hair she sheared it off in great locks. Rosita, staring, her lips parted, overawed, could not believe her eyes. The Lerrazas were not supposed to be human. This seemed human enough, and more than human. There remained now only a fluffy brush of golden dust clouded around the head of Dorotea. She was throwing off her clothes.

"See if that is a brown shoe polish there in the corner," she demanded. "Quick, Rosita! Is it? It is! Help me to put it on. I must be as brown as a peon if it's a peon's part that I'm to play. There—and there—now for the clothes."

She was rubbed brown as chestnut stain from head to foot in a moment, and Rosita gasped as she saw the silver sleekness of the body overclouded.

THE SONG OF THE WHIP

The clothes that she took were simply a pair of white cotton trousers and a long white shirt. She got a black silken scarf and tied up the remnants of her hair inside it.

"Look," said Dorotea. "Shall I pass in the street? Watch me, Rosita! Here is the walk—now I slouch—now I stop and roll the cigarette. I stick it on my lower lip. I let it bob up and down as I talk. I slink down on one hip as I lean against the wall."

"Wonderful!" cried Rosita. "But if you look up a single time and let them see the blue flash of your eyes, Dorotea—"

"I shall not look up. I am a dirty little brown thief of a boy, and I only look at people with side glances—so!"

"Now you are perfect," said the other girl. "If only no one should jostle against you and press too close to you. Men are not all curving softness like you, Dorotea."

"I shall be harder than whip leather," said Dorotea. "Are you ready?"

"Do you know what we shall do?"

"Go straight to the jail.... You can draw a crowd and keep it staring. You can draw the crowd with a song and a dance, Rosita. And once you have their eyes, I'll have a door open and get into the jail. There the keys can work for me. You understand?"

"Ah-hai, Dorotea! How I love you! What a brain! What a glorious heart!... Alas! I shall lose El Keed, but let's go on."

In fact, there were some twenty guards strolling about in the patio of the jail—the exercise-ground, as it were, excluding the milling crowd that filled the street from entrance to the proximity of the jail. The whole street was filled with the merrymakers, and just at the outside of the jail gate danced two girls, with castanets.

Rosita was instantly with them. She stood in the center of their whirling dance, passing through a dance of slow movements, and singing, and at the sound of her clear, sweet, penetrating voice, voices began to call out: "Rosita! She has come again! Rosita!"

The soldiers thronged the gate and cheered her.

"Shall we go in and dance for you?" panted Rosita. "There's nothing but dust, ankle-deep, out here. But you have a good, firm-trodden parade-ground in there. Shall we go in and dance for you?"

"No, no, Rosita. You can't come in here. What do you think? We'd be flogged for it."

"What? On a night like this? Come, come! Both of you come along with me. They won't keep us out. There's more light in there, too, and they can see our dancing."

The pair she had joined, a little hesitant, followed Rosita and saw her deliberately put her hands on the shoulders of the guards and push them aside—yes, dignified, important Rurales that some of them were! And they gave back, laughing.

The whole crowd in the street began to laugh also, and presently there was a little rush.

Not more than a dozen of the people from the street gained the entrance, to be sure, before a pair of the armed men crossed their rifles and kept back the rest with a couple of angry shouts. But among those who managed to gain the patio of the big jail was a slinking little down-headed boy who had a cigarette stuck on his lower lip.

He, when the rest of the crowd, guards and all, formed a circle to watch the dancing and to hear the singing of Rosita—how charming she was!—slipped away along the side of the court until he came to the first door.

He tried the knob with his hand, and it was locked, of course. So he leaned his back against the door, and the hand that was behind him tried, one after the other, the three largest of the keys of the big bunch that he carried.

Presently one of them fitted. The bolt slid, the door sagged open, and instantly Dorotea had slipped inside.

As she closed the door softly behind her, she found herself in one huge room, dimly lighted by lanterns that hung from the ceiling, here and there. And that light glimmered through a forest of narrow steel bars by which the great room was split into many little cells.

Dorotea, lurking in the corner, saw in every cell one or more white-clad figures. The still, foul air choked her. The heat made perspiration run on her face. Her lips twitched with disgust. And yonder she saw the brutal face of Rubriz, for two lanterns burned with wicks turned high, close to his cell, and in it was handsome young Tonio Lavery, now waiting to pay all accounts in his life when the day dawned. And around the cell lounged half a dozen well-armed men. Not heedless or careless, either, but two of them walking up and down their beat with a regular stride, decidedly on guard.

She had come all this distance for nothing, then? Perhaps what she had done had shut her away from her old life forever. But at any rate here she was—and helpless!

A voice whispered: "*Amigo*, have you a cigarette, for the love of God and all the saints?"

She had found a small sack of tobacco, and some cigarette papers, in the pocket of the shirt, and she tossed these through the bars. Two men, inside, suddenly reached for them. She threw matches in to them, too.

"The grace of God fall on you, boy!" she heard them saying.

Brutal faces—faces almost as brutal as that of Rubriz. Unredeemed by the savage brain that gleamed out under his shaggy brows. But they were men and the hands of men could do more than hers.

She went to the door of the cell and began to try the keys. She found, at the seventh trial, a master key that opened that cell door easily.

As it swung in, she whispered: "Softly! Softly! That door to the patio is open. But there are twenty armed men in the patio. And there is the guard over Rubriz to shoot you down if you move! Stay quietly till more are ready!"

A hissing whisper of reassurance answered her.

And so she went down the aisle of the cells, opening right, opening left.

The reason the jail was so full was that the Rurales had been sweeping this section of the country very clear of all suspicious characters so long as both Rubriz and El Keed were known to be in the vicinity. In the other half of the great room she could hear one of the guards talking, and the growling, great voice of Rubriz making response while she worked.

And now she stood up and surveyed her work. A whole double row of the cell doors ajar, a whole mob of men on the leash, ready for a signal.

Would they wait?

At that moment a white-clad form slipped out of a cell. Another followed. Then all the rest. Those many feet—every pair of them was naked—made no more than a dim whisper over the floor. Like a great throng of white alley-cats—ay, or of white panthers.

"What's that? What the devil—" shouted the voice of a guard suddenly.

And then came the rush.

It had started silently, and silently it flowed, as fast as desperate men could run.

Several of the guards shouted at one and the same time. A gun roared with a great, re-echoed explosion; three more crashed in a deafening volley. And then there was a sound of blows given, a hurrying, whirling, snarling noise of muffled voices.

When she reached the place she saw a uniformed man lying on his face, the back of his head crushed in. And the wave of the released prisoners swept on towards the doors.

She knelt at the door of Rubriz' cell, where he stood like a vast gorilla, gripping the bars with both hands, Tonio behind him.

And as she knelt she kept thinking that blood was like red paint—sticky, like red paint . . . or had the brains of the man been dashed out along with his blood?

Her brain swirled a little. She set her teeth to clear her vision and steady her nerves. . . . And suddenly the lock clicked under the pressure of a key which she was trying. Instantly the door was open.

"What are you, lad?" Rubriz had asked her through the door of the cell. And she had made no answer, but now, as he leaped outside into the aisle, he cast an arm about her, saying: "On with us, my brave boy—"

His voice changed to a shout of wonder: "Hai, Tonio! It's a girl that's come to us! By all the bright saints!"

They ran on together. She could hear Tonio saying: "It is Dorotea Lerraza, or else I'm a madman!"

"You *are* mad if you say that," grunted Rubriz. "But we'll do our thinking to-morrow . . . Tonight—"

At the heels of the rest of the prisoners they leaped through the doorway into the patio.

There all was an instant whirl of confusion. The guards who had been listening to the song and watching the dance of Rosita had heard the gunshots inside the jail and turned to stare. While they still were staring, the door—they could have sworn that it was securely locked—burst open, and a torrent of humanity instantly was plunged into the patio, dirty, unshaven men with wild eyes and reaching hands.

Not half a dozen shots were fired. The guards fled from that surge of yelling men. Some of the Rurales ran towards the long line of horses stabled under the open arches of the columns along one side of the patio, but the mob was keener to reach horses than to gain Heaven. Those horses were seized by the rioters in a moment. A steady stream of the liberated men, every one armed with some sort of a weapon now, poured out of the gate of the patio into the street and then fled, each man as his fancy dictated.

Only one cluster of four riders remained closely bunched together, swerving down the alleyways, twisting aside into the broader streets, and so, suddenly, gaining the cool open of the starlit night.

And Dorotea Lerraza seemed to herself to be riding through more than space. It was time also that was flowing like a wild river under the feet of her horse. She was drifting back into another age when the dare-devil spirit of the Lerrazas, those centuries before, drove them out of the mountains of Castile to seek adventure around the world.

So they came close, at last, to the lifting circle of the hills inside which El Keed and his last survivors were closed.

And around the edge of the sky the grey-green of the dawn was beginning to lift a gentle sheen. The time would not be very long now, before the gunfire opened from the ridge and searched every inch of the space beneath.

And what a host of armed men had gathered for the kill, either to take part, or to look on at the famous show. For it was to be a public execution rather than a battle!

Little fires had been built, here and there, along the outer edges of the slopes where the black silhouettes of men showed as they sat on their heels and did bits of cookery. And farther down the slopes, still, all the hundreds of horses of the fighting-force were grouped in two or three herds, watched over by random guards.

"We have come," said Rubriz, "and we see that the door is slammed in our faces."

"There will be something to do," said Tonio calmly, "or some way of dying, at least.... There's one thing first. Dorotea goes home to her people before we make a move."

CHAPTER 33

The way of Rubriz with women was not affectionate. He looked at Dorotea and growled: "Let her go or stay. What do I care?... Tonio, lend me a pound of brains and tell me what to do."

"We need a crowd to smash through the lines of them," said Tonio.

"And there's nothing but a crowd of horses," said Rubriz.

Rosita said: "If we could stampede a hundred of those mustangs right through—"

"Hush! Ah-hai! Is there a brain in women, after all?" demanded Rubriz. "Oh, Tonio, God bless the day that brought us Rosita! She makes men trouble until they need help. So you could speak of the saints—or a good lot of them, at least.... But how many are guarding the horses, there—that mob of mustangs near the trees?"

"We'll see," said Tonio. *"Adios,* Rosita."

"Adios, Tonio."

She went up to him and put her arms about his neck, and crossed her hands behind his head.

"Querido mio!" said Rosita. "Will you kiss me good-bye?"

He said: "You care nothing for me, Rosita."

"I love you," said Rosita, "because you are about to die for him. Kiss me!"

He touched her forehead with his lips.

"What a gringo kiss *that* was," said Rosita. "Well, *adios! Adios,* Mateo! You should kiss Lady Dorotea. She is the one who broke open the prison for you."

"I would kiss her a thousand times except for her ladyship and the smell of the damned shoe polish," said Rubriz. "But farewell, everyone, and enough of this silly chattering. Tonio, are you ready?"

With that they went off on foot, instantly, towards the mass of the horses that was nearest them.

THE SONG OF THE WHIP

Rosita said to Dorotea: "Can you ride?"

"Yes," said the girl.

"I'm not asking if you can sit on the back of a silky thoroughbred, but can you stay in the saddle on a bucking mustang?"

"I can try," said the Lerraza.

"Then come with me—come after them; they may need us to help. Only the two of them, and all those horses—and every horse with a devil in each hoof...."

Dorotea Lerraza waved her hand and went instantly after the two men.

They were flickering forms in the darkness now, against the shadowy slope of the hill, stealing towards the horse herd. And Dorotea heard a voice challenge, saying: "Who are you, my friends? Who—?"

Afterwards, she heard the thudding sound of a blow. And after that—she could see it dimly, the huge, squat bulk of Rubriz and the slenderer form of the Rural he had grappled. And then came a dull, muffled, and yet horribly sharp sound of bones broken inside flesh.

The Rural, his brilliant uniform glittering vaguely in the starlight, was dropped to the ground. His spurs jingled. He was still.

And Dorotea Lerraza stepped unconcerned past that broken body and came in among the lithe-bodied, dangerous, twisting, savage little mustangs. She could hear the hiss of sharp knives cutting lead ropes. The herd began to loosen, spread. Then a dark body sprang into a saddle at the rear of the herd. That was Tonio Lavery. And off to the right, a great gorilla shape mounted suddenly. That was Rubriz, of course.

Rosita sprang into a saddle; and Dorotea was instantly on the back of another mustang, a wild little horse that reared suddenly and almost unseated her. As it rocked forward it began to squeal and snort and caper.

A sudden roar came from Rubriz. He was bellowing, and shooting into the air. And with that, the entire herd of horses bolted up the hill at full speed—the two men riding at the outer edges, and Rosita and Dorotea screaming at the heels of the center of the herd.

No cavalry charge was ever half so wild as that. The lines of watchers immediately above the charge began to yell. A dozen guns were discharged at random, and then the guards fled right and left.

Off there to the side—was that a man who went down before

the front of that wave of horseflesh? And as the herd fled on, was it a human body that made the dark spot on the ground close to Dorotea's speeding horse?

She set her teeth. She was glad of her man's clothes now. For she had to grip the saddle with knees and legs and hands to make sure of her place. From the corner of her eye she saw Rosita tossing on the back of her racing horse as free and easy as foam on the crest of a wave, actually with a hand free to lash at the rumps of the running mustangs before her with her riding-quirt.

Bitter envy seized on Dorotea. She was glad that El Keed was not there to see.

Then the head of the herd dipped out of sight. In a cloud of stinging dust, Dorotea dropped over the edge of the ridge and found herself racing with the others into the hollow. Guns were crackling all around the rim of the hollow of El Circulo now, and higher still, she saw the bright green of the coming dawn. But the hollow itself was dark as a deep pool of water.

Into that darkness they were plunging.

Suddenly, in the center of the enclosure, voices roared. Guns blazed rapidly. She saw the herd split right and left, and into the cone of open ground that appeared she saw the dim forms of men lassoing mustangs, mounting. And one tall silhouette on a tall horse shouting commands. . . . El Keed!

Right onwards drove that maddened herd, and sifting into the middle of the wild horses were the riders—four to begin with, and now four more, all bent low over the saddle, all shouting like demons.

Shouting everywhere, and the roar of guns, until it seemed that the sky was splitting and thunder was pouring out of heaven. And so they drove on towards the opposite rim of El Circulo, surrounded by that living, squealing mass of horseflesh. The manes shook upwards like dust. The wild eyes glared with a phosphorescent brightness.

And Dorotea Lerraza began to laugh out of an hysterical fullness of heart.

Here, right and left, she saw the rifles of the guards flashing and then they were gone, jerked suddenly back behind her. And the rolling roar of the hoofbeats sped away through lower ground.

She looked back. She could see a score of riders coming in pursuit. Then the cañons of the higher hills received them and covered them. The main body of the stampeding herd thundered away to the west. And the eight riders turned into a north-bound cañon.

The morning was brightening. And afterwards they heard the pursuit begin to stream past them towards the west, always towards the west, following the illusion of that thundering stampede.

They left the cañon. They paused on a high shoulder of land and watched the spray of a little waterfall dazzle down the face of a cliff.

There they halted and looked at one another silently, Julio Mercado with his head bound up in a bleeding rag, because a bullet had grazed his skull during that night of waiting and enduring, and Viljoen still unharmed, keen, eager as one of his favorite sharp knives, and Tonio Lavery beginning to smile a little, and Rosita laughing silently with joy, and the huge friar, Brother Pascual, looking around him like a man dazed. And there was Rubriz walking up and down with the Kid, while Dorotea at the waterfall was washing from her face and hands the horrible brown stain that disfigured her, and taking off the black wrapping from her head, and letting the gold of her hair shine out again.

Rubriz, his vast hand on the shoulder of the Kid, was roaring out: "My God, *amigo*, what a wonderful thing it is that in such a little world there should be two men such as you and I! If there were a century between us, still it would be wonderful. . . . But to be alive in the same land, at the same time, that is enough to be put into a book, even into a Bible!"

Brother Pascual had dismounted from his mustang, and now climbed on to the back of it again, the beast grunting under that enormous weight.

He called out: "Señor El Keed, will you ride a little forward with me? I have something to show you."

"With you, Brother," said the Kid, "I'd ride to the end of the world."

He left Rubriz and followed the friar over the edge of the little plateau, and then on through a short winding cañon. At the end of this the friar halted and pointed, far ahead, to the brown streak of a river.

"Do you know that, *amigo*?" asked the friar.

"The Rio Grande?" said the Kid. "Of course I know it."

"What land is that beyond the water?"

"The United States, of course."

"Is that your country?"

"It is my country, Pascual."

"Why are you so far south?" asked the friar.

The Kid turned and looked at him with keen, wrinkling eyes.

"You must travel straight on," said the friar. "You must not turn back."

Montana was silent.

"When you come south," said the friar, "there is troubel.... Consider this.... A peon is flogged, and that was too bad ... and to help the peon you crossed the river into danger.... How many men have died since then because a peon was flogged?"

Montana could not speak a word.

"Young Tonio has left his father's ranch; a dancing-girl has been riding under gunfire," said the friar; "a lady of great place has damaged her name—who can say how much? A famous hacienda has been looted; a peon has been turned into a bandit; every Rural in Mexico has been turned into a savage beast; an outlaw has passed into fire and out again; and a poor friar has left his flock and gone wandering far into sin, I greatly fear.... Because El Keed rode south! Because he heard 'The Song of the Whip'!"

The Kid turned his head and looked darkly back through the cañon.

"As for the rest, they will take care of themselves if you are not with them. But if you are there—would you choose black eyes or blue, brother?"

The Kid rubbed his knuckles across his forehead. He sighed.

"I have to think," he said.

"Take time," said the friar. "But tell me, what have you gained for all this riding and shooting?"

"Only the horse I ride on," said the Kid, "and some spoiled clothes!"

"Well, think!" said the friar.

The Kid bowed his head. And El Capitán, finding his head free, reached for a tuft of bunch grass, sun-cured, sweet.

He cropped it, reached for another, began to wander step by step down the slope from grass to grass. The head of the Kid lifted. He did not turn it again as the horse wandered.

And the friar drew a great breath, for he saw that the Kid was looking steadily towards the north.

When he looked up again, El Capitán was at a trot, moving north, north towards the brown river.

Raw, fast-action adventure from one of the world's favorite western authors

MAX BRAND
writing as Evan Evans

0-515-08571-5	MONTANA RIDES	$2.50
0-515-08527-8	OUTLAW'S CODE	$2.50
0-515-08528-6	THE REVENGE OF BROKEN ARROW	$2.75
0-515-08529-4	SAWDUST AND SIXGUNS	$2.50
0-515-08582-0	STRANGE COURAGE	$2.50
0-515-08611-8	MONTANA RIDES AGAIN	$2.50
0-515-08692-4	THE BORDER BANDIT	$2.50
0-515-08711-4	SIXGUN LEGACY	$2.50
0-515-08776-9	SMUGGLER'S TRAIL	$2.50
0-515-08759-9	OUTLAW VALLEY	$2.50

Available at your local bookstore or return this form to:

JOVE
THE BERKLEY PUBLISHING GROUP, Dept. B
390 Murray Hill Parkway, East Rutherford, NJ 07073

Please send me the titles checked above. I enclose _____. Include $1.00 for postage and handling if one book is ordered; add 25¢ per book for two or more not to exceed $1.75. CA, IL, NJ, NY, PA, and TN residents please add sales tax. Prices subject to change without notice and may be higher in Canada.

NAME _____
ADDRESS _____
CITY _____ STATE/ZIP _____
(Allow six weeks for delivery.)

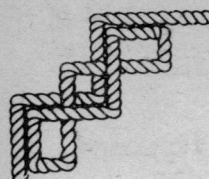

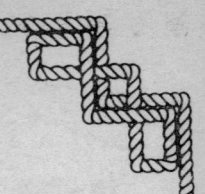

Blazing heroic adventures
of the gunfighters of the WILD WEST
by Spur Award-winning author

LEWIS B. PATTEN

__ GIANT ON HORSEBACK	0-441-28816-2/$2.50
__ THE GUN OF JESSE HAND	0-441-30797-3/$2.50
__ THE RUTHLESS RANGE	0-441-74181-9/$2.50
__ THE STAR AND THE GUN	0-441-77955-7/$2.50

Available at your local bookstore or return this form to:

CHARTER
THE BERKLEY PUBLISHING GROUP, Dept. B
390 Murray Hill Parkway, East Rutherford, NJ 07073

Please send me the titles checked above. I enclose _____. Include $1.00 for postage and handling if one book is ordered; add 25¢ per book for two or more not to exceed $1.75. CA, IL, NJ, NY, PA, and TN residents please add sales tax. Prices subject to change without notice and may be higher in Canada. Do not send cash.

NAME_____
ADDRESS_____
CITY_____ STATE/ZIP_____
(Allow six weeks for delivery.)

★★★★★★★★★★★★★★★★★★★

The Biggest, Boldest, Fastest-Selling Titles in Western Adventure!

★★★★★★★★★★★★★★★★★★★

CHARTER'S MOST WANTED LIST

Merle Constiner
_81721-1 TOP GUN FROM THE DAKOTAS — $2.50
_24927-2 THE FOURTH GUNMAN — $2.50

Giles A. Lutz
_34286-8 THE HONYOCKER — $2.50
_88852-6 THE WILD QUARRY — $2.50

Will C. Knott
_29758-7 THE GOLDEN MOUNTAIN — $2.25
_71147-2 RED SKIES OVER WYOMING — $2.25

Benjamin Capps
_74920-8 SAM CHANCE — $2.50
_82139-1 THE TRAIL TO OGALLALA — $2.50
_88549-7 THE WHITE MAN'S ROAD — $2.50

Available at your local bookstore or return this form to:

BERKLEY
THE BERKLEY PUBLISHING GROUP, Dept. B
390 Murray Hill Parkway, East Rutherford, NJ 07073

Please send me the titles checked above. I enclose _____. Include $1.00 for postage and handling if one book is ordered; add 25¢ per book for two or more not to exceed $1.75. CA, IL, NJ, NY, PA, and TN residents please add sales tax. Prices subject to change without notice and may be higher in Canada. Do not send cash.

NAME_____
ADDRESS_____
CITY_____ STATE/ZIP_____
(Allow six weeks for delivery.)

WANTED:
Hard Drivin' Westerns From
J.T.Edson

J.T. Edson's famous "Floating Outfit" adventure books are on every Western fan's **MOST WANTED** list. Don't miss any of them!

___	THE COLT AND THE SABRE	09341-7/$2.50
___	THE GENTLE GIANT	08974-6/$2.50
___	GO BACK TO HELL	09101-5/$2.50
___	HELL IN THE PALO DURO	09361-1/$2.50
___	THE HIDE AND TALLOW MEN	08744-1/$2.50
___	THE MAKING OF A LAWMAN	06841-2/$2.25
___	OLD MOCCASINS ON THE TRAIL	08278-4/$2.50
___	THE QUEST FOR BOWIE'S BLADE	09113-9/$2.50
___	RETURN TO BACKSIGHT	09397-2/$2.50
___	SET TEXAS BACK ON HER FEET	08651-8/$2.50
___	THE TEXAS ASSASSIN	09348-4/$2.50
___	THE TRIGGER MASTER	09087-6/$2.50
___	WACO'S DEBT	08528-7/$2.50
___	THE YSABEL KID	08393-4/$2.50

Available at your local bookstore or return this form to:

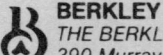

BERKLEY
THE BERKLEY PUBLISHING GROUP, Dept. B
390 Murray Hill Parkway, East Rutherford, NJ 07073

Please send me the titles checked above. I enclose _____. Include $1.00 for postage and handling if one book is ordered; add 25¢ per book for two or more not to exceed $1.75. CA, IL, NJ, NY, PA, and TN residents please add sales tax. Prices subject to change without notice and may be higher in Canada. Do not send cash.

NAME_____
ADDRESS_____
CITY_____ STATE/ZIP_____
(Allow six weeks for delivery.)